"Oh, my little Viking, don't cry."

Josh couldn't hold himself back. In two long steps he rounded his desk and drew her up out of her chair and into his arms. The late morning sun sent hazy rays into the dim library. Her eyes looked impossibly blue, and her mouth trembled just inches from his.

"Don't cry," he whispered again and touched his lips to hers. The kiss was as light as a breath, but that was all it took. A molten flare seared through his middle. A sound came from low in his throat, and he tightened his hold, deepening his search of her mouth.

Kari's lashes closed over the brimming tears. Her head was spinning. Suddenly, after days of bearing the burden of loneliness and uncertainty, his strong arms felt irresistibly comforting. "Josh," she breathed as he pulled his mouth away.

Dear Reader,

Welcome to Harlequin Historicals. We hope you will enjoy this month's selection.

From Lindsay McKenna comes *Brave Heart,* the story of Serena Rogan, a deeply troubled young woman who discovers a world of love and respect under the gentle care of a Lakota medicine man.

In *Destiny's Promise* by Laurel Pace, Lucinda Chandler hides away on a remote Georgian plantation, but must face her past when she falls in love with her new employer's son.

Ana Seymour's first book, *The Bandit's Bride,* was one of our 1992 March Madness titles. We are very pleased this month to be able to bring you her second book, *Angel of the Lake,* set in Wisconsin in the mid-1800s.

Last, but not least, *Spindrift* by Miranda Jarrett. This captivating romance features the younger Sparhawk brother, Jonathan, from *Columbine* (HH #144), as a shipwrecked seaman determined to unravel the lovely widow Allyn's carefully guarded secrets.

Next month, keep an eye out for *A Warrior's Quest,* the next book in Margaret Moore's Warrior series.

Sincerely,

Tracy Farrell
Senior Editor

Angel of the Lake

ANA SEYMOUR

Harlequin Books

TORONTO • NEW YORK • LONDON
AMSTERDAM • PARIS • SYDNEY • HAMBURG
STOCKHOLM • ATHENS • TOKYO • MILAN
MADRID • WARSAW • BUDAPEST • AUCKLAND

Harlequin Historicals first edition May 1993

ISBN 0-373-28773-9

ANGEL OF THE LAKE

Books by Ana Seymour

Harlequin Historicals

The Bandit's Bride #116
Angel of the Lake #173

ANA SEYMOUR

grew up in Minnesota surrounded by reminders of her Norwegian heritage; in fact, her mother was born on *Syttende Mai,* Norwegian Independence Day. Today she lives with her two teenage daughters in a hundred-year-old house on the edge of one of the state's ten thousand lakes.

For the real Kari,
who perished on the S.S. *Atlantic*
in the early morning hours of August 20, 1852,
and
For her great-great-great-great-great
granddaughters, Kathryn and Cristina,
who carry her heritage into the future

Chapter One

Lake Erie
August 20, 1852

In the muted moonlight an eerie haze hung out over the water. It made the night sky look solid enough to touch. Josh Lyman reached out his hand as if to grab an inky chunk of the stuff, then pulled it back, a slight smile turning up his lips.

"It's a dark 'un, tonight, sir."

The hearty voice at his shoulder startled him. He turned and recognized the sea-weathered features of Officer Garrity.

The slight smile of his reverie turned up into the genuine article—an open, friendly smile that fell naturally on his face with the ease of frequent use.

"I was just thinking the same thing myself, Mr. Garrity. The air is so thick, it's a wonder we can still breathe it."

The old seaman stood feet planted slightly apart, knees bending automatically with the roll of the ship. He squinted into the murky depths beyond the rail.

"I'll take a good blow to a night like this 'un," he said grimly. "It's unnatural—creepy-like, if you know what I mean, sir."

Josh nodded. He'd had much the same impression himself as he stood brooding on the deck. But he had figured it had been his own dark thoughts painting the mood.

The SS *Atlantic* was one of the finest of the first-class side-wheelers that crossed the Great Lakes carrying a curious mixture of upper-class tourists looking for luxury and penniless emigrants looking for a new home. "Palace steamers" they called the big ships, the interiors of which were decorated with rare woods and gold trim, marble fountains in every lounge and magnificent gaming tables, whose gleaming wood bounced back the light from crystal chandeliers and breathtaking stained glass domes. The highly touted bridal suites were sumptuous retreats lined with silk and damask, each with its own bath with hot and cold running water.

To Josh the excursion through the Lakes to Montreal and back had seemed like a perfect idea for an attempt at building a true marriage with Corinne. It satisfied his sense of adventure, and it would take them far away from the sometimes suffocating attentions of Corinne's well-meaning parents.

It had been these close attentions that had prevented him from having any inkling of the problems he would have trying to establish a "normal" marriage with Corinne. The joining of the Lyman and Pennington fortunes had been the talk of Milwaukee for months before their wedding. But once the engagement had been finalized, he had not seen her alone. He had not kissed her, even on the cheek. Not with her mother hovering so close he could have fogged her spectacles with a single deep breath.

He had preferred to spend his last days of bachelor-hood finding amusement with his fellow loggers. When his father had died in the cholera epidemic of '49, Josh had dedicated all his youthful energies and a sharp innate sense for business to administering the family holdings. With unerring timing, he had foreseen what was now open knowledge—that the lead mines were beginning to give out—and had invested the family money heavily in the new lumber industry, making in three years more than his father had in fifteen.

He controlled his burgeoning empire from Milwaukee, but each winter he had headed to the camps, working right alongside the swampers, the scalers and the sawyers. There wasn't a man among them who could outwork Josh Ly-man. His men openly boasted of it. And when the last log had been floated down the river in the spring, he had played alongside them, too.

If the play had occasionally included women, that was all right with him. Though he had every intention of be-ing a faithful husband once he and Corinne exchanged vows, he'd resolved to take all the pleasure he could get those last few months, and to endure his visits to the stuffy Pennington front parlor with good grace.

"Nothing wrong, sir, I hope?" The sailor's gruff con-cern shook him out of his troubled musings. "It's mighty late to be up."

Josh took a minute before answering. Perhaps he should tell the old man. Perhaps he should go ahead and say, "No, nothing's wrong except that tonight is the one-year anniversary of my marriage, and my wife is very probably lying wide awake in our gilded honeymoon suite bed ter-rified that I might arrive any minute to exercise my 'hus-bandly rights.'"

"I'm just not much of a sleeper, I guess," he said instead.

"No one says ya have to spend your time sleepin', son," Garrity said with a wink. "There's some folks that disappear into one of those fancy honeymoon suites and don't surface the whole trip."

Josh took a step back into the nearly black shadow of the ship's mammoth smokestack. "Some folks are lucky," he said softly.

Garrity turned away from the strapping young man and resumed his scanning of the invisible horizon. "One thing you learn out here on the water, Mr. Lyman, is that things come along in their own good time. Bein' in a hurry never got no one nowhere out here."

He pulled a tobacco pouch and pipe out of one of the pockets of his thick wool jacket. "If you just let things go along at their own natural pace, you usually end up where you want to go."

Josh smiled ruefully in the darkness. The old man reminded him of his grandfather. Grandpapa Lyman had been a master at giving advice without ever needing to know what the problem was. Josh had missed him sorely when the family had moved to the bustling new port of Milwaukee when Josh was still a boy.

The move had been good for them; his father had doubled the family fortune in Wisconsin's booming lead industry. The vitality of the frontier state was in Josh's blood now, but sometimes—like tonight—he would give almost anything to be back in Philadelphia listening to his grandpapa Lyman out on the old frame porch.

"Patience. I gather that's what you're telling me," he answered the old sailor finally.

"Aye, patience—the young man's curse and the old man's blessing."

Josh smiled. "I'll keep it in mind, Officer, and maybe I will turn in now, after all."

Garrity nodded and busied himself with his pipe. "Pleasant dreams, son."

The old mariner watched as the tall young man walked briskly away along the deck. Josh's strong legs made no accommodation for the gentle roll of the ship. He walked as though he were a man eager to get somewhere and not about to let mere fathoms of water hinder his progress.

By the time he had crossed over to portside where the most luxurious cabins were located, he had slowed his walk, and the brief lifting of his mood had disintegrated. "Patience" the old man had said. It had been a year now since Milwaukee's society wedding of the year had joined him to Vernon and Myra Pennington's only daughter, Corinne. It had been one year since the disastrous wedding night that had followed.

He continued on past the double doors to belowdecks and wandered slowly up toward the forward part of the ship. There *was* something strange about the night, he mused. It wasn't just his mood. He'd never known air could be so heavy. He reached the railing that overlooked the promenade for the steerage passengers three decks below. Had he been on his way here all along? he wondered. He peered intently down into the haze.

She was there again.

An uncomfortable tingle went down his back. He could just make out her form through the murky night, and it was almost like something supernatural. A beautiful apparition with hair the color of the moon. If he hadn't already seen her many times in daylight, blue eyes sparkling and cheeks ruddy with life, he would swear she was a phantom siren creature of the great dark lake they were crossing.

He shook his head. What in heaven's name was a lone woman doing out in the middle of the night? She was one of the emigrants, he knew that much. And he reckoned she was with the larger group, the Norwegians. The others were Russians and Germans and seemed less inclined to challenge this new land of theirs out in the open air of the badly crowded steerage deck.

If this one, the apparition, had a bed belowdecks, you'd not know it. She was always there, outside, leaning out over the rail or face turned up to the sun with a smile that had stopped Josh dead in his tracks the first time he had seen it. It had been on the pier in Montreal. She'd been sitting on a pile of luggage and laughing with a boy who had her same whitish-blond hair. Josh had been doing his best to coax some life into Corinne. He was determined not to let this trip end in total disaster.

"So where's that French you suffered over all those years with Miss Duvalier?" he had teased his wife, tweaking the ribbons of her tucked silk bonnet.

"It doesn't sound the same when these people talk," she'd answered with a small pout.

There had been a time when he'd thought Corinne's pout was pretty. In fact, it had given her a great deal of power over him as they grew up together in Milwaukee—since the first time he'd met her when he was fifteen and she only six. He'd put a frog in her lemonade. Her lips had pouted in a perfect little circle and two enormous tears had quivered on the edge of her big brown eyes.

On their wedding night he'd looked down to see those same two tears. And he'd felt even more horrible and guilty than he had about the frog.

Josh pulled himself back to the present. He wondered what the young woman down there would do if he called to her? He half opened his mouth, but the stillness of the night seemed too deep for interruption. She probably doesn't understand English anyway, he told himself.

As if answering his unspoken call, the object of his attentions turned suddenly and looked up at him. It was too dark to see her face, but he had no trouble picturing it. It had imprinted itself on his brain during the few days since he'd first seen her. He had watched her, memorized the vitality of her light blue eyes. He'd come to this rail time and again to imagine the feel of that glorious thick hair, which she left loose, heedless of the lake breezes. He wondered if she could see him through the murk. She didn't move, just stood looking up at him, as still as wax.

Josh didn't know how long they stood there, two figures frozen like stone across the quiet heaviness of the night. Suddenly, a shocking crack shattered the stillness, and the entire steamer gave a sickening, unnatural lurch to the side. Josh grabbed the rail and kept himself upright. Blood rushed into his head. God in heaven, what had happened?

He straightened up. The ship seemed to steady itself and appeared to be moving normally ahead through the dark waters. Through the resumed quiet he could hear the reassuring rhythm of the ship's engine.

Something had hit them. Josh had no way of knowing how badly the vessel was hurt, but he knew that a crash like that could not have left it unharmed. He looked around for a possible source for the collision, but could see nothing but darkness all around his side of the ship.

As his pulse slowly returned to normal, he looked down at the deck below him. There was no sign of the woman at the rail. Peering into the darkness, he at last saw her slender form lying facedown on the deck, her silver hair spread out around her like a veil.

The jolt to the ship must have knocked her down. He strained his eyes to see some kind of movement, but she lay still. She must be hurt. For a moment he contemplated jumping over the rail, down the three decks to her level.

"I'll be a lot of help to her with two broken legs," he said aloud. How the hell did one get down to steerage?

He turned and ran back toward the rear of the ship. As he neared the large double doors that led to the lower decks, crew members began appearing, all heading toward the bridge. Up ahead he spied Officer Garrity talking with two sailors who were nodding intently at his words.

Josh ran up to them. "What's going on?" he asked, his voice still calm. Down below the chug-a-chug of the engines beat like a soothing pulse.

"The ship's been hit, Mr. Lyman," the old man said, his voice a touch higher than normal. "You'd best get your missus and head out to your assigned lifeboat."

"Lifeboat? Do you mean to tell me the ship is sinking?" A wave of panic hit his stomach as the big vessel lifted on a swell.

"It's a possibility, sir. Best take no chances."

Garrity turned back to the sailors, but Josh grabbed at the rough wool of his coat. "Wait—there's a woman, a girl—in steerage. I think she's been hurt. I saw her over the rail..."

Garrity was shaking his head impatiently. "Sorry, Mr. Lyman, you'd best see to yourself now, and your wife. The folks down below will be loading their own boats there."

The ship lurched abruptly as the old man turned away. This time the movement seemed to upset some kind of nautical balance and the wood planking of the deck rocked crazily beneath them.

"Hurry, man!" Garrity shouted back at him as he and the two sailors broke into a headlong run toward the front of the ship.

Josh grasped the smooth wood of the ship's rail and tried to regain his equilibrium. The ship jerked once more toward portside, then with the sound of grinding timbers came to rest at a definite tilt. The now-open doors to the decks below skewed out at odd angles and Josh's legs threatened to slip out from under him.

Willing himself to breathe normally and think clearly, he let go of the security of the rail and started down the stairs. From the hall leading to the first-class staterooms, people were emerging in various states of undress.

In front of him the passageway was almost entirely blocked by the voluminous folds of the nightrobe of one of his and Corinne's tablemates, Mrs. Hennessey. Throughout the endless shipboard meals, the kind, portly matron had lightened the tenseness between the young married couple with her good humor.

"Mr. Lyman," she wailed, her normally florid face pale. "What are we going to do?"

Josh's reflexes were once again sharp and the powerful muscles of his legs kept him firmly planted on the sloping floor. He put a strong arm around the buxom woman's shoulders and propelled her toward the stairway.

"Go up to the lifeboats, Mrs. Hennessey," he told her steadily. "The crew will help you."

The ship lurched again, throwing them both against the side of the stairway and leaving Josh engulfed by the perfumed silk of his companion's wrap. He righted himself and pushed the clinging fabric away from his face. Then, with the same practiced ease with which he hefted massive logs at the lumber camps, he picked her up and in two giant steps had her at the top of the stairs.

Passengers pushed by them on both sides, running now, panic beginning to build. "Can you make it from here?" he shouted to her over the mounting din.

She nodded, her several double chins jiggling furiously.

"Have you seen Corinne?" he asked her.

Mrs. Hennessey's compartment was just two doors away from their own luxurious suite. "What about Corinne?" he shouted as Mrs. Hennessey tried to stabilize her hefty form on the sloping deck.

"The poor lamb." Mrs. Hennessey shook her head. "I didn't see her come out of your room." Somewhere in the distance a bell began to sound.

With a final, futile effort at helping the older woman as she began to slide along in the general direction of the crowd, Josh turned around and bounded back down the stairs. The hall to his room was clearing. Here and there a cabin door banged open with the increasingly erratic pitching of the ship.

In a skidding run he reached Stateroom 6A. He grasped the handle and tugged. The door wasn't locked, but something heavy must have fallen against it, effectively barring his entry.

"Corinne!" He pounded on the door. Surely she couldn't be sleeping through all this. Another reel of the ship and the last corridor lamp sputtered out, plunging him into total blackness.

"Corinne!" The stout timbers of the door shook beneath his fists.

There seemed to be an odd moment of quiet all at once. Josh realized that the ship's engines had finally stopped, but just as he started to think what this might mean, he was thrown violently back against the opposite side of the passageway as the vessel slipped once more and settled into a new, dangerously inclined position.

With a fleeting wish that he had on his heavy logging shoes, he braced himself against the wall and thrust his leg powerfully against the closed door of his cabin. The door finally gave and suddenly he was half falling into the room, nearly tumbling over the large chest that had slid away from the entrance.

The cabin looked pitch-black against the hazy gray circle of the porthole. He sensed at once that the room was empty, but he nevertheless groped his way across the floor to the bed on the opposite side. In the dark he felt the jumbled silk covers and stepped on a pillow, which had been tossed aside in haste.

"Corinne?" he asked the blackness. Obviously she had already gone abovedecks. Disquiet washed through him. He couldn't imagine Corinne single-handedly battling the hysterical mob of passengers he had seen on the hurricane deck. Perhaps she had someone helping her, he tried to tell himself. The only sister to the Penningtons' four boys, Corinne had *always* had someone to help her.

Josh pushed up the fallen pillow and threw it onto the bed in frustration. He had to find her. Pulling himself along the wall, he managed to get through the door and started up the slanting hall toward the barely discernible opening to the stairs. His hands traced the carved mahogany molding, which was just one of the details he had so admired upon boarding the ship only days before. Now, as the noise of the crowd up above began to be punctuated by shouts and occasional screams, Josh admitted to himself that the *Atlantic* trip had been a big mistake. Corinne hadn't wanted to leave Milwaukee. He had disregarded her wishes, determined that once away from her parents, he could make her happy.

Josh shook his head as if to empty it of the gloomy thoughts. His full lips turned up in self-ridicule. It seemed ludicrous to be brooding about personal troubles when he was on a sinking ship in the middle of a black night. The scene abovedecks brought him swiftly back to reality. People were shoving and screaming. The ship's whistle had been tied down, adding its tremendous blast to the general din.

In front of him two crew members were struggling to lift a pretty brunette into a boat that had already pushed away from the side of the ship. The young woman fought against them, hysterically calling out the name "Hiram" or perhaps "Herbert."

With his height and strength, Josh had little trouble pushing his way through the crowd. He headed toward the stern to the lifeboat station assigned to their stateroom. Along the way he searched among the scared, tense faces for Corinne.

Almost unconsciously, he found himself also looking for long, silver-blond hair. But of course, that was crazy, he told himself. The young emigrant wouldn't be up here. The steerage passengers had their own lifeboats down below.

By now it was eminently clear that the ship was going to sink. Many of the boats had already been dispatched, and it became a desperate priority among those remaining on board to find some other form of support before the ship was swallowed up by the dark waters of Lake Erie. He worked his way around a group of passengers who were tying deck-chair mattresses into what they evidently hoped would serve as a life raft.

Looking down into the water, he could see quite a few passengers bobbing along singly in the newfangled "lifechairs" with tin bowls attached to the bottoms. The flimsy-looking contraptions seemed a poor match for the broad, black expanse of lake that spread out beyond them.

He reached the end of the row of lifeboats without seeing any sign of Corinne. The boat assigned to him was already over the side, and panic-stricken people clamored to jump in as it was slowly winched down to the water. The passengers who already crammed the boat to overload made futile attempts to push it away from the side and discourage further entry. Josh scanned the group; Corinne was not among them.

Toward the back, nearly buried by two stout men on either side of her, Mrs. Hennessey waved a hand and called out to him. "Corinne's not here, Mr. Lyman. I didn't see her come up."

"I'll find her," he shouted back, not in the least bit certain of how he would do so. Perhaps she hadn't made it up to the hurricane deck. She might be still trapped below. But if she wasn't in their cabin, where was she?

Ignoring the increasingly poignant screams as more and more people splashed into the insecurity of the dark waters below, he started back toward the stairway. The ship was now practically vertical, slanting toward the prow. How much longer before the mammoth vessel would slide entirely into the water?

For the first time Josh began to think about rescue. He stopped a moment and looked over the rail into the distance. Around him people were gesturing in one direction and there, barely discernible, he could make out the lights of another vessel coming toward them. He felt a surge of elation. They weren't to be abandoned to the black waters after all. Now all he had to do was find Corinne.

A young sailor stopped him. "You're heading the wrong direction, sir. Get to the stern and hang on, or find something to jump in with."

"I can't find my wife."

The crewman shook his head. "Sorry, sir. The entire front end of the ship is underwater, and if she's still below, there's not much hope."

Josh felt panic arise again in his stomach. He shouldered his way around the burly sailor and ran toward the stairway opening. Throwing open the closed doors, he prepared to jump down to the next deck, but held back at the last minute. The passageway below him was filled with swirling water.

For a moment he clung to the heavy door and closed his eyes. The ship slid another few feet. He *had* to find her. It was his fault that she was on this ship—little Corinne, who for the first time in her life had been forced into something against her wishes.

If she wasn't belowdecks, the only choice was to cross to the other side of the ship and look there. He let go of the stout door and started to ease himself down the treacherous slope of the deck to the crossway. Suddenly, the entire vessel did a sharp, abrupt turn toward portside. Josh made a desperate grab for the rail, but a wave of water rushed out at him from the stairway opening, rolling him over the rail and down to the lake below.

He plunged deep into the lake, icy water slamming his senses. The surprise left him stunned, but his natural abilities took over and in moments he was swimming strongly back up to the surface. He had grown up with lakes, and later had survived many a dousing in rough river waters as he and his men fought mile-long logjams.

His concern as he broke through the surface was not the water, but the position of the ship above him. It loomed like a great towering monster in the dark night. Willing himself to breathe deeply, he took several strong, even strokes in the direction away from the half-submerged vessel. All around him he could see the jetsam of panic—

debris, chairs, bedding, a few boats—too few boats, he surmised, to bode well for many of the more than four hundred people who had been aboard.

He pried off his shoes and rid himself of his heavy jacket. Treading water with a natural ease that calmed him from the shock of his plunge, his thoughts went to Corinne. Damn, but he had apparently failed her once again.

His jaw clenched as an unfamiliar sense of defeat overwhelmed him. Granted, he had not tried very hard in the months before their wedding. Along with the rest of their families and friends, he had treated the match as a foregone conclusion, predestined from childhood. He had *assumed*—that had been his biggest mistake—he had assumed that all would be well between them.

He had a normal, healthy body. Extremely healthy, he had been told a time or two by women in a position to know about such things. He had always thought Corinne a pleasant enough little thing. Her sometimes-petulant demands on him as they grew up together had never caused him much hardship. And she certainly was pretty, a tiny sugar confection of honey brown hair and deeply lashed eyes.

He had had no idea that years of spoiling, years of sheltering, would leave Corinne so incapable of an adult relationship with a man that she would actually come close to physical illness.

Josh looked up at the faltering ship with a frown. Had his wife gotten off? Had someone helped her? *Where the hell was she?*

With a stronger kick of his legs, he boosted himself higher in the water and searched the darkness for the second ship he had seen from up above. There it was—steady, cheerful, promising lights approaching from the west. It appeared that if everyone could just hang on for a while, there was hope for rescue.

He looked about for something to attach himself to. Though completely at home in the water, he didn't want the continued flooding of the ship to drag him under again. A few yards away he saw a large steamer trunk, top open, pulled along slowly with the still slightly forward motion of the ship.

In a few strokes he had drawn near enough to see that it seemed to contain clothes. He reached a strong hand up to grasp the side, intending to sacrifice its contents in favor of a steadier vessel for himself.

Shockingly, it was not cloth his hand touched, but an arm—a wet arm, as cold as the lake around them—but definitely an arm. He stretched to the other side of the trunk and boosted himself awkwardly above it. Inside was a woman, lying lifeless and crumpled. The sight was startling in itself, but what had riveted his attention was the unbelievable sight of long hair shrouding the entire upper portion of the torso—magic, silver hair such as he had only seen on one other person in his entire life. *It was she.* It was his apparition of the night, and if she had looked a ghost before, he now feared that his nighttime fantasy may be all too true.

His arms gave way and he dropped once more into the water. A shout came from behind him. One of the ship's lifeboats was approaching, offering him help. He hollered back and waved. When he was certain the boat was heading in his direction, he once again climbed up around the edge of the trunk. Balancing precariously, he reached down and tried to gather the inert form of the girl into his arms. She was soaking wet and deadly cold.

Half pulling himself into the trunk, he managed to lift her from the bottom. With increasing horror he began to fear that he was holding a corpse in his arms. Was it possible for living skin to be this cold? He put his head down to her chest, trying to detect some movement, a sign of breath, but the girl seemed lifeless, an icy rag doll with a woman's body.

His mind went quickly to the logging camp last spring when they had pulled Lucky Gibson from the Chippewa River after what had seemed an interminable search. Josh's foreman, Holstein Ericssen, had picked the half-dead man up out of the water by the waist, turned him over and actually *blown air* into his mouth. Neither Josh nor his men had ever seen the like.

Should he try such a thing with the woman in his arms? Josh wondered desperately. Experimentally, he pushed a little on her chest. The effort was futile. With a shake of his head, he finally leaned over and put his mouth against her chilled and stiffened lips. Prying her teeth open with his own cold fingers, he blew into her mouth, first gently, then with more strength.

There was no response, and he pulled back, trying to get a good look at her. In the deadened moonlight, her face could have been carved for a statue, features beautifully formed, serene, and so very still.

Damnation, he raged, as a swift vision of that same face alive with laughter crossed through his mind. It was a vision that had guiltily filled his thoughts all too often this voyage.

He lowered his mouth once more to hers. It had worked for Lucky Gibson, he said to himself fiercely. He would damn well *make* it work for her.

In his fury Josh had not even noticed that the lifeboat had now pulled up close behind him. "Is that you, Mr. Lyman?" a voice from the rear called. It was Mrs. Hennessey again.

It occurred to Josh that what he was doing to a complete stranger might look exceedingly peculiar to the lifeboat passengers, some of whom had now actually grabbed the side of the huge trunk. But he couldn't stop. Had that been a slight movement in his arms, or was he imagining things?

"It *is*. It's Mr. Lyman." Somewhere in the back of his consciousness he could hear Mrs. Hennessey's voice. "Is that Mrs. Lyman he's holding?"

Suddenly the girl in his arms gave a gasping cough. Josh's heart leapt and he struggled to lift her more fully upright. Her head lolled back and forth on her slender neck, then she stiffened and water gushed forth from her mouth.

Her eyes fluttered open. They were glassy and confused, but to Josh it seemed that the night had suddenly grown a little brighter, a little warmer. He smiled down at her.

She coughed again and struggled against him.

"Shh, easy, quiet." Josh took his own deep sigh of relief. "You're all right now, do you understand?"

She looked around awkwardly, her big eyes fearful.

"Do you understand English?" he asked her.

"Yes," she whispered, her voice hoarse.

Josh gave her a little hug of gratitude. She *was* all right. She had answered him. She understood him.

"Can we help out, sir?" a voice called from the lifeboat.

He looked back down at the girl. Her eyes were closed again, but she was definitely breathing now. Against his soaked chest he could feel the pressure of her firm breasts rising and falling with reassuring regularity. He gathered her to himself more closely, reluctant to let her go.

"There's room here on the boat. It'll be safer for you both." Hands were reaching for him and, still in the daze of victory to have her breathing again, he let them lift her away from him, then forced his body to cooperate as they helped him, too, into the relative security of the sturdy yawl.

"This one's hurt," he heard someone say.

"I don't think she was breathing when I found her," Josh said shakily. "But she's going to be all right now." He collapsed gratefully into the bottom of the boat between two seat benches and put his head down on his knees.

"She's breathing fine, but there's blood all along the back of her head."

Josh sat up abruptly.

"Looks like she's taken a nasty hit on the head."

He looked over at the girl, now lying across the laps of the first row of lifeboat passengers. She had spoken to him. She had to be all right.

"She spoke to me," he said weakly.

An older man was holding her head between two big hands. He looked grave. "It's cut here. Must be four, five inches. Is this your wife, sir?"

All at once Josh felt incredibly weary. He shook his head slowly and then let it drop once more to his knees.

"No. I...I couldn't find Corinne," he mumbled. "I couldn't find her. I've lost my wife."

Chapter Two

Many hours later, dry and warm now in new clothes, Josh still couldn't believe it. Of all the carefree travelers and eager emigrants who had shared the voyage of the *Atlantic*, only a small number of fortunate ones had survived. Josh had wandered back and forth between the hastily put together shelters, but Corinne was not among the survivors.

Then he had begun the grim tour of the makeshift morgues. The body count was inaccurately small. The SS *Ogdensburg*, the same propeller ship that had dealt the *Atlantic* its death blow, had been the rescuer ship. Its crew, horrified at the havoc their ship had wrought, worked tirelessly throughout the rest of the long night. But they had concentrated their efforts on the survivors; the dead had been mostly left to rest forever in the peaceful blackness of the vast lake.

Josh rubbed his hands over his eyes. It was a nightmare. The sick feeling in his stomach that had started as he'd stood last night outside the empty stateroom was with him still. He hadn't eaten. He couldn't remember if he'd had anything to drink.

The people of Erie had rallied to help the shipwreck victims with amazing efficiency. He had a new set of clothes within minutes of his arrival, and the emigrant girl he had helped had been whisked away—he supposed for medical attention—before he could say a word. She had appeared to be still unconscious, and he now wondered in the midst of his misery how she was doing.

He thought about his family and Corinne's. He should wire, let them know he was safe. But what could he say about Corinne? What in God's name could he say to her parents?

It was Mrs. Hennessey who roused him. He had fallen into a restless sleep sitting upright on a hard chair at a shelter that had been set up in a dockside tavern. The hearty gray-haired woman seemed little the worse for wear after the long ordeal.

"Mr. Lyman, you poor, poor man. They've set up cots in the back. Why don't you go lie down?"

"I have to look for Corinne," he said groggily.

"I know, dear. But there's really nothing anyone can do just now. They said they would be bringing in more—you know—more of them, as many as they can."

He looked up at her angrily. "I'm looking for *her,* not her body. She wasn't in our cabin. She must have gotten out. She could be anywhere."

The elderly woman patted a hand on his shoulder gently. "She could be anywhere, Mr. Lyman, that's right."

She hesitated a moment, then pulled over a wooden chair. Carefully balancing her bulk in the middle of the narrow seat, she leaned toward him. "It's just . . . my dear man, they're saying that the majority didn't make it, maybe as many as three hundred . . . still out there in that awful water."

She paused a moment to wipe away a tear that was making its way down her fleshy cheek. Josh had already discovered that Mrs. Hennessey's heart was as big as her person. He reached out and took both her hands in his.

"I tried," he told her brokenly. "I tried to reach her. I tried to go down again in case she hadn't made it up. I couldn't find her."

"I know, dear. You can't blame yourself."

Josh felt as if one of the massive iron pulleys they used to move lumber in the camps had fastened itself on his heart. "She can't be dead."

Mrs. Hennessey's tears now rolled down unheeded. "Is there anything I can do, Mr. Lyman?"

Josh let his head drop into his hand. He swallowed hard over a great lump that had lodged in his throat. "I don't even know what to do myself. I should send a wire back home . . . I should . . . I don't know . . ."

Mrs. Hennessey pulled herself upright in the tiny chair. "How can something like this happen?" she asked indignantly. "How can two ships simply *bash* into each other in the middle of that huge lake? It's horrible. Somebody ought to answer for it."

Josh lifted his head up, spurred by the energy of this plucky woman who was more than twice his age. "It *is* unbelievable. The water was as smooth as a looking glass."

"It was that Captain Pettys. They ought to string him up. Some say he was hurt scrambling to be among the first to get on a lifeboat. He abandoned his ship!"

Josh found he could not summon anger. If it was true that Corinne was dead, anger wouldn't bring her back.

"For a while after the crash, I thought everything was going to be all right," he said distractedly.

Mrs. Hennessey nodded. "The *Ogdensburg* was already two miles away before they got the radio message of the damage they had done to us. We're lucky we were able to get through to them. They could have just left us all there to drown.''

''You mean *some* of us are lucky,'' Josh said wearily.

''Of course...I didn't think...." Mrs. Hennessey was immediately contrite, her expression stricken.

Josh reached over again to pet her plump hands. ''That's all right. I'm glad you made it, Mrs. Hennessey. Milwaukee wouldn't be the same without you.'' He mustered the ghost of a smile, then stood. ''I guess I'll go make the rounds again.''

Mrs. Hennessey pushed herself up off the chair. ''I'll go with you, if you like, Mr. Lyman. Two pairs of eyes are better than one.''

Josh shook his head. ''You should get some rest, Mrs. Hennessey. It hasn't been an easy day for any of us.''

After fending off her protests, Josh managed to get her situated a bit precariously in one of the narrow cots that had been set up for survivors. Then he started walking along the waterfront again, stopping wherever he could to ask for news of any more victims of the wreck—dead or alive.

Finally, he worked his way over to the impressive new brick city hospital where the most badly injured had been taken. In the first rush of disaster, the emigrants and millionaires had been pushed together with no regard for rank or fortune. But by now, Josh's third visit to the modern facilities today, the large wards were crammed full of emigrants, and the first-class passengers had presumably been moved to the relative luxury of private rooms.

It was in the second of the large ward rooms where he came across the girl he had helped last night. He spotted her easily from the far end of the room, her chaff-colored hair unmistakable.

Josh slowly made his way around the beds that had been placed in the center aisle. As he approached her, she turned her head, and her vivid blue eyes met his. They were no longer dazed, as they had been when he had held her in his arms.

He took a little unnatural breath. Damn, she was beautiful. Her normally rosy complexion was still pale, but her hair cascaded around her shoulders like liquid silk. It ended just at the tips of her perfectly formed breasts, which were covered now only by the soft cotton of a hospital gown.

His gaze must have lingered there, because she hastily pulled the rough wool blanket up around her as he reached the side of her bed. Her eyes widened and for a moment a touch of the confusion he had seen in them the previous night flashed through them.

"I didn't mean to startle you, miss," he said quickly. With visible effort he forced his face into a smile. "You look a sight better than you did last night."

He was at the edge of her bed, close enough to reach out and touch the soft perfection of her cheek. His hand tingled as he remembered how cold that skin had been against him in the dark waters of the lake.

"You do understand English, don't you?" he asked her gently.

It seemed a long time, but was perhaps only seconds before she softly replied just as she had last night. "Yes." This time it was not the hoarse whisper of a half-drowned woman, but a lovely, almost musical tone, with an odd cadence to the word that made it evident she was not American.

"Are you with the Norwegians?" Josh asked, hardly believing he was actually speaking to her at last.

"Yes."

Belatedly, Josh realized that he was tense and staring, which must not be exactly comfortable for a girl who had gone through what she had the past day and night. He tried to relax his body and voice.

"I wanted to see if you were all right. They said you had quite a cut on the back of your head." Sitting would help him feel more natural, he thought. His eyes searched the crowded ward for a chair.

"You are the one who saved me, no?" Her English was perfect; there was just that slightly off rhythm that indicated it was not her native tongue.

Gratitude and admiration shone out of her bright blue eyes. To his chagrin and slight amusement, Josh felt himself flushing. "A lot of people helped. They pulled us into one of the lifeboats."

She struggled to sit up higher in the stark iron bed. She winced as her head scraped against the bare wall behind her. "But, I mean . . . *you* are the one who saved me. They told me about it. They said you were blowing . . ."

She touched slender fingers to her mouth and now *her* pale face reddened. Josh had automatically put his hand out to steady her as he saw her trying to sit up. He grasped her shoulder, his face just inches from hers, then went stock-still. He hadn't feared the black waters of Lake Erie last night, but with a sense of tumbling, he felt all at once that he could drown in those bright blue eyes.

He straightened abruptly, took a step back from the bed and made an effort to slow the whirring in his head. "You were inside a steamer trunk, and you weren't breathing. My foreman once saved a drowning man by blowing air into his mouth, so I decided to try it on you."

"I'm extremely grateful to you, sir."

"Josh," he said automatically, as though it didn't occur to him that they wouldn't be on first-name terms.

"I'm very grateful, Mr. Josh."

Her voice was lovely. The slightly strange pattern made you listen to every word. Josh gave his first genuine smile of the day. "No, just Josh—Josh Lyman."

Dark golden lashes swept downward. "Oh, I'm sorry...I don't know many American names."

"Don't be sorry," he replied softly. "Or grateful, either. I'm just glad I was there to help. You were in pretty bad shape. I can tell you that I was never so relieved in my life as when you coughed up about half of Lake Erie all over the two of us."

"Oh, dear." The red returned to her cheeks. "How dreadful."

"It wasn't dreadful at all." He reached out again and put his strong hand gently on her shoulder. "It was wonderful, a miracle."

She smiled at him then, and it was as if he had been waiting for the sight an entire lifetime. A liquid rush coursed through his body.

"What's your name?" he asked her shakily.

Her wonderful smile faded and a hint of moisture gathered along the bottom edge of her bright eyes.

"I'm not sure," she said, her voice a whisper.

She was *almost* sure it was Kari, but her head started to ache so dreadfully when she tried to pin it down, to think of it with absolute surety. Her own name!

She shook her head—slowly, so as not to start the nauseating dizziness again—and tried to answer the tall, handsome man at her bedside. "I think it's Kari."

The man's warm smile faded, and she was inordinately sorry. Without the smile he looked so weary and sad. She wanted to put it back on his face.

"Well," she said, forcing a little laugh. "Now you know the kind of shape I'm in. I'm not even sure of my own name."

"You don't remember?" The man was strong, almost too big and muscular for the fine-cut clothes he was wearing. He could put many of the strapping Norse fellows back home to shame, she thought to herself. Back home...where? The name was right there—on the edge of some kind of cloud in her brain. Her visitor's grave brown eyes were regarding her as if she were insane.

"I'm having a little trouble. The doctors say it's probably just confusion from the knock on the head. I should be all right soon."

Josh's expression remained troubled. He looked so tired, Kari thought, this man, who had last night miraculously blown the very life back into her.

"What can you remember?" he asked.

Kari smiled for real this time, a natural, sunny smile that grew broader as she watched some of the tenseness leave the man's face. "At the moment everything is a little confused. I feel like I've had too much *akevitt*. You know *akevitt?*"

Josh shook his head, mesmerized again by that smile.

"My *Onkel* Einar, he used to drink too much of it sometimes and then he would talk crazy. Like I'm feeling." Her smile dimmed. "I remember about my *Onkel* Einar and the *akevitt* ... but I don't remember my own name."

Josh wiped a tired hand across his face. Though she appeared to have recovered from her ordeal in the lake, it was evident that the beautiful girl on the bed in front of him had serious problems. Where was her family? Surely if they had survived the wreck, they would have found her by now; they would be here, helping her remember, helping her find out who she was.

"Your family?" he asked.

She shook her head again. "I don't know. You're the first person I've recognized all day, and when I saw you, I thought you had been part of some kind of bad dream."

Josh gave a rueful chuckle. "That's not exactly the kindest thing I've ever been told by a woman."

Kari reached out a hand to touch the fine serge of his jacket. "Oh, no, please. I did not mean . . . it's just that I remember looking up and seeing you watching me. It was dark, I think. I remember thinking you were tall . . . and very beautiful."

Josh laughed once again. "Can't say I've ever been told that by a woman, either."

Her eyes were wide and serious. "I don't know, maybe it was just a dream."

The light left his face. "It was no dream. You must be remembering last night out on deck. I saw you standing there, just before the other ship hit us."

"I don't remember the ship hitting us. I don't remember any of it."

"It looked as if you were knocked down. I saw you lying there on the deck. I wanted to get down there to help you." He paused. He had been on his way to help her, but instead had had to look for Corinne. He should be looking for her now.

"And you did help me." Her smile was pure sunshine.

Josh shook his head. "I couldn't get down to your deck. It was later I found you . . . in the water."

"I wish I could remember." She massaged her temples with slender, long fingers.

"If the doctors tell you not to worry, then I would take their advice." He gave her a brief, distracted smile. He was remembering his duty again. "I have to be going." Perhaps another search ship had arrived back at the harbor.

Her eyes clouded, and there it was again, that look of confusion. It made Josh want to reach out and hold her as he had last night.

"I'm sorry," he said, faltering. "I . . . there's something I have to do." He didn't want to add to her troubles by burdening her with his own.

"Will you come back?" It was barely a whisper.

Josh ran his hands through the tangled waves of his dark hair. "If you want me to," he said at last.

"Please. I don't know anyone here."

Back on the deck of the ship, her tall, lithe body had looked strong and comfortable with the elements. But now, lying there in her white hospital gown, she looked utterly fragile and alone.

"I'll be back," he said, with more conviction this time.

Her smile lingered at the edges of his mind as he turned and left the room.

It was evening before he was back. And this time there was no pretense of a smile, no doubt about the exhaustion etched into his face. Each passing hour of no word made the verdict more inevitable: Corinne was gone. She lay somewhere at the bottom of Lake Erie, along with some three hundred other victims, along with the wreck of the "floating palace" where they had danced and gambled.

Josh had waited until just minutes before the office of the Mississippi Valley Telegraph Company was to close to send one of the newfangled telegrams to his mother and brother, Davey. He wasn't in any hurry to send on the bad news, but with modern technology, he knew that soon they could very well be reading about the disaster in the newspapers. He had asked them to relay the news to the Penningtons. He didn't know how to put the words down on paper.

Then he had planned to get some badly needed sleep at one of the shelters, but instead found himself once again at the door of the second ward of the city hospital. The Norwegian girl had seemed so alone, and he couldn't get over his feeling of responsibility for her. He had, after all, brought her back to this world. He supposed the least he could do would be to see her safely reunited with her family.

He was almost sure that didn't include a husband. On the ship he had only seen her with the one young boy—young, but surely too old to be her son. He had assumed it was a brother. But where was he now? And where were the parents? What if they, too, had never made it out of the water?

She appeared to be sleeping, and he hesitated. She probably needed sleep more than she needed a visitor. But just as he turned to leave, her long lashes fluttered open, and once again those clear blue eyes brightened at the sight of him. The heaviness around his heart lightened just a bit.

"You came back." Her voice was stronger now, and had a definite lilt of happiness.

Josh tried to smile, but found his features wouldn't cooperate. His expression remained strained, and hers lost some of its radiance.

"I told you I'd come. How are you feeling? Have you remembered anything more?"

Her perfectly shaped lips pursed into a frown. "I feel fine. It's just that my head, it goes—" she made a graceful little motion with her hand "—*swimming* when I move too much."

"Like the *akevitt*." Josh felt a little foolish as his tongue tripped over the strange word, but was rewarded as the smile came back to her face.

"*Ya,* like that—like *Onkel* Einar." She laughed then for the first time and Josh felt as if his heart would crack. He wanted to laugh with her. He wanted not to have this horrible ache inside him about Corinne, about going back to face her family. He wanted to be able to laugh with the beautiful girl in front of him and talk to her and share everything about her life and his.

"You've heard nothing about your family?"

She shook her head slowly. "Nothing. You are the only one who comes."

Josh felt a rush of frustration. Why hadn't anyone come to help her? Didn't these people take care of one another? He called to an orderly who was helping a patient in a bed across the aisle.

"Do you know what's being done to identify this patient?" he asked the man, whose stained uniform and day's growth of beard testified to long hard hours at his task.

The man gave a sympathetic look at the girl in the bed and then addressed Josh. "We've had our hands full just trying to patch them up, sir. But a while back, some of the people from the shipping line were through here trying to get names. They say the purser lost the passenger lists in the wreck."

Josh rolled his eyes in exasperation. "Aren't there other Norwegian passengers around who might know this young woman?"

The orderly picked up a tray from the bed where he'd been working. "They're all just bodies to me, sir. I wouldn't know a Norwegian from a Chinaman."

"I haven't heard anyone speaking Norwegian," the girl's musical voice interrupted.

"Where can I find these people from the steamship line?" Josh asked the orderly.

"I heard they've set up an emergency office down by the wharf." The man was impatient to be about his business, and Josh waved him away with a quick thank-you before turning back to the girl.

"You *do* remember your own language?"

"Of course I remember Norwegian just fine—and *engelsk*—English, too. It's very strange, is it not?" Her eyes had that look of dazed hurt again.

Josh reached over to pat her slender hand. "Don't worry about it. I'll head down to the waterfront and see what I can find out."

She turned her hand over in his so that their palms pressed together. Her touch jolted his overtired senses and he pulled away abruptly. She looked up at him, her sky blue eyes uncertain.

Angry at himself and the world, Josh's words were curt. "Try to get some rest, and I'll be back as soon as I learn something."

She gave him a tentative smile. "Once again, I am very grateful to you, Josh Lyman."

He turned on his heel and left her.

Up to his wedding night, failure had not even been a word in Josh's vocabulary. In Milwaukee they said that once Josh Lyman set his mind to something, you could be sure it would get done—quickly and successfully. But now, as he left the steamship office, he felt as though nothing would ever be right in his life again.

First there had been the wrench of seeing Corinne's name in bold block letters on the list crudely titled at the top: Bodies Not Recovered. Though the passenger lists were gone, they did have the names from the first-class staterooms, the harried clerk had informed him, and, no, they were no longer holding out any hope. The area had been thoroughly searched by rescue ships all day long. There was no one left out in the lake. No one *alive*.

Then had come his fury over the indifference about the plight of the young woman in the hospital. The Norwegian survivors had been shipped on by train to Chicago, the clerk told him hastily, and would then take another steamer to Milwaukee, since most were heading to Wisconsin or the newer settlements of Minnesota. "If the girl had had any family, surely they would have made inquiries?" the man had asked with just an edge of impatience.

"Do you think a young woman like that would come by herself all the way from Norway?" Josh had asked the man angrily.

The clerk had merely shrugged and busied himself with his lists. Horrible lists, condensing into a cramped page the dreadful loss of life, marks on a page signifying the end of the hopes and dreams of hundreds of human beings. Lists of survivors, like Josh, who could go about their business and love and laugh and live to see their grandchildren at play. And lists of the dead, like Corinne, who would never do any of those things. Josh's shoulders drooped. He was so tired. It seemed to him all at once as though human destinies were being determined by the methodical stroke of the clerk's pen. He suppressed an urge to choke the little man.

Kari Aslaksdatter. The name, at least, was clear to her. She had awakened with a wonderful certainty. Sun was streaming in through the high windows of the hospital room and for just a moment it seemed that the events of the past two days had only been a dream.

Then she sat up, and the dizziness came, and that awful sense of things missing, a world out of place, the unknown. An unfocused fear clutched at her stomach. She lay back down on the hard hospital pillow and forced herself to breathe deeply and relax.

She was safe, she told herself. She was in a hospital in America. She had had a knock on the head, but would soon remember. Like a litany, she silently repeated: soon she would remember everything.

It didn't take her long to calm herself. Her face took on its naturally serene lines and she was able to smile without effort when the doctor came to check on her.

"How's your head today, miss?" he asked her, his bass voice deep with professional authority.

"Better, I think, Doctor. And I have remembered my 'last name,' as you call it. It's Aslaksdatter. That means, you know, that my father is—" she faltered a moment "—was, I don't know—his name was Aslak. Do you think that will help find my family?"

The bewhiskered medical man leaned over to examine the cut on her head. "I would think so, Miss Kari." He straightened and smiled down at her. "The wound looks fine. If we could only get you remembering things a bit more clearly, we could let you out of here."

Kari answered slowly. "I would like to leave, Doctor, but . . . I have nowhere to go."

The doctor gave a great sigh. He hadn't slept in two nights. "Perhaps the steamship company could help you, my dear. I know they'll be taking care of the hospital bills, if that helps any."

Tears prickled behind her eyes. In dealing with the dizziness of the past two days, she hadn't thought much beyond remembering her name and trying to feel better. Now the doctor was telling her that she was free to go—free to return to a life she couldn't remember in a country she didn't know.

Over the edge of the doctor's shoulder, she could see a familiar tall form walking toward them. Kari closed her eyes in relief. It was Josh. Though she had only met him yesterday, somehow she knew that he would make everything all right. He would know what she should do. Perhaps he even had news of her family. She struggled to sit up.

From the carefully neutral expression in his dark brown eyes it did not appear that he had good news to share. He shook the doctor's hand and introduced himself.

"You know this little miss?" the doctor asked him.

Josh looked over at Kari's wide, hopeful eyes and smiled. "Our acquaintance has been short, but of a rather intimate nature."

"Mr. Lyman saved my life."

As always it was a surprise to hear her voice. How could any human sound be so lovely? On impulse Josh reached over and took her hand. The fingers that were so slender felt strong in his.

The doctor looked at their clasped hands and smiled benevolently. "Well, I'm glad to know this pretty young lady has someone to look out for her."

Josh dropped her hand and took a step away from the bed. He didn't know what he was thinking. He was giving the doctor, and perhaps the girl, too, the wrong impression.

"I undertook to make some inquiries on her behalf," he said stiffly. "But unfortunately, the *Atlantic*'s records are gone, and no one seems to know anything about a lone

Norwegian girl. The other Norwegian passengers who survived have already left the city."

Kari sat up straighter and pounded her hand against the bed next to her. "*Why* can't I remember?" she said, her soft voice suddenly furious with frustration.

Josh looked at the doctor. "Can you shed any light on that question, Doctor?"

The man took a moment to answer. "There are just some things that medical science doesn't know much about, I'm afraid, and memory is one of them. Why do any of us remember anything? Or why do we forget anything? We just don't know. All I can say is that she appears to have suffered no lasting hurt, and her mental abilities don't seem to be affected. Her English is beautiful."

"Maybe that can tell us something," Josh said eagerly. "Do you know, Kari, why you speak such good English?"

Kari closed her eyes as if trying to squeeze the thoughts into her brain. Finally she shook her head. "It just seems natural to me."

"In most cases of a light blow to the head, the memory loss doesn't last too long."

"How long?" Kari and Josh asked in unison.

"A few days—a few weeks. It's hard to say."

Her blue eyes held a bit of fire in them for the first time since Josh had pulled her from the bottom of the trunk. "And what am I supposed to do while I'm waiting?" she asked indignantly, looking from one man to the other. "I have nowhere to go. I have no money. I suppose I don't even have any clothes." She pulled angrily at the shapeless sleeve of her hospital gown.

The doctor looked uncomfortable and shifted nervously from one foot to the other. "Perhaps I can talk with the hospital board," he said halfheartedly. "You may be able to stay here for a while longer."

Kari's anger died as quickly as it had come. "I'm sorry," she said softly. "You both have done all you can to help me. This is my problem, and I will work it out on my own."

Josh had been surprised by her short outburst of anger. It was as if his angel had suddenly taken on flesh and blood. Color had flooded back into her face, and he felt the same hollow in his gut that he had the first day he had seen her on the pier.

"Perhaps—" He cleared his throat. This was insanity. He had enough to deal with coping with Corinne's death, the complete and utter failure of his marriage. "Perhaps you could travel with me as far as Milwaukee. That's where the Norwegian emigrants were heading. You might be able to find someone who knows you."

Kari looked guardedly hopeful. "I'm sure if I could find my people—" She stopped and looked intently into Josh's face. "But I couldn't ask you . . ."

"Milwaukee's my home," he told her gently. "I'll be going back there anyway."

"But I don't have any passage money. I . . ." She turned to the doctor. "Can I get that from the steamship company, too?"

Josh gave an impatient wave of his hand. "I'm not worried about that. I have plenty to cover our fares."

Kari tightened her lips, but instead of making them look prim, the expression only emphasized their fullness. Josh felt a little flutter inside him. "I must pay my own way," she said firmly.

"When we find your family, they can repay me."

The doctor smiled kindly at the two attractive people in front of him. The solution made perfect sense to him. "So it's settled, then?" he asked happily.

Josh raised his brows in a question to Kari. She leaned back on the bed and gave a small sigh of satisfaction. "Mr. Lyman," she said contentedly, "I think here you say...'you have a deal.'"

Chapter Three

It was crazy, Kari thought to herself, but she was actually *happy*. She was in a strange land with no money and no memory. She had no idea what had happened to her family—or if she even had a family. Yet she was feeling remarkably like singing.

She looked around the now half-empty wardroom a bit self-consciously. Josh should be coming for her any minute. For the first time she would greet him in a proper-looking dress, with her hair combed and her face scrubbed. She wished suddenly for a mirror, and at the same time came to the realization that it was an unusual wish for her. Back in Stavanger, she had never been one to be concerned about the way she looked.

Her eyes widened. *Stavanger!* She remembered the name...and all at once a flood of images—a gray stone farmhouse with a red roof, the chickens scratching at the flower garden, a boy flinging open the shutters and calling her name...and then, sharp black rocks leading down to the dark waters of the sea...the sea...the sea...

She sank onto the bed, her head swimming. Suddenly the dark waters were not the fjord at Stavanger, but a vast, black lake, and she was choking, she couldn't breathe...

"Kari!" It was Josh. His strong hands were gripping her shoulders. "Are you all right?"

The waters receded, and her eyes focused on the handsome lines of his face, bent toward hers with a worried expression. She took a deep breath.

"It's…I'm fine." One of his arms had gone around her, and she leaned into him. His body was hard and warm and immensely comforting.

"You looked so pale. I thought you were about to faint." Josh pulled her closer. It had given him a good scare to walk in and see her like that. Though he had told himself he was going to keep his distance, the overwhelming protectiveness he had felt toward her the past couple days had come back to him full force when he had seen her sitting there in such obvious distress.

"No, really. I'm fine now. I had just remembered the name of my town back in Norway. It's good, no?"

Josh looked down at her excited face. Without moving out of the reach of his arm, she turned slightly toward him. Her breasts pressed into his side. They were firm and lean, like the rest of her long body. The thought came unbidden—Corinne's had been soft and plump. He jumped back as though burned.

He tried to concentrate on what she had just said. "Your town? Well, that's just fine. It's as the doctors said—soon you'll remember everything."

He stood up and looked down at her. She was wearing a new dress, complete with petticoats that made the skirt bell out gracefully from her slender waist. Her white-blond hair was twisted into an intricate kind of braid that he had never seen before, and framed her perfect face like a golden wreath.

The way he had compared her so automatically to Corinne throbbed at his conscience. It made his voice rougher than he intended. "Are you ready to go? Is there anything more we have to do here?" He looked around for some sign of the doctor they had talked with yesterday.

Kari stood. It had felt good to be held close to him, but he had turned cold so abruptly. What was wrong with him? She remembered how he had pulled his hand sharply away from hers yesterday. Perhaps in America it was bad for people to be close. She would be careful not to anger him that way again.

"I'm ready to go," she told him, her voice low.

Neither spoke as they made their way out to the carriage he had rented for the ride to the railroad station. Kari was surprised to see a round, elderly woman already ensconced in the plush back seat.

"This is Kari Aslaksdatter," Josh told the woman. Kari hid a smile at the careful way he pronounced each syllable of her name. "Kari, this is Mrs. Hennessey, a fellow survivor of the disaster. She'll be traveling to Milwaukee with us."

Kari gave the lady one of her brilliant smiles, but was met with a look of disturbed surprise.

For a moment Mrs. Hennessey regarded the beautiful girl in front of her. "This is the emigrant you are helping, Mr. Lyman?" she asked Josh finally.

His brown eyes met hers steadily and he answered with just a hint of challenge. "Yes."

Mrs. Hennessey turned back to Kari and extended a hand to help her up into the carriage. She finally returned Kari's smile. "Forgive me, my dear. I just wasn't expecting anyone so young—" her eyes darted once more to Josh "—or so lovely."

Kari climbed up next to the older woman and gave a musical laugh. "I'm very pleased to meet you, Mrs. Hennessey, though I can't imagine that I deserve your compliments after the past few days. I feel like I have—how do you say—gotten much older in a short time.''

Mrs. Hennessey patted Kari's hand. ''Believe me, you are the loveliest thing I have seen in a long time. And such a pretty voice. Now I want you to tell me just exactly what the doctors have said about your condition.''

Josh had climbed up next to the driver and signaled him to leave. He groaned inwardly. He had forgotten just how solicitous the well-meaning Mrs. Hennessey could be. And how talkative. He had a feeling there were some things he should have discussed with Kari before they started this journey.

''...and we'll both take good care of you, won't we, Mr. Lyman?'' Mrs. Hennessey was beaming at Kari now and had assumed that motherly tone Josh had come to recognize. He didn't bother to answer as Mrs. Hennessey's cheery voice continued. Turning his head from side to side, he tried to relieve the ache in his neck. He felt as if he hadn't slept for weeks.

Kari was tired, too. She wished she were sitting alongside Josh. He looked so worn-out. She wished she could sing to him. Her father had always loved it so when she sang to him. Or was it her grandfather? The memories still darted just at the edge of her mind.

She liked the big woman at her side. But she didn't want to talk anymore. She was tired of concentrating on the English words.

''...and that's part of the reason I was surprised when I saw you, my dear—what with Mr. Lyman's wife and all—''

Kari's brain snapped to attention. *His wife?* Mrs. Hennessey stopped in midsentence at the young woman's stricken look. Josh whipped his head around to look at them both, his eyes troubled. Kari felt her new, happy world begin to dissolve like a sugarcake in the rain.

Chicago. The name seemed to give a little nudge to that cloud that was still so firmly in place over her memory, obscuring her past, her family, her very identity. What was it about Chicago? Kari pressed her fingers against her temples.

She stared anxiously out the side of the open carriage, as though expecting the bustling streets to tell her something about herself. It was alive, this place. Everyone was moving so *fast.* Everyone seemed to have places to go in a hurry—important places.

They passed a street corner where a group of men gathered in heated argument around a tall, gangly man standing on a crate. Down the next block was a marketplace, and young boys scurried up and down the aisles with their little wooden carts like so many ants on a hill.

It was the *America Book,* she thought abruptly. That's where she had heard about Chicago. Back in Stavanger. Ole Rynnig's *America Book.* They all had read it, all had dreamed about coming to the new land it talked about—a land where the sky blue lakes teemed with fish and the pines filled the air with the scent of freedom and abundance.

She could remember now...sitting on the straight-backed bench that always jutted out just so from the big stone fireplace so that you could warm yourself nicely against the winter chill without roasting on one side. She remembered long hours of sitting on that bench reading the *America Book.* Had she read it alone?

The now-familiar frustration pricked at her and she abandoned the attempt to remember more. Better to look ahead, she said to herself. They were nearing the wharf.

She could smell it in the air, not salt-sea air like home, but the definite scent of water... and fish, perhaps. She felt a strange unsettling sensation in her stomach, and knew at once that it had to do with this smell in the air and the thought of getting back on a ship. Her hands gripping the carriage rail were bloodless white.

Take a deep breath, Kari, she told herself firmly. How many times have you sailed up and down the fjord in no more than a little sailboat? She didn't like this nervousness—no, it was more than nervousness. It was fear.

She pulled her hands from the rail and placed them resolutely in her lap. That was enough of that! Why, she couldn't remember ever having been afraid of anything in her entire life. At this last thought she let out a little musical giggle. How did she know if she had ever been afraid? She could hardly remember her own name.

Josh turned toward her at the sound of her laugh. He was relieved to hear it. The girl had been so quiet during the entire train ride to Chicago. Of course, it was somewhat hard to be anything else when in the company of Mrs. Hennessey. Though Josh had welcomed the garrulous woman's presence at the ship's table with Corinne, he found himself resenting her total control of the conversation with Kari. He would have liked to have more time to talk with the Norwegian girl himself, perhaps help her to remember more about her family.

But now that it was just the two of them—Mrs. Hennessey was staying for a visit with friends in Chicago—he couldn't think of a thing to say.

"What are you laughing about?"

"Oh... just laughing at myself. I was thinking that I'm not too anxious to get on that steamer today, and wondering if back in Stavanger I was a...you know...how do you say it? In Norway we say *en reddhare*—a fraidy-rabbit?"

Josh grinned. Just seeing her smile again gave him renewed energy. He still hadn't slept much. They hadn't been able to get sleeping accommodations on the train. And the little bit of sleep he did get was troubled, full of images of Corinne with her pouting lips and two big tears running down her face . . . and then she would open her mouth and scream his name and he would try to go to her, but he was drowning, and his nose and mouth were filled with water so he couldn't move, couldn't breathe. Then he would awaken in a sweat, not at all rested, feeling more exhausted than ever.

But hearing Kari's laugh was like magic. "I can't imagine you as a 'fraidy-rabbit.'"

"I don't know. . . ." Her voice trailed off and her smile died. Something was wrong, Josh decided. Something more than the reserve she had adopted since learning that Josh had just lost his wife.

"Are you all right?" he asked her, his sense of alarm urgent and surprising. He couldn't remember ever having felt so protective toward anyone. But then, he told himself, he'd never saved anyone's life before.

"It's the ship, I guess." Kari gave a wavering smile. "I don't know if I can get back on the water again. I feel so strange."

In fact, Josh noted, little beads of sweat were forming at the edges of her wheat blond hair. Without thinking, he slipped a comforting arm around her.

"It's only a short trip," he told her. "In six hours we'll be in Milwaukee."

Her tongue ran nervously over suddenly dry lips. He could see the faint movement in her slender throat as she swallowed with effort. He had an abrupt impulse to gather her up in his arms as he had in the water that night. He hugged her closer to his side, her slim body molded to his.

"You'll be fine," he said, trying to think of the right words. "Why, you've come such a long way to be here in this country. And now, maybe you're only a few hours away from finding your family. It's no time to give up."

She straightened her back but did not pull out of his arms. "I know." Her voice was soft. "But maybe I am a little bit 'fraidy-rabbit' after all."

"Nonsense. I used to watch you out on deck in the worst of the wind, when everyone else had gone below. You looked like one of your ancestral Vikings out to conquer a new land. You weren't afraid of anything."

The words were out before he had time to think about them.

"You watched me?" Her eyes, just inches from his, were troubled. The unspoken question hovered between them. Where was your *wife* as you watched me?

Kari forced herself to leave the consoling arm and move to the cold leather corner of the carriage. At least Josh's admission had distracted her from thoughts of the impending voyage. The pounding that had begun in her head was slowing, and she could feel warmth creeping back into her fingers.

"You used to watch me on the ship—*before* that night?" she asked again.

Josh colored under the stubble that had grown since the night of the shipwreck. "I enjoy being outside a lot myself and I couldn't help noticing you. You were the most beautiful passenger on board."

He said it deliberately. If he had embarrassed her, at least it had taken away that look of fear in those bright eyes. But the confession had brought back some of his own guilt, and he was glad that the carriage was already at the checkpoint to enter the waterfront area. They could walk to the ship from here, since neither one had any luggage to worry about.

Josh helped her down from the carriage, his hands almost spanning the waist that seemed entirely too tiny to belong to the sturdy Viking he had watched at the rail of the *Atlantic.*

"Are you feeling better?" he asked her, carefully touching her arm and nothing more to escort her along the pier. He wanted to see the wariness leave her eyes.

"I think so." It was true. The beat of her heart had slowed to near-normal. Physically, she felt back in control. Thoughts of the endless lake water were gone. Instead, she was remembering the feel of Josh's arms around her in the carriage, the warmth of his body against hers, his pleasantly deep voice teasing her tenderly about being a "Viking." She had felt relaxed, happy... whole. For the first time since she left Stavanger so many weeks ago, she had felt like she was home.

Vernon and Myra Pennington were considered "old money" in the young town of Milwaukee. The Pennington fortune had unknown roots in the East, and Vernon had made it prosper, not missing an opportunity to take advantage of the rapid growth of this western gateway city.

Besides the town's biggest mercantile, he owned land all along the outskirts, which was fast being purchased for new homes. He had sizable shipping interests and had invested heavily in the Wisconsin lead mines. Josh had for some time been trying to get him interested in his lumbering operations, but so far Vernon hadn't followed his son-in-law's lead into the arena of big risk and bigger profits.

Three of the Pennington boys now worked for their father, all except Phineas, who at fifteen was still a student. Myra Pennington had wanted to send Phineas back East for his studies, since Milwaukee had yet to develop its own prep school system, but in a rare instance of opposition, the male members of the family had stood up to her, and Phineas was allowed to continue at the brick public school downtown, which Josh's brother Davey also attended.

Both boys were dying to be free from it. Phineas begged his father to let him work down at the store like Emmett and Chester. That, at least, would be better than school, Phineas told Davey with annoying regularity. Davey knew that Phineas certainly did *not* want to be cooped up in a tiny room poring over numbers all day at the Pennington offices like his brother Thaddeus. The two friends agreed that they'd done enough numbers in Miss Throckton's class to last them a lifetime, and they'd resolved that once they were finished with school, they'd not touch another one in their lives.

They really wanted to be sea captains. Phineas had given his father some hints about getting him a job with the shipping line the Penningtons partially owned, and Davey had pestered Josh about putting in a good word with some of the captains he did business with. The boys spent hours gazing out at the unknown expanse of Lake Michigan and spinning tales of what they would do once the world beyond Milwaukee opened up to them.

Of course, now all that might get delayed after what had happened to Corinne, Davey was thinking as they stood waiting at the pier for Josh's ship. Phineas said his mother hadn't stopped crying since they'd heard. Davey and his mother had gone to the Pennington house in person to bring them the news. His mother had gotten out of the carriage all by herself and had stood there looking not much heavier than a dried-up leaf. And she and Phineas's mother had hugged and hugged and hugged. It was dreadful.

He and Phineas had slipped off eventually and had headed automatically down to the waterfront. Neither boy brought up the fact that Josh's coming out of the shipwreck unhurt seemed a little odd. Weren't they supposed to save the women and children first? And the captain should be the last to leave the ship. Davey waited for Phineas to mention the rule about women and children, but he only talked about the captain. They had both solemnly agreed, as they stood looking out at the lake that terrible afternoon, that, as captains, they would definitely be the last to leave their ships, if it came to that.

The Penningtons had brought Davey with them to the dock this afternoon, as his mother was too sick to make the trip. She was mostly too sick to do anything these days, Davey reflected glumly. He knew that Phineas felt sorry for him sometimes. His mother was a lot different from Mrs. Pennington, who was *never* sick. While Mr. Pennington ran the business, working sometimes till way after dark, Mrs. Pennington ran the house—and the four boys.

Some of the boys at school were afraid of their teacher, Miss Throckton, but not Phineas. Miss Throckton was a *cupcake* compared to Mrs. Pennington, Phineas had told his friend. The Pennington children had to mind, all except Corinne, of course. With Corinne it had always been different 'cause she was a girl.

As usual, it was Phineas who spotted the ship first. Davey had often told him that if they couldn't both get ships, he'd sign Phineas on as first lookout. Phineas could spot a four-leaf clover in a whole hillside of threes, without so much as a squint.

"There she is," Phineas said quietly. Usually when Davey and Phineas came down to the docks to wait on a ship, they'd let out a whoop when they saw it coming, but

Davey didn't feel much like whooping today. Everybody looked so solemn. The four Pennington boys were all dressed in those brown serge suits they wore on Sundays, and each had an identical thick black mourning band around the right sleeve. Mrs. Pennington's cheeks were puffy, and every now and then she'd dab a crushed hanky at her eyes.

Davey tried to put himself in the Penningtons' place. What would it be like if they were all there to meet Corinne and it was *Josh* who would never be coming home? He blinked hard several times and self-consciously put his arm across Phineas's narrow shoulders as they watched the steamer pull in.

Josh was nervous. At the lumber camps he handled a dozen crises a day without breaking a sweat. He batted away problems as easily as a cow swished flies off her rump. But he'd be darned if he knew what he was going to open his mouth and say when he came face-to-face with the Penningtons.

Kari had weathered the steamer trip just fine. In fact, she looked as calm as he had seen her since they'd left the hospital in Erie. Though he noticed that she avoided looking down toward the water, she had stood bravely out at the rail and let the wind pull at the tight coils of those intricate braids she wore.

"Well, Viking, you made it. We're almost there." His smile gently teased.

Kari turned toward him—away from the water. She had been daydreaming, or remembering, perhaps...emerald green hills dotted dark with pines. It was easier than thinking about all that water below her, easier than paying attention to the constant lift and fall of the ship, which urged her stomach to revolt on every swell. She was disgusted with herself. She may not be able to remember much, but she was absolutely sure that before the shipwreck she had never been seasick as much as a moment in her entire life.

She tried to answer Josh's smile. "Have you ever heard of a seasick Viking?"

Josh laughed. "Erik the Seasick? It doesn't quite ring true, does it?"

"I may be the first one, then," she said wanly.

He was about to reassure her when the grin froze on his face. He'd just spotted the Penningtons and Davey, and what was worse... they'd spotted him.

"Who's he talking to?" Josh could almost read Phineas's lips as he turned with the question to his mother. They must all be wondering the same thing, he thought to himself guiltily. He should have thought of this before and asked Kari to wait belowdecks until he had explained the situation. Now it was too late. They'd seen him with her, *laughing* with her, for God's sake.

The normal docking delays seemed interminable, though it was less than half an hour before they were allowed to disembark. Kari held back as Josh's long legs made short work of the big step up onto the gangplank. She had seen his face when he had looked out at his relatives. At his wife's relatives, she corrected herself. He had explained to her who they all were. The Penningtons—a grief-stricken family that had lost its most cherished member.

She watched as Josh made his way down the wooden walkway toward them. He pulled back his broad shoulders and looked straight ahead at the little group awaiting him.

She didn't belong here, Kari thought sadly. Perhaps she should just melt into the crowd and make her way on her own from now on. Now that she was in Milwaukee, surely she could find some of her fellow countrymen to help her. The other passengers jostled against her as she clung to the rail in indecision.

Josh stepped briskly off the gangplank. Steeling himself against the coldness in her eyes and the traces of tears on her cheeks, he went first to his mother-in-law.

"Myra, I'm so sorry." Even to himself, the words sounded hollow. He grasped her shoulders through the fine silk of her shawl and bent to give her a kiss that was meant for her cheek but ended up in the air.

Turning, he put out a steady hand to Vernon, who returned his grip warmly after only the slightest hesitation. One by one he shook hands with the four Pennington boys. His eyes were drawn to the four black bands—five with Vernon's—and he self-consciously ran his fingers along his own bare coat sleeve. How could he have neglected to get himself a mourning band back in Erie?

The uncomfortable and formal greetings stopped when Josh reached the end of the line where Davey was standing looking young and shaken. By mutual consent the two brothers clasped each other in a tight embrace. Davey crushed his face into the shoulder of Josh's woolen coat, embarrassed to lift his head and reveal the tears streaming down his cheeks.

Josh choked back tears himself and ran his hand roughly through Davey's hair, the same rich mahogany brown as his own. "Hey, little brother" was all he said.

Phineas broke the tense wave of emotion that had gripped them all. "Who was that girl with you up on deck, Josh?" His voice quavered on the verge of manhood.

Josh pulled away from Davey and turned back toward the solemn row of Penningtons. He took a deep breath. He had to tell them about Kari. He looked around in sudden confusion. Kari—where was she? Finally, he spied her standing forlornly at the ship's rail. He raised one hand and motioned to her to join him.

"She's Norwegian—one of the surviving emigrants from the shipwreck."

The front of Myra's plum-colored dress puffed out a tad. Her eyes behind the wire-rimmed spectacles had gone from misty to steely. Josh directed his explanation to her, hoping for some maternal sympathy.

"She's lost her memory, and apparently all her immediate family were lost in the wreck. No one came to help her, and no one seems to know who she is."

It was not Myra, but Vernon who responded in his clipped tones. "How dreadful."

"Lost her memory—for real—like in the stories?" Phineas's face had brightened a shade and both he and Davey were looking up in awe at the angel-haired beauty at the rail.

"What's she doing here, Josh?" Myra asked, her shrill voice a notch higher than normal.

"I...she hopes to find some of her family, or at least some fellow Norwegians. They were all shipped here directly following the disaster."

"She ought to head over to Henrik House. That's where most of them are." Vernon, as usual, was the planner.

Myra pulled at her shawl. "She ought to head back where she belongs. There are already too many of those people here. And they don't even speak English."

Josh looked at Myra in surprise. He knew, of course, that his mother-in-law had a sharp tongue, but her present lack of charity was unusual. To him it only served as proof of what he had told himself over and over again on the way back to Milwaukee. She was devastated, perhaps altered forever, by the loss of Corinne. He couldn't imagine her ever getting over it.

"Kari speaks very good English," he said gently.

"Kari?"

"The girl—her name is Kari Aslaksdatter."

"It doesn't even *sound* American," the plump little woman said under her breath.

Josh gave his head a little shake. Poor Myra. He sighed and turned toward the gangplank. Kari had not moved from the top. With a mumbled "excuse me a moment" to the group behind him, Josh made his way toward her with long strides.

He could see at once that she was again experiencing one of those strange periods of distress. She was still gripping the side rail, but now her eyes were riveted to the water, which lapped rhythmically against the weathered wooden dock. Her face was ashen, and her chest rose and fell in quick erratic movements, as if she couldn't get enough breath.

For a moment he forgot the Penningtons and everything else except the girl in front of him. "Kari! It's all right. You're fine—I'm right here with you."

He pried her icy fingers loose from the rail and pulled her forward up onto the narrow gangplank. Kari's eyes were wide with terror as she looked over one side of the walkway, then the other. Water surrounded them.

Josh tugged her hand firmly, wanting to get her quickly down to land. He looked back toward her and felt his own panic build as he saw the deep blue pupils of her eyes dart wildly, then suddenly seem to float upward into her head. Her hand went limp in his and he almost sent them both tumbling over the side of the gangplank reaching out to catch her as she collapsed into a faint.

Using every bit of the power in his thighs, he managed to both right himself and lift her into his arms without falling over. He settled her into a comfortable position in his arms, then started slowly down toward the dock.

Almost instantly the golden lashes fluttered open. "What happened?" she asked in a near whisper.

"You fainted, Viking," Josh said gently.

"I don't faint."

He didn't argue with her. He was well aware that their little scene had made them the center of attention on the dock. He wanted to get her away from the ship, away from the water, which seemed to distress her so. He wanted to take her home.

"What are you doing with her, Josh?" Myra had planted herself firmly at the bottom of the gangplank.

"She fainted. She's still not well from a blow on the head she got in the wreck."

"Are you going to take her to Henrik House?"

"Maybe... later. Right now she needs to rest. I'm taking her home with me."

"You're taking her home! Well, I never..."

Josh stepped carefully around his mother-in-law, whose tear-swollen cheeks had developed two bright red spots. He looked down the line of astonished male Pennington faces to his brother. "C'mon, Davey. We'll hire a cab."

Kari was regaining her senses and murmured a protest, but Josh just joggled her a bit in his arms as one would a babe and told her, "Shh."

Davey stepped away from Phineas, who in a stage whisper told him, "Come over when you can."

"Thank you for coming to meet me," Josh said to the group in level tones. "I'll talk to you later, when we're all a little more settled."

Before he started toward the line of waiting rental carriages, he turned once more to Myra Pennington. Her dark brown eyes were sad and reproachful. They were Corinne's eyes.

Chapter Four

"Oh, Mr. Lyman, we're ever so glad to have you safely home again."

The maid, Daisy, had opened the big wooden door that Josh's father had had carved from native Wisconsin pine. Her sprightly little face under a hopeless tangle of curly brown hair brought a half smile to Josh's lips. Though, God knows, he didn't feel like smiling.

The meeting at the pier had been even more disastrous than he had imagined. Why hadn't he stopped to think about how he would handle Kari's arrival? Why wasn't he prepared with a proper mourning band on his suit? His last view of Myra's shaming eyes had haunted him all the way home.

Kari was quiet and still pale. He hadn't tried to talk with her, and except for a few exchanges between her and Davey, the entire ride had been silent. He could tell that she felt unwelcome and embarrassed by the encounter with the Penningtons, but he was too sick with his own remorse to offer any comfort.

Daisy's grin was like a tiny piece of sun peeping out from behind a cloud, but even it scuttled quickly behind when she took a good look at Josh's long face.

"I'm so very sorry, sir, about...Mrs. Lyman." She ducked her head and the curls bobbed.

Josh nodded. What did one say? What were you expected to say when people gave you sympathy for losing a wife—a wife of one year, whom you had completely failed to please in every respect? A friend from a carefree childhood who had taught them both that the reality of adulthood could be shattering.

"Where's my mother, Daisy?" Josh asked.

"I think she's sleeping, Mr. Lyman. She's been doing poorly...since the news."

By now Davey had pulled Kari across the brick porch and up through the big door. Daisy's brown eyes widened, and Josh sighed. "Daisy, this is Miss Kari Aslaksdatter from Norway. She'll be staying with us while we try to find some of her family here in the city."

Daisy looked in wonder from Josh back to the lovely young woman standing next to him. "Miss Ahs-lahg..." she faltered.

"Just Kari, please—if I might call you Daisy?" As usual, Kari's smile and lyrical voice had its effect. Daisy's worried expression melted into a grin of welcome.

Kari forced her tense shoulders to relax. Not everyone in this place was going to look at her with the censuring eyes that had watched her at the pier. It wasn't *her* fault that Josh had lost his wife. Or that she had lost her memory. She hadn't wanted any of this to happen. But now that she was here, she was determined to find out who she was, and get on with whatever plans had brought her halfway around the world to this strange country. She wouldn't be a bother to Josh for long, she resolved. By tomorrow she would be gone from his life. She would leave him alone to mourn his wife in peace, and he could deal with his in-laws then.

Feeling as though she had come to some kind of resolution, she once again returned Daisy's smile, then turned to Josh. "I want you to know that I understand how difficult it must have been for everyone today down at the dock. I don't intend to be a problem to you for long. Perhaps tomorrow you could take me to this Henrik House your mother-in-law mentioned, and I can see if I can stay there."

Her declaration did not appear to make Josh any happier. "We'll talk about it later."

"You can't leave so soon, Kari." Davey's newly found bass voice didn't seem to go with his gangly fifteen-year-old body. "I want to hear about the *shipwreck!*"

"Leave Kari alone, Davey," Josh snapped. "She needs to get some rest." He glared at his younger brother, who glared right back, neither one remembering that a short time ago they had wept in each other's arms.

Kari put a gentle, slim hand on Josh's right arm and Davey's left, linking them in a calming kind of circle. "Don't worry about me, either one of you." She looked up at Josh. "I'm fine now, Josh. I'd be happy to talk with Davey."

Josh felt a pounding begin in his head. His glance went from her vivid blue eyes to the mouth that was speaking in the soothing tones of a mother speaking to a child. But her full, moist lips did not make him feel as if she were his mother. All at once her light touch on his sleeve seemed to burn him, and he pulled away.

"Do whatever you want," he said curtly. "I have things to see to at my office. I'll be back later for supper."

Without another word he turned and left, pulling the big pine door shut behind him, leaving Kari, Davey and Daisy staring at it in surprise.

* * *

The soup bubbled cheerily, filling the kitchen with the rich smell of chicken and onions. Kari stepped back in satisfaction as the last of the dumplings dropped perfectly off her fork and into the pot. After days in bed at the hospital and the long trip home, it felt wonderful to have something to do again.

When Josh had left so abruptly this afternoon, an embarrassed Davey had mumbled something about needing to go find Phineas, and had run off. This left Kari with Daisy, who looked a bit at a loss as to what to do with her.

"Don't worry about me, Daisy. You go ahead and do whatever you were doing when we arrived."

The young servant girl's confusion turned to something approaching fascination as she followed the lilting words of the lovely foreigner.

"I was just about to fix Mrs. Lyman's soup." She shook her curls. "The poor lady hardly eats enough to feed a mouse these days."

"Could I help?"

Daisy looked doubtful. "Mr. Lyman said you was to rest."

"Please, I'd much rather be busy. I feel as if I rested enough in that hospital bed to last me a lifetime."

"Mrs. Lyman's soup" turned out to be a pallid broth with just enough chicken to flavor the hot water. After only a bit of gentle persuasion, Kari had convinced Daisy to let her doctor it up some.

"It can't be very interesting to eat exactly the same thing every day," Kari had said, deftly dicing a sprig of parsley. In what seemed no time at all, the soup was thick and savory, and Daisy's fascination with the new houseguest had turned to awe.

A bell jingled next to the number three in the box on the kitchen wall.

"That's her," Daisy said, jumping up from the stool where she'd been sitting, watching Kari's sure hands work with the pork rolls she had offered to prepare for dinner. She was pounding the meat flat with the heel of her hand, then soaking it in the thick cream she had scraped off the top of the milk jar and rolling it in a mixture of crumbs and spices.

Daisy took a heavy bowl out of the crockery cupboard and put it on a tray.

"May I take it up to her?" Kari asked.

Daisy looked over at her in surprise. "You really want to?"

"Yes, please." She couldn't remember, but some instinct told her that she had done this before. She had taken care of someone who was sick. Someone in her family? All she knew was that she had an overwhelming urge to meet Josh's mother and help her.

Daisy finished ladling a bowl of Kari's soup and handed it to her on a tray.

"Be my guest," she said with a grin. "One less set of stairs I'll go up and down today."

The first thing Kari thought as she opened the door was, yes, this is what it smells like—sickness. A vague touch of menthol, unwashed human odors and above all that staleness of air not stirred, breathed into only by weak lungs or hushed voices.

The room was so dark she could barely see the frail figure half-engulfed by the big feather bed. As she got closer, a face materialized through the gloom of the room, a finely boned face devoid of wrinkles. Except for the gray hair that wisped out around her in total disarray and the look of tired resignation around her light hazel eyes, Mrs. Lyman could be a young woman.

"Who are you?" The voice, too, was still young.

"I hope I didn't startle you, Mrs. Lyman. I'm helping out Daisy by bringing you your supper."

The hazel eyes lit with a spark of interest. "You don't sound American."

"I'm from Norway. I came on the same ship as your son Josh."

"Josh! Is he home?" She tried to sit up, pushing against the bed with arms that were no bigger around than a child's. Kari set the tray on the bureau and went to her side to help her. She slipped her arms around the older woman and lifted her easily into a sitting position. So many pillows crowded the bed board that Mrs. Lyman sank almost as deeply as into the feather bed. It made Kari feel claustrophobic.

"Yes, but since you were sleeping, he left to take care of some business at his office."

The sick woman smiled benevolently. "That's my Josh . . . he works so hard. He takes such good care of us all."

Kari didn't feel quite in the mood to discuss Josh with his mother. "Are you going to eat your soup in bed?"

"Yes, I usually do. By this time of day I don't have any strength left to get up to the table anymore." The resignation had come back into her eyes.

Kari eyed the soft lounging chair that sat near the closely shuttered bay window. "How about if tonight we try it over there?" she asked with just a touch of coaxing in her voice.

"You have a lovely voice, my dear." The older woman looked at her in wonder. "Who did you say you are?"

"My name is Kari. I . . . I lost track of my family in the shipwreck. Your son has kindly agreed to help me find them here in Milwaukee."

"You're going to stay here with us?" Mrs. Lyman sounded distressed as the ramifications of this surprise visitor started to come to her. "Oh, dear," she ended faintly.

Kari smiled at her calmly. "Only until tomorrow. I'm sure I'll find someplace with the other Norwegian emigrants by then. Now let's try to get you over here to eat something."

It took urging more than help, really, to get Mrs. Lyman situated in the chair. But it didn't take urging to get her to agree to let Kari open up the window. She pulled back the shutters which creaked from disuse. A fine afternoon breeze blew lightly at the tatted curtains. Mrs. Lyman looked out with pleasure at the rustling leaves of the huge oak tree that sheltered the window on all sides.

"Everyone always says I have to keep it shut, keep the drafts out," she said wistfully.

"Nonsense," Kari said briskly. "Back home we say that fresh air cures all ills."

A bit of pink had come into Mrs. Lyman's cheeks as she bent over the bowl of soup. "What is this?" she asked in wonder.

"Daisy let me make your soup tonight. I hope you don't mind."

"Mind? It smells like heaven." Moving her arm with much more strength than she had in the bed, she began to bring large spoonfuls of it to her mouth. "It's delicious."

Kari beamed. "I like to cook." The smile died. "I *think* I like to cook."

At Mrs. Lyman's questioning look, she sighed and plumped herself down on the feather bed. "I might as well tell you, Mrs. Lyman. I seem to have lost most of my memory in the shipwreck. I can remember my name, some things about home, but not much. I can't remember my family."

Mrs. Lyman looked as if she was going to say something like "how dreadful," as Mr. Pennington had on the pier today. But after a moment's hesitation, she looked Kari straight in the eye and said gently, "Well, you certainly haven't forgotten how to cook, my dear. This is the best soup I've ever eaten."

Grateful not to face any more sympathy, Kari smiled back at the older woman. "Now, you tell me about yourself. What is it that keeps you here in bed?"

Mrs. Lyman continued eating her soup for several moments before she answered. "It started after my Homer died. It's my heart, dear. I get terrible pains when I try to do too much. So I stay here shut up in this room." She closed her eyes. "And sometimes the pains come anyway."

Kari frowned. "Well, if the pains come anyway, maybe it doesn't help that much to stay all cooped up in here."

Mrs. Lyman gave her a sweet smile. "Maybe not, but nowadays I don't seem to have the strength to do much else."

Kari stayed silent. It seemed like common sense to her that if Mrs. Lyman stayed in bed all day and ate nothing but poorly flavored hot water, she wasn't going to have much strength. There didn't appear to be a problem with her appetite. She had finished the rich bowl of soup in no time at all. Kari resolved to try to get her to eat something heartier for breakfast.

"Maybe if you ate a little more, your strength would come back to you."

"My land, child, it seems that all I do is eat. I doze all day, then wake up to eat. The days can be mighty long sometimes."

Kari jumped up and pushed back the little table that held the now-empty supper dishes. Impulsively, she grasped Mrs. Lyman's hands, the fragile bones feeling like mere twigs in her strong fingers. "Would you like me to sing to you?"

Kari didn't know where the impulse had come from. She only knew that she had given comfort before during long, tedious days of sickness. The older woman's smile was answer enough and Kari sank to her knees, still holding the frail hands.

The voice that came from her throat was of such crystalline purity that it startled them both. Mrs. Lyman looked down at the young woman with amazement.

The song was a *vandringsvise,* a wandering ballad, Kari remembered, one of her favorites. The clear minor tones sounded like a flute played by a mountain creature in the mystical days of old. Her eyes closed as the haunting melody plucked painfully at chords of memory from deep within her, chords of childhood and family and love.

As the last note faded into the complete silence of the room, Kari opened her eyes, surprised to feel her lashes wet with tears.

"My Lord, girl. That was the most beautiful thing I've ever heard."

Now there was definitely pink in Mrs. Lyman's smooth cheeks, and her eyes held a sparkle that belied her invalid state. Kari felt a glow of pleasure. She had known, somehow, that her voice could bring this kind of solace. She gave Mrs. Lyman a brilliant smile.

"I'm glad," she said simply, giving the woman's cold hands a squeeze.

Before either could say more, the door to the bedroom thundered open and a breathless Davey tumbled into the room, followed by Phineas, not half a step behind.

"Was that you, Kari?" Davey gasped. "I knew it was you—we could hear you all the way out on the front stoop! Was that Norwegian? Do you know lots of songs like that? Gee whizbang, you sing like an *angel!*" At this last he shot a furtive glance at his mother to see if the slang he had used had put that "look" into her eyes. But all he saw was his mother looking happy and interested and almost *healthy* for the first time in ever so long.

Both boys straightened up in surprise to hear Davey's mother speaking to them in sturdy tones. "Mind your manners, boys. Give our visitor a chance to answer, Davey, if you're going to be pestering her with questions."

Kari let go of Mrs. Lyman's hands and gracefully stood. "It's no bother, Mrs. Lyman. I'll be happy to talk with two such handsome young men."

She smiled first at Davey, then at Phineas, who held back, a creeping flush starting at the base of his still-downy cheeks. Taking in their reaction, she turned back to Mrs. Lyman with a wink that left the older woman chuckling.

"Perhaps we should let you get some rest, now, ma'am," Kari said in a more serious voice.

"You know, my dear, I think I'll just sit here a while more and look out at my oak tree. I'd forgotten how beautiful it is."

Kari gathered up the tray and, with a nod at Mrs. Lyman, ushered the two boys out of the room. She closed the door gently behind her, then paused to smile as through it she heard the faint humming of the Norwegian *vandringsvise.*

* * *

The stable boy was nowhere to be seen, and Josh sighed as he hefted the saddle off his big black gelding. He was bone tired and still disturbed about his encounter with the Penningtons that morning. Now, he supposed, he had the household to deal with—as usual. His mother had been less and less able to handle the duties of mistress of the house since the death of his father and the beginning of her failing health. And bringing his new bride into the house had not helped matters appreciably. Corinne had spent the majority of her time back at the brick mansion over on State Street where life could revolve around her instead of the needs of an invalid mother-in-law. Josh had not objected—at least spending time with her family made her happy, which was something *he* wasn't able to do.

But it left the burden of running the house, as well as the business, to Josh. Daisy was better than some of the hired help he had worked with. At least with her, he knew his mother would be seen to. Daisy was quite fond of his mother. In the rest of the house, the fires may not be lit, and Davey might be scrounging the kitchen for his supper, but Josh could rest assured that Mrs. Lyman would have been served the weak chicken broth that seemed to be all her delicate stomach could handle these days.

Josh walked out of the Lyman carriage house and looked down the hill toward the town stretched out below him. The new gas lighting gave it a merry glow—like the candles on a Christmas tree. It was late. He hoped that Davey had for once started in on his lessons without prompting.

Daisy was in the kitchen. She hadn't yet left to sneak the back way down the hill to meet the Fultons' driver, Charles. There was, then, at least hope that he might get some hot food. In fact, he noted as he shut the flimsy kitchen door behind him, something bubbling on the stove smelled *wonderful*.

"Good evening, Daisy. What *is* that you're cooking?" He moved toward the savory smell like a wild animal stalking prey.

Daisy turned with a grin. "You're home, Mr. Josh. Just in time." She pulled her shoulders up in mock dignity, and affected her idea of a British accent. "Supper will be served at eight."

The pose made her starched apron ride up ridiculously around her neck, and she ended with a giggle. Josh merely stared in wonder. Normally by this time of day, Daisy was either gone to spark with her beau or, if she had been requested to stay, was out of sorts with the world. The pattern over this last long year had been that he arrived home to find the house dark, the kitchen barren and cold, Corinne already shut up in her bedroom, Davey hungry and his mother tossing restlessly in a disturbed sleep, which only calmed when he spent a few moments stroking her forehead.

"Where's Miss Asla—our visitor?" The beautiful Norwegian hadn't been off his mind all afternoon.

"She's in the parlor helping Davey with his sums, I think. And your mum's tucked away sleeping like a babe. I declare, she ate enough of Miss Kari's soup to feed one of your lumber camps." She beamed at him and the curls, which by this time of day snarled in confusion around her head, swayed from side to side.

Josh shook his head in wonderment, went through the swinging door to the hall and headed toward the front parlor. He could tell from the flickering glow coming through the parlor's glass French doors, which had been his mother's pride back when she cared about such things, that a fire had been lit against the early fall chill.

It took him a moment after quietly opening the doors to the room to find its occupants. The parlor was furnished with an elegant sofa, settee and chairs that his father had ordered from Boston just before the epidemic of '49. They had arrived in time for his funeral. At the moment, all were empty.

Finally, his eyes drawn to the fire, he saw Davey and Kari, each curled up on the floor like a kitten, their two heads bent together over one of Davey's schoolbooks.

He had just a moment to admire the graceful curve of Kari's back and imagine the curve extending down below all those petticoats before Davey looked up.

"Josh, look! This is where Kari comes from...Sta-van-ger. It's right here on the map in my book. She had to cross the whole ocean and it took ever so long and she'll probably never go back, never see her home again. Can you imagine? She's been telling me all about it!"

Kari straightened up, the firelight heightening the slight flush that crept over her cheeks.

"Are you remembering more?" Josh asked her.

She shook her head. "Little pieces. I remember Stavanger. I can picture the hills, the farms. *Our* farm, I think. But not more."

"She doesn't remember much, Josh, but she's *real* smart. Smarter than Miss Throckton, even."

Josh smiled. Davey had long nourished tender feelings for his attractive young teacher. "I thought you were going to rest," he said chidingly to Kari.

She stood and shook out her skirts. "I wasn't tired."

Davey jumped up beside her. "She wasn't tired, Josh," he parroted. "Golly, she made soup and some rollie things for supper and a *pie* and she helped Daisy scrub the whole kitchen and she sang to mother—holy moly, Josh, you should hear her sing—and then she helped me and Phineas with our geometry, and it wasn't that hard after all, and then—"

Josh put up a hand. "All right, Davey, I get the idea—she wasn't tired," he said dryly. "Now how about if you gather up your books and take yourself off to bed. There'll be chores in the morning before school."

Davey's smile dimmed, but he turned back to Kari with a look of adoration. "G'night, Kari," he said, a little shyly now after his prior enthusiasm.

Kari had the impulse to give him a good-night kiss on the cheek, but she held back, uncertain about Josh's reaction. He still stood by the parlor doors, out of the immediate ring of firelight, and all she could see was his tall frame and his dark hair falling in a disheveled wave across his forehead.

"Good night, Davey," she said softly, smiling at the boy as he scooped up his books and clattered out of the room. The silence he left behind him quickly grew awkward. Kari wished Josh would say something, instead of just looking at her in that intense way she had noticed once or twice before.

"I've fixed you some supper," she said finally.

Josh moved then, stepping into the circle of light. "It appears that I owe you some thanks," he said quietly. His dark eyes gleamed and the reddish glow of the fire flickered over the strong lines of his face.

Kari's breath caught in her throat. "I . . . it was nothing," she managed to say.

Josh was only inches from her. He reached a hand out to her flushed cheek. "Are you feeling all right now?"

"Yes, thank you. I don't know what happened there on the pier. But now I'm fine." Her voice sank to almost a whisper. Her cheek burned under the touch of his cool fingers. "Just fine."

The blood was pumping again in his loins. Josh moved his eyes from her lustrous blue ones down to where the fabric of the store-made dress she'd been given in Erie strained across her firm breasts. The modest neckline gave him just a glimpse of soft, white neck. His body pounded.

Self-consciously, Kari took a step back. "I should be fine now to try to make my way on my own," she said. "Tomorrow I'll be leaving. I don't want to cause you any more problems...like today at the docks." Her full mouth turned downward. It looked moist and red in the firelight, and Josh wanted fiercely to taste it.

"Are you hungry?" Kari said falteringly, when he didn't speak.

A rough chuckle escaped him. "Yes, Viking," he said sardonically, "I am. But let's go have supper instead."

Kari looked perplexed at the twisting of words, but made no comment as Josh held the doors for her to pass before him across the hall to the dining room.

Picking up matches from the sideboard, Kari lit the table sconces. They flared to life revealing a table elegantly set with his mother's sterling and leaded crystal. Josh couldn't even remember the last time they had used them. A dark red wine was already decanted and Josh reached for it immediately upon taking his seat. His hand shook slightly as he poured them each a glass, and he tried to convince himself that it was from fatigue.

The words Kari had spoken in the parlor sifted into his consciousness.

"So what's this about leaving tomorrow?" he asked her.

Kari looked up at him, her golden lashes darkened in the candlelight. "I feel I should go, Josh. You've been more than kind to me, but now I must find my people, try to find out about my family."

"Of course, that's why you're here. We'll start inquiries tomorrow. But in the meantime, you're staying here."

Kari didn't reply for a moment, then said sadly, "This is a house of mourning, Josh. It's not proper for me to be here. Already, I think, I have been the cause of more hurt to...to the family of your wife."

Josh finished his wine in a long swallow. "It may be a house of mourning, but it is *my* house. I'll say what's proper." Faced with her irrefutable logic, he perversely changed the decision that he had made during his long hours at his office—which had been to find a place for her the next morning at Henrik House. Now, suddenly, he was determined that she would stay. At least until they found out something about her family.

Kari smiled, treating Josh to that singular radiance that started at her mouth and gradually spread over her entire face. "You are a very special man, Josh Lyman."

Josh didn't feel special. He felt tired and confused and underneath it all, the vague frustration of thwarted desire. Was he crazy to insist that she stay with him? Could he live in the same house with this woman who so stirred his senses, and still honorably give Corinne the time of memory and mourning that was her due?

He sighed. "It's settled, then. Tomorrow we'll pay a visit to Henrik House and see what we can find out."

Perhaps, he thought as he reached for the wine bottle, they would find their answers immediately. Perhaps by this time tomorrow night she would be with her family—laughing and loved. And he would be left in peace to mourn the ghost of a marriage that should never have been.

Chapter Five

Henrik House was a rambling clapboard structure that looked much better put together from inside than out. The receiving parlor was scrupulously clean, the pine floor gleaming almost white around several small rugs with cheerfully colored Scandinavian designs.

The middle-aged woman who had answered their knock looked with bright curiosity at the attractive couple as she ushered them into the parlor. She listened to the brief explanation Kari gave in Norwegian, then smiled and motioned them to take a seat and wait.

"What did you tell her?" Josh asked. He hadn't anticipated that the people here wouldn't speak English. He was so used to taking charge of every situation that it put him ill at ease to have Kari handle everything. Not that he doubted her ability to do so. The tone of her words to the woman had sounded calm and direct.

Kari smiled at him, and gave his gloved hand a pat, as though sensing his discomfort. "She's going to bring a Mr. Grindem. He lives here, and appears to be some sort of leader of the Norwegian community."

Snowy-haired and pink-cheeked, Mr. Grindem resembled a Dickensian woodcut of Father Christmas. He smiled at Kari and shook hands with Josh, adding a jovial greeting in Norwegian. Josh bit his lip in chagrin that he couldn't even reply to a simple salutation.

For the first few minutes Josh felt almost as lost as he had in the cold waters of Lake Erie. Kari and Mr. Grindem were carrying on a lively conversation. Kari was leaning forward eagerly, her face lovely in its animation as she plied her countryman with questions.

Finally the old gentleman held up a hand to halt her interrogation. He looked over at Josh and spoke in English. "You do not speak Norwegian, sir?"

Josh shook his head and tried to ease the frustration out of his reply. "No, I'm sorry."

"No reason to be sorry, young man. This is your country, after all. We're the ones who have to learn." His English was heavily accented, unlike Kari's, but the cadence of his speech sounded much like hers, which Josh had grown to enjoy during their days together.

"I wouldn't mind learning a bit of Norwegian myself," Josh replied. "I've just never thought about it before."

Mr. Grindem's faded blue eyes twinkled. "Now you're thinking about it, eh? Wonder why that is?" He glanced at Kari and gave her a wink. "Well, anyway, back to business. This pretty lady here is telling me that she needs to find out about her family."

The older man's smile faded and the mouth tucked in the wispy white beard became grim. "Terrible tragedy— that *Atlantic*. There are a lot of families who lost loved ones on that ship. 'Twas a terrible tragedy."

For a moment the man seemed lost in a dream as he sat shaking his head slowly from side to side. Josh shifted his feet impatiently. "But what about the survivors? We heard they came here to Milwaukee. Where can we find them?"

The old man looked at Kari, his eyes full of sympathy and the mistiness of age. "The ones I know about moved directly on to Madison and some of the other settlements thereabouts.''

Kari's face fell and Josh felt a strange constriction in his chest. He wanted to reach out to her, but instead addressed himself to the old man. "None of them stayed in Milwaukee?"

"Oh, well, I suppose some did—I just don't know of any. There aren't any here at Henrik House, that's for sure. Most of them took their subscriptions and moved right along to their new homes.''

"Their subscriptions?"

"Didn't you know? The city of Milwaukee gave each of the survivors eleven dollars. 'Twas a kind and generous thing, for the poor devils had been left with nothing, nothing at all.''

The head started to shake again and Josh felt the old man slipping away. They waited politely in silence for several moments, then Kari sat up straight with a determined look on her face. "I was one of those people who lost everything, Mr. Grindem. Can I get this 'subscription,' too?"

"I don't see why not." He stopped shaking his head.

"And would it be enough to get me out to the settlements?"

"You wouldn't need even that. The *Atlantic* survivors were allowed to go west free of charge on the steam train."

Kari's lovely cheeks took on the flush of excitement. "That's what I need to do, then."

Josh reached over and took one of her slender hands. "Hold on there, lass. You still don't know where your family went or even—" he paused to stroke the back of her hand gently with his thumb "—if they survived. You can't just take off west without knowing anyone there, without knowing exactly where you're going."

"Well, I'm not finding out any answers here." Her full lips pressed together firmly.

Mr. Grindem forestalled Josh's further protest. "Perhaps we could send word about your case out to the settlements, my dear, see what we can find out."

Josh looked gratefully at the old man. "That's a very sensible suggestion."

Calmly and with a quickness belying his years, Mr. Grindem took Kari through all the information she could provide. He promised the couple that before the week was out, he would have messages sent to each of the new little communities that strung out to the west in a trail of Scandinavian footprints reaching all the way to Minnesota.

With Mr. Grindem's and Josh's assurances that the inquiries were sure to produce some results, Kari reluctantly agreed to return to the Lyman house and wait. The carriage ride home was quiet. Josh knew that Kari was disappointed that they hadn't found out more information. As they settled together at his desk in the back parlor to discuss their morning, he set himself to cheer her up.

"I felt like an idiot there at the beginning," he said, trying to inject humor into his voice. "I guess I've heard some of the fellows at the camp talking Norwegian amongst themselves, but I was never part of the conversation. It's disconcerting to have someone talking to you in a normal, human voice, and you can't understand a word they say."

"I know. I'm sure many of the people coming to this country feel the same way, as if you've suddenly gone to another world—everything is alien." The determination that had been in Kari's voice at Henrik House was lacking.

"We'll find out something soon, Kari," he said gently. "I know it." She looked so beautiful sitting there across from him. Her shoulders were pulled back in a heart-breaking facade of bravery, but her big blue eyes were swimming. All at once a teardrop escaped its trough and made its way down her cheek.

"Oh, my little Viking, don't cry." Josh couldn't hold himself back. In two long steps he rounded his desk and drew her up out of her chair and into his arms. The late-morning sun sent hazy rays into the dim library. Her eyes looked impossibly blue, and her mouth trembled just inches from his.

"Don't cry," he whispered again and touched his lips to hers. The kiss was as light as a breath, but that was all it took. A molten flare seared through his middle. A sound came from low in his throat and he tightened his hold, deepening his search of her mouth. Feelings that had lain dormant the past long year of his marriage ran riot through his body.

Kari's lashes closed over the brimming tears. Her head was spinning. Suddenly, after days of bearing the burden of loneliness and uncertainty, Josh's strong arms around her felt irresistibly comforting. Then, as his lips expertly opened hers, all the sensation of her body seemed to converge on her mouth and tongue.

Her limbs went limp and she felt herself held up by the warm pressure of his body against hers. A slow heat developed at the center of her abdomen and began radiating downward in steady strokes. "Josh," she breathed as he pulled his mouth away. Without her knowing, her arms had gone around him and her hands spread flat against the hard muscles of his back.

In the dim light, his features looked angular and stern, his hair richly dark. His brown eyes flashed with a fire she'd never seen before. He watched her like a seabird waiting to swoop, then caught her up even more closely against his rock-hard chest and claimed her mouth once more.

This time Kari found herself answering his demands as his tongue awakened hers in a primeval call. She couldn't remember, of course, she thought to herself, if she had ever experienced this before, if she had kissed . . . or loved. But the havoc being wreaked throughout her body was at once as new as a sunrise and as old as the sky.

Josh knew with absolute certainty that he had not in his entire life felt sensations like the ones now racing through him. He had known lust—arousal and swift, fierce pleasure. But this was . . . need, raw senses laid open to the elements, bare to the abrasions of life, which now sought succor and release and . . . peace.

He moved his mouth along her high cheekbones, then down, following the fine line of her jaw. Between the spirals of her braid his fingers sought entry to her silken crown of hair. His heart pounded a tattoo of desire.

"Lordy!"

Kari and Josh jumped as though hit by a bucket of water.

Daisy was at the door, face flaming. "I—I'm sorry, Mr. Josh, Miss Kari. The door was ajar and . . ."

Of the three, Josh was the first to regain his composure. He dropped his arms and took a long step back from Kari, willing his blood to resume its normal pace through his veins. "What is it, Daisy?" he asked evenly.

"Y-you have a visitor. In the front parlor."

Josh frowned as he looked over at Kari, whose head was tucked down in embarrassment. He couldn't see her eyes, and he somehow desperately had to know that she wasn't angry with him. Even with the sensations they had felt together still running rampant through his body, he recognized that he had been wrong to kiss her. He had taken advantage of her unhappiness over not finding her family. He hadn't meant to—it had happened without thought, but it had been wrong.

He longed to move close to her, to turn her face up to his and look into the endless blue of her eyes. He wanted to see her smile and know that things were still well between them. "Who is it, then?" he said with a touch of impatience.

"It's your father-in...ah, that is, it's Mr. Pennington, sir."

Josh's eyes closed. He could well imagine what his father-in-law had come to see him about after the scene at the pier yesterday. Josh had planned to visit the Penningtons today to pay his respects and smooth over any hard feelings. But he had felt that it was more important to get Kari to Henrik House first. Now Vernon was here in his house, just a room away from where he had been that close to dishonoring Corinne's memory in the most direct possible way.

"Tell him I'll be with him shortly," he told Daisy.

Kari had straightened up, her shoulders pulled back in that stiff way he had come to recognize when she was facing something disagreeable. But her eyes still did not meet his.

"I'm sorry," he said softly.

She shook her head.

"It was my fault." Josh fumbled for the words. "I shouldn't have...I'm sorry," he ended finally, running his fingers back through his thick hair.

He knew his apology was inadequate. He *was* feeling sorry and guilty as hell, but he wished he could also tell her what it had felt like to kiss those full pink lips that were now clenched so tightly, as if holding back a sob. He wished he could tell her that she made his insides turn to

warm tallow and swelled his heart so that his chest felt as
if it would burst. But telling her would only make things
worse. He had no right to tell her, had even less right to
touch her.

"I guess I'd better go and see what my...visitor wants."
He made one last attempt. "Please don't fret yourself,
Kari."

He waited a moment for her to look up with a glance of
forgiveness or regret or understanding...or even anger. But
she only stood there, the sun's rays catching just the tip of
those long golden lashes as they hid her eyes from his view.
To hell with it, then, he thought in sudden exasperation.
He turned on his heel and left her standing there in the
middle of the room.

Several minutes later the heat had still not dissipated
from Kari's cheeks. She had fled to the privacy of her
bedroom—the room that had been Corinne's—and sat
perched on the high bed, her shoulders sagging under the
weight of her gloom.

Josh's kisses had been wonderful. She would never forget them...or him, she admitted to herself. But for this
next year of mourning he, his house, his family—they all
belonged to the memory of another woman. She had no
place here, no *honorable* place, she corrected herself as her
cheeks flushed anew, remembering how easily she had responded to him. She had not even protested when he'd
kissed her, had instead welcomed his caresses, had actually returned them.

For a fleeting moment she wondered if she had been,
perhaps, a woman of easy virtue back in her own country.
Her surrender had been that immediate. But deep inside
her she knew, somehow, that she had never before known
this feeling with another man. It was *because* it was Josh

that she had lost all sense of propriety and dignity. She tried to tell herself that she had been vulnerable, depressed, and that he had taken her by surprise, but she knew that none of those things had mattered when his lips had touched hers.

She couldn't speak for what might happen if they ever touched hers again.

She jumped off the bed, her resolution stamped on her face. Her first decision yesterday had been the right one all along. She couldn't stay here. She could well imagine the scene that was occurring right this moment in the parlor between Josh and his father-in-law. Josh had his obligations, his family, his world . . . and she had to set about finding hers.

She paced nervously, trying to decide how to proceed. Her first thought was to return to Henrik House and ask them to help her obtain the subscription money and passage west. The only problem with that plan was that Josh might look for her there. She didn't want that, didn't want to be any more trouble to him. She needed to simply disappear from his life completely and allow him peace to deal with his grief.

Finally she decided to walk to town, find out directions to the city offices and ask for the subscription money herself. With eleven dollars she could find lodging for the night and buy herself some clothes and personal items to supplement the little she had been given at the hospital back in Erie.

She crept downstairs and quietly crossed the hall. She hesitated for several moments at the big wooden front door. Perhaps she secretly wished that Josh would appear and stop her from leaving, she thought to herself. But the drone of male voices coming from behind the glass doors to the parlor rose suddenly in intensity and without further deliberation she twisted the ornate handle and slipped outside.

"Did you love my daughter, Josh?"

Josh was taken aback by the direct question, though his father-in-law had never been one to mince words.

"Of course." Josh saw no point in trying to cage his reply in terms that would have made it closer to the truth. He *had* loved Corinne in a way. She had been a part of his life almost since he could remember. Petite, pretty Corinne. There hadn't been a male under sixty in town who hadn't put an eye on her as she flounced along downtown in her ruffled dresses, her dainty, imported bonnets ensuring the protection of that peaches-and-cream complexion. He'd been proud to know that he was the one whose glances she returned—mighty proud to think that one day she was going to be *his* wife.

Where had it started to go so wrong? When she had turned him out of her bedroom, that first night, could he have done something to change things? Should he have let her continue to bar their door night after night as he slept on the cot in the dressing room so that the rest of the family wouldn't know their secret? Perhaps he should have smashed down the door and forced her to acknowledge their marital relationship instead of finding excuses and taking off to spend most of that long winter at the camps.

"It's just that . . . sometimes I found myself wondering, Josh. Corinne was a very delicate girl, very special, and she—" The older man's voice cracked. "Sometimes I just wondered, is all."

Josh looked down at his callused hands, the hands Corinne had recoiled from time and again. "Corinne was not always as happy as I would have liked during our time together, Vernon. I'll always regret that. But I can assure you that I . . . I cherished her."

Mr. Pennington pushed himself up out of the oversize cushions of the fancy Eastern sofa, stood and turned to face Josh. He looked stooped and older than his fifty-two years. "I know, son. I believe you did. If I thought otherwise I . . . I don't know what I'd do. But if you cherished Corinne, what in *tarnation* are you doing with that foreigner you brought back with you?"

Josh felt at a disadvantage seated, staring up at the distraught man. "I didn't *bring* her back with me." Even to himself, his tone sounded defensive. "I explained at the docks . . . she's looking for her family. She just needed a place to stay. That's all there is to it."

Vernon looked at his son-in-law without speaking, his gray eyes steady, sad and accusing. Josh felt himself flushing. Just moments ago in the library there had certainly been a lot more *to it* than that. He felt as if the older man could read his mind. Standing, he faced his father-in-law directly.

"Miss Aslaksdatter will only be here until we find out where her relatives or friends are settling. Then she'll be moving west to join them. I have no wish to make you and Myra unhappy, but it seemed to me that helping this girl was simple, human decency."

Self-consciously he rubbed the black band that he had hastily donned before joining Vernon in the parlor. It burned like a brand around his sleeve. He spoke slowly and forcefully. "This household is in mourning for Corinne. I will regret until the day I die that I was not able to bring her back to you."

Pennington seemed to find a degree of satisfaction in Josh's words, but his voice remained reproachful. "Myra took to her bed after we met you at the docks yesterday. She's some upset.''

"Yes, I could see that, and I'm sorry. I was planning to pay you a call today."

"I'd appreciate it, Josh." Again the older man's voice took on an uncharacteristic quaver. "We still consider you one of our sons, you know."

A lump had formed just below his Adam's apple, and Josh felt a sudden need to get out of the stuffy parlor and breathe some fresh air.

"I'll head back with you now, if you like."

For the first time all morning, Pennington's straight lips turned upward. "I'd like that, Josh," he said.

Kari was exhausted, and halfway ready to admit that Josh had been right—the shipwreck and blow on her head *had* taken a toll on her. It was true she had been walking all afternoon, but she had those vague memories of scampering up and down the mountains around Stavanger and in none of them did she remember feeling this tired.

It had been a discouraging day. The good people of Milwaukee, who had so warmly pooled their resources to help the survivors of the *Atlantic,* had by now, as was only human, returned to their everyday lives, leaving discussion of the disaster to the old salts in the taverns around the waterfront, who were the self-appointed minstrels of the tales of the Lakes.

At the city offices, after telling her story time and again, Kari had been relegated to the desk of an ascetic-looking young man who swore that he knew absolutely nothing about any subscription money for *Atlantic* survivors. He suggested, rather pointedly, that there might even be some question about the legality of her being here in Milwaukee on her own, and that she had better as soon as possible find herself a *male* guardian, a husband or otherwise responsible person to take her in hand.

Her last hope was the newspaper office. If they could not give her any information about the city's generosity to the shipwreck victims, she would have to give up and make her way to Henrik House. There she was sure Mr. Grindem would at least give her a place to stay. And if Josh came after her, she would just have to deal with it. The truth was that after an afternoon on her own, feeling foreign and out of place, the thought of Josh's friendly smile made the tears smart in her eyes.

With the final deadline for the morning edition still a couple of hours away, the offices of the *Milwaukee Daily Sentinel* were quiet. The man at the reception desk looked idly up as the door jingled open, then straightened in his chair at the sight of the tall, attractive blonde with no bonnet on her strangely styled hair.

"Can I help you, miss?" His eyes swept down the length of her shapely figure. With plump fingers he rolled a pencil back and forth across the blotter.

"I'm looking for some information."

"This ain't the library, lady." He stood, his considerable bulk settling around his waist. "What didya wanna know about?"

"Um—it's about the shipwreck—" She had just started to launch into her tale for what seemed like the hundredth time today, when the door of the room directly in back of the clerk smashed open and a boy ran out, followed in irate haste by a man in shirtsleeves.

"Thompson—it's that kid again! Caught him sleeping back behind the printing presses. Grab 'im."

Kari stood in bewilderment as the chaotic scene played itself out in front of her. Two grown men chased after the slight form of a boy, whose wheat-colored hair stuck out every which way from beneath a battered sailor's cap.

The youth disappeared under the flimsy wooden rack that displayed the week's papers. Flying newsprint marked his progress toward the front door where Kari was still standing, a strange whirring beginning inside her head.

His shoe dragging a torn piece of newspaper, the shirt-sleeved man pushed her aside and positioned himself to meet the fugitive as he emerged from the pyramid of papers. "I've got him!" he cried, his big hands closing around the stick-thin arms of the boy.

His shove put Kari off balance, and she swayed. The buzz in her head grew louder as she looked over at the obviously scared youngster now held firmly in the man's grasp. She felt sick, confused—the way she had in the hospital in Erie, and again on the ship. She could feel her eardrums pulsating.

The boy wriggled helplessly, his grimy hat spinning off to the floor. He glared furiously as he looked up at his captor, then dropped his jaw in astonishment as his gaze shifted to the young woman standing by the door.

"Kari!" he breathed.

The name sounded in her head as though from far away, competing with the throb in her ears. For an endless moment she looked into the boy's cornflower blue eyes...then let the darkness take her as she fell heavily backward against the solid frame of the door and slid to the floor.

Josh's well-ordered life, which had started to skew one year before the fatal night on Lake Erie, seemed to have completely turned upside down in the last few days. He stood in the street next to a horse trough, heedless of the busy downtown traffic, and admitted to himself that for once he didn't know what to do next.

He had been sure that Kari would be at Henrik House. But even with the language barrier between them, there was no mistaking that the stout little woman, the same one who had greeted them earlier in the day, had told him that Kari had not returned there. With vehement shaking of head and hands, she had most emphatically denied any knowledge of the girl.

Then, in response to an unknown impulse, he had decided to make inquiries at the newspaper office, but though they had all been speaking English at the *Daily Free Democrat,* it seemed he was communicating even more poorly than he had with the Norwegian woman back at Henrik House. The reporters he talked to looked up and down the tall, well-dressed gentleman and gave him polite smiles under cynical eyes. He was looking for a young woman who had—ah—run away from him? You say she was attractive, sir? And exactly what was your relationship to this—ah—young woman?

Damn! Where could she have taken herself off to? It was all his fault, of course. He had practically forced himself upon her this morning as she stood there in tears, unhappy and lonely. He ought to be shot.

The rival *Milwaukee Daily Sentinel* was just down the block, but Josh doubted he would have any more success there than he had had at the *Democrat.* Still, he wandered toward it aimlessly, berating himself, and vowing that if he did find Kari, he would not get within six feet of her until he saw her safely reunited with someone who knew her.

Lost in thought, it took Josh several moments to realize that there was some sort of commotion going on at the door of the *Sentinel* offices. A police officer was standing just outside, listening patiently to a man in shirtsleeves, who waggled a finger inches from the officer's nose. Inside the door, another man was kneeling over something and at the same time trying to hold back a young boy whose grimy face was streaked with the cleaner trails of fresh tears.

"My sis-ter, my sis-ter." The lilt of the boy's words caught Josh's attention.

Around the bulk of the kneeling man, Josh recognized a pale blue dress, and all at once the picture snapped together in his head. With several long strides he ran up to the group.

There, half in and half out of the front door, lay Kari, her face pale, her eyes just beginning to flutter open. Josh pushed aside the kneeling man and lifted her against his chest. His heart thudded. She had fainted again, or had had one of her spells, or whatever the hell they were. But she was breathing. Even now the color was beginning to return to her satin-smooth cheeks.

The shirtsleeved man had stopped his monologue and he and the policeman were both staring down at the newcomer. The boy had renewed his struggles against the bulky man. Without any noticeable effect, he beat a small fist against his captor's hamhock forearm. Suddenly, with a quick twist of his slender body, he was free and turned his attention to Josh.

"Leave my sis-ter. I say leave her." The ineffectual blows now rained on Josh's back. Josh smiled. The high-pitched words matched Kari's cadence exactly. The world which had been so off kilter just a few moments ago seemed to be righting itself. Kari was safe…and they had, evidently, just found her a brother, someone to open doors, solve the mystery that had plagued them.

Without loosing his hold on Kari, he half turned toward the boy. "Whoa there, son. I'm a friend of your sis-ter."

If there had been any doubt about the relationship, it was erased as he found himself looking into clear blue eyes with dark gold lashes—Kari's eyes, the same eyes that had haunted him since that day in Montreal when he had first laid eyes on her. And this, then, was the boy he had seen her with. Her brother.

"Kari's my friend," he repeated, as those blue eyes glared their hostility.

The blows slowed, then stopped. The glare softened marginally. "What's wrong with her, then?"

Josh put all his considerable charm into a reassuring smile. "I think she'll be fine. She's just fainted. It's from hitting her head in the shipwreck."

"What's goin' on here?" The heavyset man grabbed the boy's bony shoulder with a grip that made the youngster wince. "This kid's been hangin' around here, sleepin' in the back. We want him turned over to the law."

The police officer watched placidly. His expression held the forbearance of one who dealt day in and day out with such skirmishes.

Josh had shifted his attention once again to Kari, whose eyes were now open, still dazed, but coming quickly back to reality. Her voice was husky. *"Arne?"*

A smile broke over the young boy's face and he let loose a flood of Norwegian. All four men listened in bewilderment, but Kari struggled to sit up, her face lustrous.

"Arne!" she said again as the boy slipped once more from his captor's grasp and sank down to throw himself into his sister's arms. The two bright blond heads rocked in unison at the force of his embrace.

Josh sat back, a grin of satisfaction on his face, feeling as though he had just untangled the worst logjam of the season.

Finally, Kari pulled away and turned her face toward him. "Josh, this is my brother—my brother Arne!" The radiance of her smile sent tingles along his skin.

"What's goin' on here?" the man who had been holding Arne growled once more.

Josh turned to him with a silly grin on his face. "He's her brother!"

With a sorting out of legs and elbows, the three people on the floor managed to rise, the shirtsleeved man began speaking in a much lower volume and the police officer tipped his hat to the pretty young lady and said, "Are you all right now, miss?"

The various parties took turns relating their versions of the recent events, and finally Josh turned to the shirtsleeved man and in his most authoritative voice asked brusquely, "Is the boy responsible for any damages?"

"Well . . . I guess not, but he's been pesky as a—"

"Then, Officer, if we are free to go, I will take Miss Aslaksdatter and her brother to my home, where they are presently my guests."

The police officer shrugged and nodded, and before anyone could argue, Josh took Kari's arm in one hand and Arne's in the other and led them firmly down the street. He stopped only when they were out of earshot of the group still gathered in front of the newspaper.

"Are you feeling all right, Kari?" he asked her then. Her cheeks were unnaturally flushed.

"Oh, Josh, it's wonderful. We've found Arne, and I remember! I remember leaving home, getting on the ship back in Norway, and what a long way it was." Her melodious voice bubbled with happiness.

On his other side, Arne fidgeted in Josh's grasp until he let him go. The boy gave a surprisingly forceful shrug against Josh's chest and stepped past him to once again enfold his sister in his pint-size embrace. Josh was taken aback for just a moment, but he was so pleased by the turn of events that he stepped back with an understanding smile and let the brother and sister have their reunion in peace.

The Norwegian words sounded strangely musical, especially in Kari's beautiful tones—the boy-soprano voice of her brother somewhat less so.

Finally, the flow stopped and the boy took a reluctant step toward Josh. He held out a small hand. The pitch dropped several steps as he said solemnly, "Kari says I must to thank you for helping her."

Josh shook the boy's hand firmly and without a smile. In spite of the foreign sound to the words, the lad looked not much different than Davey during one of those oh-so-serious times when he was giving manhood a trial run.

"I was happy to help, Arne. And we're both mighty happy that we found you. Your sister has been very lonely these past few days."

The boy nodded, his duty done, then moved deliberately between Josh and Kari and took the arm that Josh had been holding. He came just above her shoulders, but held himself straight and proud and Josh bit back any comment. Kari looked well enough to walk on her own now, and, even if she weren't, it seemed that she had found herself a new protector.

Chapter Six

Kari didn't know if it was the fainting spell or all the memories that tumbled over one another within her head. Something had made her utterly tired. She could hardly mount the stairs to the brick porch when they reached the Lyman home.

Finally Josh had insisted, after ironically asking permission of her little brother, on lifting her in his arms and carrying her up to her bedroom.

"There's time enough to talk later," he had said with a no-argument look in his eyes.

And, much as she wanted to help Arne with his introduction to this new household, Kari couldn't manage to resist the soft comfort of her bed.

Now she was feeling better, feeling better actually than she had since before the disaster. No more cloud. Her life stretched out behind her with a kind of crystal clarity, which she now realized that she had never before appreciated.

With the memories came renewed pain—those last months by her father's bedside. His dying request that his children fulfill his dream of reaching America. It had been her father who had sat with her by the fire reading the *America Book* hours upon end. Her father who had insisted that she was the natural one to take English lessons. Her innate gift for sound, music, mimicry, anything requiring a finely tuned ear, was well-known in Stavanger. She had learned quickly, perfectly. And then she had taught others who were equally mesmerized by Ole Rynnig's description of this fabulous land of freedom and riches.

Well-worn copies of the *America Book* had been passed from household to household, and had created an emigration fervor that had turned into a veritable river of hopeful, eager pioneers stretching from Oslo to Wisconsin and beyond.

Kari sat up in bed. The slight rustling of the covers brought a response. The door to her room opened a crack and a white-blond head peeked carefully through. Arne broke into a smile when he saw her awake and bounded across the room to flop himself next to her on the bed. Obviously he had been waiting just outside for her to wake up, and Kari felt guilty that she had left him alone in a strange house. She reached out to affectionately ruffle his bright hair, which looked as though it hadn't seen a comb in several days.

More sedately behind Arne came Josh. Had *he* been waiting for her to wake up, too? He smiled at her and Kari felt her heart thump once out of place.

Arne started in with his stream of Norwegian, but Kari stopped him with a gentle hand on his arm. ''We're in America now, Arne, you must speak English as I taught you, as we have prepared all these many months.''

Impulsively she hugged the boy to her. ''We're really here, little brother. We're really in America!''

Josh's smile died. He was, of course, happy that Kari had found her brother, but peculiarly, he was feeling a sense of loss. No longer was Kari the magical lost creature he had breathed the life into in Lake Erie. No longer was she the girl without a past who belonged only to the present ... and to him. She was one of the emigrants—with a family and aspirations for a life in a new land.

"How are you feeling?" he asked abruptly. He felt a need to reestablish the connection between them.

Kari relaxed her hold on Arne and turned to Josh with a brilliant smile. "I feel wonderful! I remember everything, Josh. It's almost like being born again."

Her excitement pulled him out of his odd sadness. "I'm very happy for you, Kari." And he was, he said to himself firmly. Very happy.

It took Kari only a few minutes to hear that Arne had already begun to feel at home in the Lyman household. Davey Lyman, only a year or so older, was pronounced to be, after some searching for the English word, a *splendid* fellow. Somehow Arne's face and hands had gotten scrubbed, and Josh put in that the boy had eaten enough to feed the entire crew of a Norwegian whaler.

This last comment brought a brief flush to the boy's cheeks. "I haven't eaten much in the past few days," he mumbled, looking down at the bright yellow coverlet on Kari's bed.

Josh immediately regretted his remark, which had only been said to put the boy at ease.

"Where *have* you been eating?" Kari asked, her voice full of motherly concern.

"Here and there" was all Arne would say. He had told them that the Norwegian families they had come over with had insisted that Arne continue traveling with them to Minnesota. Kari and Arne had planned to join their aunt and uncle on the farm they had established two years before near St. Paul, which, fortunately, was now officially known by its new name. The original name of the settlement, still listed in some editions of the *America Book,* much to the Norwegians' amusement, had been Pig's Eye.

"I tried to tell them that I *knew* you weren't dead, Kari, but nobody would believe me. Every day I went down to the lake and I'd talk to you. I'd tell you to come back to me...."

Kari gave him another hug, her eyes filling.

"And you did!" The tip of Arne's turned-up nose was pink. Neither brother nor sister spoke, and Josh found his own voice a trifle husky as he broke the silence.

"What did you tell your friends, Arne? How did you get them to leave you behind?"

Arne's dark gold eyelashes swept downward in the same way Josh had come to know so well with his sister. "Um... I... didn't exactly tell them anything."

Josh and Kari waited for him to continue.

"I sort of ran away. At the depot. We all got on the train together, then I told them I wanted to look out the back. So I moved to the next car and got off."

"Oh, Arne," Kari chided. "They must all be worried about you! Who were you with—the Pedersens and the Johansens?"

Suddenly, the boy's expression became adult and very grim. "The Pedersens and Jacob Haugen. The Johansens... nobody knows what happened. They were lost, all of them."

Kari gasped. "The children, too?"

"All. And Jacob's cousin Harold. And Eric and Maria Steinmark. So many, Kari. It was awful. And they told me that you were gone, too." His young voice cracked. "But I *never* believed it."

Kari took him back into her arms, silent now at the enormity of the loss. All those bright young families who had come with such wonderful hopes for the future. To have their long, difficult journey end at the bottom of an endless lake. It was almost too much to bear.

Josh felt it, too. Their grief brought his own sharply into focus. He should go, he thought, and leave these two to comfort each other for their losses. He should go have supper with his in-laws. Theirs was the grief he should be sharing.

He thought back to the uncomfortable visit when he had returned there with Vernon earlier. No one had mentioned Kari, but the existence of the Norwegian girl had hovered like a brooding spirit in the Penningtons' front parlor. Even that had been strange. He had headed for the familiar family parlor in the back of the house, but Myra had led him into the formal receiving room as if he were the minister come to tea. Then she had asked the servant to fetch Chester and Emmett, who were home from the store for midday dinner. The five of them had sat like strangers in the stiff ornate chairs and tried to reestablish to some degree the bond that had linked them over the past year.

Josh had declined the invitation to dinner, sure that he would have trouble getting even a morsel of food to slide down his dry throat. He had told them he had to see to things at his office... perhaps later... perhaps for supper.

And that's where he should be heading now, he told himself again. His loss and mourning were as clearly divided from the Norwegians' as first class had been from third back on the ship.

But Kari was smiling again now, through tears, which made her eyes shine as blue as an autumn sky. "So we will never forget them, Arne," she was saying. "We will live their dreams for them. We will build a wonderful life in this new land for all those who were lost—'' her voice dropped ''—and for Papa.''

"Especially for Papa," Arne agreed, his blond head nodding in absolute determination.

Kari looked up at Josh. "America was our father's dream, his obsession, actually," she explained. "It is because of him we are here. For years he planned to come, but in the end, his heart was not strong enough. He died last year."

"We promised him we would get to Minn-e-sota," Arne said fiercely, as though expecting to face an argument. The look he shot Josh was distrustful.

"And so you will, Arne," Josh said kindly. "As soon as we're sure your sister is well enough, I'll help you get there."

Minnesota, Kari thought. The word had had such a magical sound on her father's lips back in Stavanger. Now, suddenly, it seemed alien and faraway. Far from Milwaukee. Far from Josh.

She could feel Arne's hostility toward her American rescuer, and wished she could think of something to say to make him relax his guard.

As each sat immersed in his own thoughts, the door popped open and Davey pushed himself halfway through.

"Hey, Arn', come on. Let's go meet my friend Phineas. We'll show you where we can climb up on the Fultons' porch roof and spy on Daisy sparking with her beau, Charles."

"Davey!" Josh admonished, but his lips turned up in a grin.

"Go on, Arne," Kari said gently. "I'll see you later, before bed."

Glad of a chance to escape the emotion of the last few moments, Arne dashed a quick hand over his eyes to erase any telltale traces of unmanliness, jumped down off the bed and followed Davey out the door.

"He's a fine boy, Kari," Josh said softly after they left.

"Davey, too," she replied. "It seems we're both raising a little brother."

Josh nodded. "A mixed blessing at times. These past couple of years Davey has missed both a father and a mother's care. I had hoped things might change when Corinne…" He stopped himself with a shake of his head. "What about your mother, Kari?"

"She died when Arne was born. I had just turned seven, but I can still remember thinking, 'All right—I'm the mother now.'"

"That's quite a burden for a little girl."

Kari gave one of her dazzling smiles. "Oh, no, I loved it! I really did love taking care of Arne and my papa. Keeping the house and doing the cooking were like games for me. And I could sing while I worked. I was always singing."

"Yes, my mother was quite impressed with your song last night. She asked if you would sing to her again this evening, if you're feeling up to it."

"I'd love to."

Josh walked over to the bed, trying to see for himself if she had, indeed, recovered. Her cheeks had returned to their natural, healthy rose. Her hair fell around her in waves of spun gold. Josh felt once again the clamor deep in his middle. He reached for her hand.

"I have to talk to you first, Kari. You know how foolish it was for you to run away today?" He tried to make his voice sound detached and normal.

"I wasn't exactly 'running away,' Josh. I was just continuing on my way west—the way I have to go."

His grip on her hand tightened and his dark brown eyes clouded, but he didn't speak.

"Nothing has changed, Josh. I still don't belong here. Getting my memory back and finding Arne has just made it easier for me to head out to find my people."

Josh sank down beside her on the high bed. "What about the spell you had today? Suppose you had fainted on some stranger's doorstep? Suppose Arne and I hadn't been there?"

The muscles tightened along his jaw. Kari reached out to touch them with her free hand, as though she could soothe his anger with the gentle stroke of her fingers. But you *were* there, Josh, my wonderful rescuer, just as you have been over and over these past few days. And now I must leave you...and I am starting to realize how lost that is going to make me feel.

The satin touch of her fingers against his day's growth of beard heightened the churning in Josh's stomach. His head was a jumble of feelings. He was angry with her for not recognizing the danger her fainting put her in, hurt at her casual talk of leaving, and, he admitted, jealous of the happiness she had found with her brother. Once again, he told himself that he was a bounder. He should step out of her life now, before either of them was hurt. But even as the thoughts tumbled haphazardly through his mind, he was reaching for her.

Clad only in the loose wrapper she had borrowed from his mother, Kari's body was soft and warm and molded amazingly to his, sending immediate and urgent messages to vital parts of his body. Her mouth opened to his instantly—no hesitation this time—and it seemed as though they had been lovers before, always.

He pulled back just enough to speak. "You can't imagine how I felt when I saw you lying on the ground this afternoon." His voice was husky. "You have to take care of yourself...please...."

Then his body decided for him that touch was more effective than speech. He renewed his onslaught of her mouth, nibbling, sucking, tasting, drawing back from her a measure of the life he had breathed into her that night on the lake. Passion surged through the lower part of his body with a power he had never known.

Kari couldn't explain to herself why it felt so right to be in Josh's arms. With her memory fully established, she now knew that it wasn't past experience that made her feel so instantly alive to the sensations he brought to her. She had been kissed before. The pastor's son, Per, had courted her until her care of Papa left little time for such things. But she and Per had been children, really. Their kisses had been inexpert, hurried attempts to establish a bond between two people who had nothing more in common than proximity of age and location. Per's kisses had made her stomach flutter, but had left her feeling guilty and odd.

She didn't have time to feel guilty with Josh. Her mind was too awash in erotic sensation. With his mouth centering attention on hers, Josh's hands were slowly moving the silky wrapper against the smooth skin of her back and sides. Now, with a slight shift in position, his right hand had reached the sensitive outer reaches of her left breast. Her nipples hardened in unknown anticipation, and the intensity of feeling stabbed through her like a shard of glass.

She murmured something low in her throat. It was not a protest, but it caused Josh's hand to go abruptly still, and in the next instant, before he had actually moved, she felt the chill and the withdrawal.

Josh kept his eyes closed, waiting for the pulsing behind them to subside. He bit back an oath. Hadn't he sworn that very afternoon never to touch her again? What was it about this girl that put every other thought—of decency, of prudence, of family, of responsibility—out of his head?

He bowed his head to avoid seeing those luminous blue eyes as he opened his. Instead, he saw the frilly yellow comforter... Corinne's comforter. Damnation! He was in Corinne's bed, days after her death, a hairbreadth from losing his soul completely in the body of another woman.

He let Kari go and sat back, his eyes blazing with self-reproach. "I'm sorry," he said stiffly.

It wasn't what Kari wanted to hear. The taut words set a slow heat burning up her cheeks, a very different heat from the one she had been experiencing just moments ago. *Now* she could feel guilty. Shame and embarrassment warred for top priority.

"I..." She stopped, not knowing what to say. She wanted to tell him not to be sorry, that for those few moments she had never before in all her life felt so wonderful. But she couldn't say it. Obviously, he was mortified by what they had shared. He hadn't meant it to happen. He wasn't interested in getting involved in that way with a poor emigrant girl. He needed to concentrate on putting his life back together, mending fences with the Penningtons, taking care of his own family.

She bit her kiss-swollen lip and forced herself to speak. "Now maybe you will believe me when I say I have to leave. I will go talk to Mr. Grindem in the morning. I'm sure he will have some ideas on how Arne and I can reach Minnesota."

"I said I was sorry, Kari, and I meant it. My... animal behavior shouldn't put you in danger. I want you and Arne to stay here until you are completely well, and until you have found a safe way to reach your relatives. I promise there will be no repetition of tonight's ... mistake."

His eyes were dark and unreadable, and his words made tears tingle inside her head. He called it *animal behavior,* this wonderful thing they had shared? A mistake? Is that all it was to him? A quick flare of anger stabbed her. "I've made up my mind, Josh. Arne and I leave tomorrow."

Josh pushed himself up off Corinne's bed and looked down at Kari. Her hair was tangled from their embrace and the wrapper hung loosely open around her magnificent body. Her eyes snapped blue fire. He wanted to get out of the room, too shaken to trust himself near her any longer.

"We'll talk in the morning, Kari. You need your rest. I'll tell my mother you're not up to seeing her tonight."

Before she could protest, he had crossed the room in his brisk, long strides and disappeared through the door.

Kari's head hurt. She had awakened with the dull ache before dawn and had spent the rest of the night in a disturbed sleep. She had dreamed horrible images of bloated bodies bobbing along in endless water, which slowly turned from black to green to blood scarlet.

After dressing, she descended the stairs, her pace sedate in deference to the throb at her right temple. Suddenly the swinging door to the kitchen banged open and three furies raced by her, one by one coming into focus as her brother and his two new American friends. They stopped just short of the front door and stood straight to face her, their faces beaming with inner mischief.

"Good morning, Kari."

"'Mornin', ma'am."

"Goot morn-ing, Kari."

The last was Arne, and the grin on his face put her in mind of the days before their father's death, when he was a fun-loving, good-hearted boy with nothing more to worry about than how soon the ice would be thick enough for strapping on the silver blades he and his friends lived in all winter long. These last few months had been hard on both of them, but especially on Arne. He'd had to grow up too soon.

"Good morning, boys." She found herself smiling broadly in response to their youthful ebullience. "What have you all been up to?"

"Nothing, ma'am." It was Phineas who answered—too quickly. Davey and Arne looked down at the Persian hall carpet and grinned.

Kari waited a few moments, but could see the conspiracy of silence was too strong to break when it was three against one. "So, Arne...you have made new friends?"

Her brother looked up, his eyes glowing. "They're taking me with them to *school*."

Kari felt a wave of guilt wash over her. That was another thing Arne had missed. After her father died, they had both agreed that every *kroner* would be saved for the trip to America. Arne had given up school and helped out by earning a few coins working on the neighboring farms. That money and what Kari earned teaching English to others who planned the journey went into the stiff leather pouch hidden in the floorboards under her father's empty bed.

"Can't see why he's so all-fired excited about school," Davey grumbled, picking up from the hall table the end of a strap that bound together three schoolbooks. He was about to hand a similar bundle to Phineas when a shattering scream came from behind the swinging door to the kitchen.

"What in the world...?" Kari was pushing her way through the door before any of the boys could move.

Inside, Daisy was sitting on top of the wooden cooler. Her curls danced wildly as she rolled her eyes and pointed across the room. There, a tiny pink creature squealed in fear, rivaling Daisy's shrieks in volume. Four little legs, nearly hidden by the plump, shapeless body, scrambled in desperation against the slippery tile floor.

After taking a minute to assess the scene, Kari walked calmly across the kitchen and picked up the little intruder. Its skin felt naked and warm, with just a touch of bristly hair beginning to sprout here and there.

"It's all right, Daisy. It's just a little baby pig."

Daisy's screeches subsided to whimpers and then silence, and the piglet quieted, too, with the soothing stroke of Kari's hand. Making a strong effort to look severe, Kari called, "Boys!"

The swinging door pushed slowly inward, and three grinning heads poked through.

"Come in here!" Kari said, the smile she could no longer hold back belying the severity of her tone. The piglet squirmed in her arms. "What do you know about this?"

Davey spoke finally when it seemed that neither of the other two had any intention of doing so. "It's a piglet."

"I can see that. Poor thing...it's frightened to death."

The smiles dimmed a little as the three trooped into the kitchen. Davey shot an embarrassed glance up to Daisy, still perched on the cooler. "I'm sorry, Daisy. I didn't think it would scare you so bad."

"Where did it come from?" Kari asked him.

"Johnny Hofmeier brought it to school yesterday. I traded him my slingshot and twenty pellets," Davey replied sheepishly.

"You boys ought to be in jail." Daisy's normally sunny nature had been jolted too badly for her to be charitable.

Kari sighed. "Let's have an apology from each of you to Daisy. Then I want you to take this little thing and make a pen for it out in the stables. Hurry, you'll be late for school."

She held the round little animal out to Davey, who took it gingerly as it protested with a tiny squeaking sound.

"Honest, Daisy, we were just having fun. I'm sorry," he said again.

"Sorry," Phineas mumbled, and Arne echoed, "Sorry."

"All right now. Off with you."

The kitchen seemed remarkably empty minus boys and pig. Kari helped Daisy down from the cooler. "They didn't mean any harm, Daisy."

Daisy, who had never been one to let bad humor last for long, grinned. "I know. Sure gave me a start, though, finding a critter like that in my kitchen."

Kari returned her smile, and before long the two were laughing so hard they clung to each other for support. It was this way that Josh found them as he swung through the door, his broad frame filling the opening.

"Is breakfast too much to ask for around here?"

"Not if you want some bacon, sir," Daisy hooted, which set both women laughing again, leaving Josh to wonder if it perhaps was true that the entire world was going crazy.

Kari was still smiling later that morning. It warmed her heart to see Arne so carefree. He had missed much of his childhood in the last couple years. The long trip had taken a toll on his growing body, too. He had been a sight this morning. It seemed these days that his pants were always inches too short for him as he continued sprouting, promising to be as tall as their father. With the poor rations they had had on the crossing and his days of not eating while he was looking for her, the clothes hung on him like an old suit set out on a stick to scare the blackbirds.

How tempting it was to agree to stay here for a while. To let Arne make friends, play, go to school, eat all the good food he wanted from the limitless Lyman larder. And, she admitted to herself, it was not only for Arne that she wanted to stay. But, of course, that was the problem.

Her thoughts went back to the scene in her bed the previous evening. If Josh had pursued the matter, she didn't know what her response would have been. How could she stay here when she knew that he had that kind of power over her?

She tossed the question back and forth in her head as she swiped a last shine into the gleaming kitchen counter. In Stavanger her house had been spotless, as had the houses of her neighbors. She had been appalled at the haphazard housekeeping at the Lyman household. Of course, Josh's mother stayed mostly in her bed. But what about his wife?

When the last speck of grime had disappeared from the big kitchen, Kari put aside her apron and made her way slowly to the library, hoping to catch Josh at his desk. She had made up her mind.

By the time a still-giggling Daisy had brought his breakfast, Josh was in no mood for talk. He had scarcely slept. His body had still been racing from its contact with Kari's, and his mind had swung from thoughts of her, sleeping that very moment in the bedroom next to his, to thoughts of Corinne. Poor, lost Corinne, lying somewhere in the depths of the lake.

By morning he had almost come to the conclusion that Kari was right. He was making her miserable. She was *definitely* making *him* miserable. And her presence in his house was making his in-laws miserable. Perhaps he should make arrangements today for her and her brother to stay at Henrik House until more information could be obtained about their friends and relatives in Minnesota.

He could drive them over there this morning and be rid of the whole problem by the noon meal. The morning sun strengthened its approach through the leaded windows of the library and the day began to look brighter to Josh in more ways than one. With the air of a difficult decision wrestled with and conquered, he whistled as he made the latest entries in his accounting journal.

The knock was so light, he had to stop the aimless tune to be sure he'd heard it. "Is someone there?" he questioned.

Slowly it opened and Kari walked into the room, her face serious and beautiful in the golden morning rays. Josh felt his newly won peace of mind splinter like a badly cut log.

"About last night..." Her face reddened in the flush he had come to know, starting at the fine line of her jaw and spreading upward to heighten the blue of her eyes. "I've been doing some thinking about what we said last night."

Josh passed his hand across tired eyes. "Doing some thinking" was an understatement for him. He'd been able to think of very little else.

"Yes?" His reply was impassive.

Now that she was sitting across from him again, that half-pleasurable tension was back, and Kari once again had to ask herself if she was making a mistake. But she took a deep breath and plunged ahead.

"I'd like to take you up on your offer of staying here until we can head west. For Arne's sake," she hastened to add at the end, as his dark eyes widened slightly.

"For Arne's sake," he repeated dryly.

"Yes." The words tumbled over one another. "He's gone to school with your brother and Phineas, and they all looked so happy together, and it's been such a long time since I've heard him laugh like the three of them were after putting the pig in the kitchen...."

"The pig?" Josh was having a little trouble following her tumble of lilting words.

Kari's nerves calmed as she told Josh the story of the errant piglet, and by the time she had finished, his strong features had relaxed into a smile and his eyes held the first warmth of the morning.

"Anyway," she finished, "I would like to stay here, but on one condition."

Josh shifted uneasily in his chair. He felt as if he had stepped back onto a rolling log—unsteady, alert and exhilarated. She would not be out of his life by the noon meal, then ... perhaps not for a long time.

"What's your condition?" He kept his voice mild.

"That I can help out around here, help take care of your mother, get the house in order, that kind of thing." Her sharp eyes searched out the corners of the cozy room, which looked as if they had not seen a good cleaning in many a day. "I'll cook, too."

Josh let his exasperation show. "I told you that you are welcome in this house as my guests, Kari, you and your brother. You don't have to *earn* your keep."

"I just want to make myself useful. Please, Josh, it's what I'm used to." Her great blue eyes watched him pleadingly, the same eyes that had snapped with passion last night. A passion he was duty-bound to forget.

"Fine," he said briskly. "Do whatever you want. You won't be troubled by me. I have more than enough work to catch up on at my office."

Kari nodded. Though his indifferent tone cut, she knew that it was for the best. If Josh stayed out of her way, she could provide a good interim home for Arne without having to suffer from a guilty conscience.

She stood. "So then, that's settled." She shook out the skirts of an old yellow organdy dress Josh's mother had given her last night after she had, after all, gone in to sing to her. Her movements were full of unconscious grace, and Josh felt the squeezing in his chest again.

"I will, of course, appreciate any comfort you can give my mother." He tried to soften the words, but they come out sounding stiff.

"Yes, of course. As I said, it's settled. I would be obliged to you if you would send word to Mr. Grindem about our circumstances and ask him to continue with his inquiries."

"Certainly."

It was a business deal, concluded with nods and polite words. And this is the way it will stay, Josh resolved. "Is that all?" He glanced up at her from his journal without rising.

"That's all," Kari said firmly. With one last long look from her vivid blue eyes and a swish of yellow organdy, she was gone.

Chapter Seven

Josh stayed away until dark each night, as if the blackness would protect him from the sudden sunshine that had filtered through his household. But the changes were too obvious to miss.

The food was the most dramatic change. Josh had grown used to the ways of the lumber camp where the only important feature of food was its quantity, bulk enough to keep a strong body working at top capacity for several more hours. Now he found himself salivating the minute he walked in at night and smelled the delicious odors emanating from behind the swinging kitchen door.

Kari prepared her favorites from the old country, *skinkeboller*—the tasty, deep-fried balls of potatoes and ham, juicy meatballs swimming in a tangy sauce that Josh couldn't recognize, spicy and succulent home-ground pork sausage, and fish, fresh from the lake, served in a seemingly endless variety of savory dishes.

Davey's gangly teenage body was filling out with the new diet. And Arne had completely lost the pallid, hungry look he'd had when they'd found him on the streets. But the biggest change, Josh reflected, was in his mother. Frequently, now, when he came home late, his mother was not only awake, but dressed and downstairs, sewing or just watching quietly as Kari helped Davey and Arne with their schoolwork while a big fire burned cozily in the parlor. The room was taking on a lived-in look that it hadn't had for years.

Josh didn't make it a habit to join them. He ate his late dinner alone, then went by himself to the library to shut himself away with his books and accounts. Though the nights had now grown quite cold, he didn't bother to light himself a fire. The cold and the occasional laughter he could hear from the front room served as some kind of perverse penance for everything that had gone wrong with his life.

His other penance was his regular visit to the Penningtons. Three times a week he mounted the fancy wrought-iron stairway, the only one of its kind in Milwaukee, to their big brick house and shared the noon meal with them. The discussion inevitably turned to Corinne, and Josh considered himself lucky the days they were able to make it through the meal without Myra pulling out one of her lace-edged hankies to dab at her eyes.

Tonight was particularly cold, Josh was thinking as he stared gloomily at the numbers in front of him. It had snowed for the first time that morning. Perhaps he would light the fire, after all. He half rose to do so when a knock on the door made him sink once again into his chair.

"What is it?" His voice was frostier than the room.

The door opened slowly, and Kari slipped inside. He recognized an old shawl of his mother's around her shoulders. The thought crossed his mind that he would like to buy her something pretty and new of her own. But instantly he knew that Kari would not allow him to do any such thing.

"It's dreadfully cold in here."

He had hardly spoken to her in several days, and had almost forgotten the effect of her beautiful voice. He smiled and relaxed. "It's warmer now that you're here," he said softly.

She was in the shadows, but he knew exactly the route the blush was taking up her cheeks.

"I came to see if you want to join us in the parlor."

She sounded hesitant. And why wouldn't she be? Josh asked himself angrily. Night after night he had shut himself up alone, barely speaking to her, even to thank her for all the work she was doing for his family.

"Why?" he asked abruptly.

Kari stepped into the circle of light surrounding his desk. "Davey and your mother wanted to show Arne and me about . . . pop-corn."

"Popcorn?"

"Yes, isn't that how you say it? They told us that you always used to make it in the fireplace these fall evenings."

Josh had a swift, painful memory of happy family evenings around the big parlor fireplace. He remembered the first time his father had solemnly passed the long-handled popper to Josh to let him make the favorite treat. Josh had felt grown-up that day, though he'd been younger than Davey was now. They had not made popcorn since his father had died.

"Don't you have popcorn in Norway?" He felt a terrible reluctance to be pulled from his cold books into the warmth and laughter of the next room. Here he felt in control.

Kari's face glowed. "No. I have not heard of such a thing. You will come and make it for us?" The truth was, she didn't really care much about the popcorn, though it did sound intriguing. What excited her was the thought of, for once, pulling Josh out of his solitude.

She had enjoyed her time with the Lymans, had grown very fond of Davey and Mrs. Lyman, but Josh's conspicuous absence from the family gatherings weighed like a stone on her heart. She told herself it was better for her; the less she saw of him, the easier it would be for her to leave. But as she stood there watching the memories flicker behind his expressive brown eyes, she couldn't help clutching her hands together in anticipation. Please come, Josh, she prayed silently. Please don't shut us out one more night.

"All right." Josh stood. "You've been sharing enough of your Norwegian dishes with us. It's time we showed you a good old American food."

His grin transformed his face and made him look years younger. Kari wanted to reach out and smooth back the wave of chestnut hair that fell over his forehead. "Let's go, then," she said happily, reaching out a hand toward him. After a moment's hesitation, he surrounded it with his, which was warm in spite of the temperature of the room.

Their entry into the parlor was met with exuberant shouts from Davey and Phineas, who had taken to spending more and more time at the Lymans. Arne was more reserved and shot a frowning glance at Josh's and Kari's linked hands. Helen Lyman raised an eyebrow slightly, too, before Josh quickly dropped Kari's hand and took a step away from her.

"Will you make popcorn, Josh? It's been ever so long since you've made it," Davey asked. From where it had lain tucked away to one side of the fireplace, he had already retrieved the old pewter popper that their mother had brought from Pennsylvania.

Josh grinned at his brother, happy to see him enthusiastic, happy to see that tight thinness gone from his cheeks. "I would think it's about time *you* did the honors, little brother. A man's got to know how to pop popcorn."

"Really? Can Phineas, too?" Both boys were on their feet.

"I don't see why not. Just mind the fire."

Josh settled himself on the floor next to his mother's chair and watched as Davey and Phineas set to work shucking kernels from a basket of dried ears. After another somber look at Josh, Arne turned to join them.

"How are you feeling, Mother?" Josh asked, looking up into Helen Lyman's soft hazel eyes. They had a sparkle in them tonight that had been missing for many months.

"It's about time you remembered to ask, son," she chided gently, letting him know that his long absences had been noted. "I feel wonderful. The pains haven't come for days now."

She smiled at Kari, who had taken a seat on the nearby sofa. "I think it's because I have music back in my life."

Davey looked up from the corn. "Yes, Kari. Why don't you sing us something while we're working? Sing us a *vandringsliede.*" He paused for a moment. "Ah...*vær så snill.*"

Josh looked at his brother in amazement. "That means 'please,'" the boy said proudly. "Kari's teaching us Norwegian."

"*Vær så snill,* Kari," Phineas repeated, and Arne giggled at his friends' stilted pronunciation.

"It seems I've been missing out on something," Josh said dryly.

His mother reached over and patted his shoulder. "Yes, you have, son," she said softly. "I've been telling you that for a long time."

The singing was put off as the corn was ready for popping. The boys passed the popper among themselves as they endured the agonizing wait for the first muffled explosion. It came soon enough, and before long the room was filled with crackles and pops that had Kari laughing and Arne's eyes wide with amazement. "It sounds like when I shoot at the squirrels," he said, awed.

And there was more wonder when the pan was opened to reveal the puffy white kernels. They were all laughing by the time the hot butter had been mixed in and they competed for big greasy handfuls. Finally, the three boys ended up with the heavy wooden bowl nestled among them in front of the fire, and Josh took a seat at the opposite end of the sofa from Kari.

"So how about that song?" he asked softly. "It seems that everyone has heard you sing except me."

Kari turned toward him. Her cheeks were flushed from the fire and the shared merriment. Her braid had loosened and corn-silk tendrils of hair framed her face. "I'd be happy to sing for you, Josh."

Her words subtly changed the mood. Josh listened in rapt fascination as she unerringly chose an opening note and began a haunting melody in a minor key. He couldn't understand the words, but the purity of tone caught at his heart. It was as if she was sending vibrations of her soul straight into his.

She finished on a high note that soared then faded like a bird in flight. Only the crack of the fire broke the silence of the room.

"Whew," Davey said at last. "How do you do that, Kari? Sing some more."

Kari's eyes were on Josh, but when he merely nodded at Davey's words, she began another song, livelier this time. And following that, she coaxed Helen into joining her for a song together in Norwegian, which brought an exclamation of surprise from Josh.

"I've been learning, too, Josh," his mother said smugly.

Then they all sang in English, with Arne doing his best to keep up. Until finally, Kari laughed and said, "No more. It's time you boys were in bed. Phineas, you should have been home long ago."

To Josh's surprise, the three were up from the floor instantly without so much as a pout.

"God natt!" Davey hollered as they headed out the door.

"Good night, boys," Kari answered. She began cleaning, gathering the remnants of the popcorn feast, and Josh jumped up to help her. His mother stood and faced them both with a tired, happy smile.

"I need to be turning in myself," she said. "Thank you for joining us tonight, Josh. It seemed almost like old times, didn't it?"

Josh walked over and gave his mother a hard kiss on her cheek. "Yes, it did, Mother." There was more he wished to say to her, but the words wouldn't come out.

She waited a moment. "Good night, then," she said finally, and with a last smile at Kari, she left the room.

When they were alone, Josh crossed the room to Kari and reached for the dishes in her hands. "Let me take these to the kitchen," he said. "You've worked enough for one day."

She murmured a protest, but let him take the things from her. "I enjoyed the evening, Josh," she said.

He nodded. "So did I. Your singing is extraordinary, Kari, and I haven't seen my mother this happy since my father died. Davey, too. I want to thank you for all you've been doing around here.''

Kari was surprised at his compliment. In the past few weeks, it hadn't appeared that Josh had even noticed she existed, much less the work she had done around the house. Her first job had been to tackle the sadly neglected housekeeping. With a little coaxing, Daisy had agreed to help, and after several days' work, the two had the house sparkling down to the last brass doorknob. Then each day Kari had racked her brains to come up with a different new dish, trying to combine the cooking she had learned back home with the ingredients she could find here in Milwaukee. In most cases, the outcome had been completely satisfactory. She had enjoyed seeing the boys wolfing down her dishes with their teenage appetites. Both they and Helen had praised her cooking highly, but she had heard nothing from Josh.

''I've been happy to do it, Josh. You have a wonderful family.''

Josh was watching her with an intent look. ''I know,'' he said. ''You still have butter around your lips.''

Kari flinched as he smoothed his thumb along one side of her mouth. His hand lingered there just a moment longer than necessary, and a flutter went through her middle. He was still holding the big wooden popcorn bowl. If he's going to kiss me, Kari thought, he'll have to put it down, or lean over. She moved a step forward so that only the width of the bowl separated them.

''Yes, well.'' Josh reached down to retrieve the tin cup that had held the melted butter. ''Anyway, thank you. I appreciate your help.''

She didn't even have to look at the expression on his face to see his withdrawal. Feeling disappointed and foolish,

she snatched the wooden bowl and other utensils back out
of his hand.

"I'll take these," she said briskly. "You undoubtedly
need to be getting back to those important books of
yours." Without waiting for a reply, she marched out of
the room, slamming Helen Lyman's prized glass parlor
doors behind her.

Kari had only seen Mrs. Hennessey once since the garrulous woman's return from Chicago. As victims of a
shared disaster, the two had greeted each other as if they
were family. Mrs. Hennessey had been delighted to hear
that Kari had regained her memory and found her brother,
and she had been politely, but avidly, curious about the
lovely young Norwegian's relationship with Josh Lyman.
She seemed disappointed when Kari explained that the
master of the house was seldom to be seen in it.

By the end of their meeting, Kari knew that she had another true friend in Milwaukee, so she wasn't surprised
when Daisy announced that Mrs. Hennessey was waiting
in the parlor to see her the morning after the popcorn
party.

The elderly woman's eyes danced with suppressed excitement. "Kari, my dear. I've such good news for you."

Kari had already had a long morning of cleaning and
cooking. Some of her natural vitality was missing today.
Spending the evening with Josh had had the opposite effect from what she would have wished. But she smiled
pleasantly at her new friend. "Good news would be nice,
Mrs. Hennessey."

The women took a seat on the same sofa Josh and Kari
had shared the past evening. Without bothering about
preliminaries, Mrs. Hennessey burst out with her news.
"I've found some people who know your aunt and uncle

in Minnesota. They're heading there themselves this very week and have agreed to take you and Arne with them."

The smile melted from Kari's face like a snowflake on a warm window. "Take us to Minnesota?"

"Yes! They'll take you right to your aunt and uncle's farm, if you wish. It's what you've been waiting for, isn't it?" Mrs. Hennessey looked confused, as if Kari's reaction wasn't what she'd expected.

"Yes, of course. We want to go to Minnesota. It was my father's dream for us." Kari stood and walked a few paces away. "It's just that ... the Lymans have been so good to us. And Mrs. Lyman is getting so much better, and she says her pains go away when I sing to her...." Her voice trailed off as Kari had a sudden and forlorn realization of just how reluctant she was to leave this first home in her new land. In a few short weeks, it had become as dear to her as her own back in Stavanger.

Mrs. Hennessey's bright eyes grew soft with understanding. She struggled a moment to pull her ample body from the soft cushions of the sofa, then walked over to put an arm around Kari's shoulders. "My dear," she said softly. "You told me how things were between you and Mr. Lyman. There just isn't a place for you here." She took a deep breath and continued. "It's not a respectable situation."

Kari closed her eyes to shut in a tear. She remembered last night as they had stood together over the popcorn bowl. She had taken a step forward, as if she expected Josh to kiss her, as if she actually wanted it. She remembered his withdrawal, his stiff good-night. Mrs. Hennessey was right. There wasn't a place for her here.

She blinked hard, firmly banishing any threatening tears. She gave Mrs. Hennessey a little hug, then faced her with a determined smile. "You are right, my friend. This

is the opportunity we've been waiting for.'' She walked
across the room and picked up the fireplace broom to ab-
sentmindedly sweep the cinders from last night's party into
the fireplace. She could feel Mrs. Hennessey's sharp eyes
on her back. Finally, she turned and said brightly, "So
tell me more about these new traveling companions of
mine...."

In the weeks since Kari had joined his household, Josh
had seldom come home for the midday meal. He had
never, until today, come home early for dinner. But the
scene in the parlor last night had been on his mind all
morning. He remembered Kari taking that tentative step
toward him, her full lips glistening in the firelight as he
gently wiped the butter from them. He had wanted to kiss
her. He had wanted to do more than kiss her, he admitted
to himself. And in trying to restrain his own desires, he had
ignored hers. Given their circumstances, there wasn't too
much he could do about that, but at least he could talk to
her this morning. At least he could see that sunny face with
its halo wreath of white-gold hair.

His first reaction upon seeing Mrs. Hennessey through
the glass doors was disappointment. He had envisioned
having Kari to himself this morning. But, reminding himself once more that it was unwise for the two of them to be
alone together, he let his face assume its inherent, friendly
smile and went in to greet his erstwhile ship companion.

As the two women looked up in surprise at his entry, he
crossed and kissed Mrs. Hennessey on her plump cheek.
It seemed only natural. Hadn't he, after all, carried her in
her nightclothes? She had made quite an armful. His grin
grew at the memory, and he realized that it was the first
time he had been able to think of that night with anything
other than horror.

Mrs. Hennessey colored and beamed at his greeting, but his eyes were on Kari, whose smile hid sadness in its depths. He straightened and asked her directly, "What's the matter?"

Kari only shook her head. She bit her lower lip, and her long fingers played nervously in the lap of her bright yellow dress.

Josh looked over at Mrs. Hennessey, his eyes questioning. The older woman nodded reassuringly. "Nothing's wrong, Mr. Lyman. I've just been telling Kari that I've found transportation for her and Arne to Minnesota with a very nice emigrant couple from her hometown who already know her aunt and uncle."

Josh dropped down into a chair. "Oh," he said dully.

Mrs. Hennessey looked sharply from Josh to Kari and back again. "I understood that this was what everyone wanted," she said defensively.

Kari answered. "Yes, of course. Arne and I are very anxious to get to Minnesota. We're grateful to you for finding these people, Mrs. Hennessey."

The gray-haired woman visibly relaxed. "Then it's all settled. I'll tell the Olsens you will be ready to leave . . . tomorrow, shall we say?"

"Tomorrow?" Josh's voice hid none of his agitation. "Are you sure this is what you want, Kari?"

Kari gave him a long, even look. "This was my father's dream for us. Arne wants to go, and so do I." She'd be darned if she would tell him the real reason she had to leave, she thought to herself angrily. If he couldn't see for himself, if he hadn't seen for himself last night, she wasn't about to tell him.

"Perhaps they would wait until next week. . . ." Mrs. Hennessey ventured lamely, distressed by Josh's obvious irritation.

Kari reached over and patted her friend's soft hand.
"Tomorrow will be fine, Mrs. Hennessey. The sooner we
start, the sooner Arne and I will be able to begin our new
life in Minnesota."

Josh stood and began to pace. "Who are these people?" he asked Mrs. Hennessey with a frown.

The older woman's round face looked flustered.
"Why... as I said, they are from Kari's hometown."

"But you've never heard of them?" He turned his bel-
ligerent tone on Kari.

Kari shook her head. "I don't think so. But Olsen is a
very common name in my country."

"Well, I'm not about to send you off into the wilderness with strangers."

"Josh," Kari said gently. "Up until a few weeks ago *you*
were a stranger. At least these people are from my homeland."

Josh looked from Kari to Mrs. Hennessey, who had a
look of sympathetic understanding in her faded blue eyes.
"It's perhaps for the best, Mr. Lyman," she said.

Josh felt a stab of frustration so sharp it made him want
to gasp. "Do whatever you want," he said angrily, and left
the room.

Davey slammed the library door behind him and
marched up to Josh's desk with a thundercloud face.
"What did you do to Kari?" he shouted at his brother.

Josh put down his pen. "What are you talking about?"

"Kari—what did you do to her?" Davey's teenage bass
voice softened, but the angry glare stayed in his brown
eyes. "Arne says they're leaving tomorrow. And he says
it's 'cause you make his sister unhappy."

Josh sighed. "Why don't you sit down for a minute,
Davey?"

Davey scowled and slumped into the chair across the desk from his brother. "Is it true?"

Josh met his brother's accusing gaze. "It's true that they're leaving tomorrow. They're going to Minnesota, which is what they set out to do when they left Norway. They never meant to stay in Milwaukee."

"Why does Arne say you've made Kari unhappy?" Davey persisted.

Josh regarded his little brother thoughtfully. The extra pounds the boy had added during the past few weeks had made him look older suddenly. For the first time, Josh noticed there was a faint dark shadow of hair at the base of his brother's chin. Little Davey was growing up.

"There have been some difficult moments between me and Kari, because she is an attractive young woman, and I'm still in mourning for Corinne."

Davey straightened in his chair and shifted uncomfortably. "You mean . . . you and Kari . . ." His face grew red.

Josh gave a brittle smile. "I mean that there can not be anything between me and Kari. I have other responsibilities right now."

Davey sat for a minute considering this new side to his brother and Kari. It hadn't occurred to him before, but the idea of Kari and Josh falling in love sounded perfect to him. "But Corinne's dead," he said matter-of-factly. "Of course, nobody wanted it that way, but now that she's gone, I don't see why you can't be with Kari."

Josh shook his head. "It's a little more complicated than that."

"Why?"

It was hopeless. If he couldn't explain it to his own satisfaction, how could he expect to justify it to a fifteen-year-old, whose view of life was still governed by the simple blacks and whites of youth?

"You'll just have to accept it, Davey. It's better for everyone if Kari and Arne leave."

Davey's eyes narrowed. "It's better for you, is what you mean. It's certainly not better for Mama. Why, she's happy for the first time in years, and healthy, too."

Josh had no argument and reverted to the time-honored adult answer when faced with the irrefutable logic of youth. "Maybe you're still too young to understand. . . ."

Davey leaned over and pounded a surprisingly strong fist on the desk. "Mama's happy, and Daisy, and me and Arne. Even Kari's happy. I know she is. She goes around singing all day long. You're the only one who's not happy with the way things are, Josh." He stopped and drew a big breath before he continued with a wisdom that belied his tender age. "And I think that should be your problem, not ours."

Josh leaned back in his chair. Was he the only one who found this situation precarious? No, he knew in his heart that Kari felt it, too. She had said this morning that she wanted to leave, wanted to get to Minnesota. They had both felt it last night. It was no longer possible for them to be in the same household. Unless he could stay away from her. Maybe Davey was right. Maybe it was his problem.

"I'll talk to Kari," he said. "But I'm not making any promises. They have to leave sooner or later, you know."

"Maybe not." Davey grinned. He looked as though the battle had been won. "Just tell Kari that winter's no time to be heading off into the wilderness. And, who knows? Maybe it'll be a really long winter."

As Davey bounced to his feet and left the room, Josh stared into the floating stream of dust motes that danced aimlessly across his desk in a beam of sunshine. Davey had one thing right. If he and Kari were to continue sharing the same house, it would definitely be a very long winter.

* * *

The Olsens had come and gone—an earnest, serious couple with the high cheekbones and harshly planed features of the Far North. Kari's heart had been torn in two. She hadn't wanted to leave. But the frosty words with which Josh had invited her to stay through the winter did nothing to ease the guilt she felt at delaying once more the fulfillment of her father's wishes.

Arne's behavior had been puzzling. While initially reluctant to leave behind his new friends and the first school he had known in almost three years, he had at the end become vehemently opposed to staying.

With a worried glance at Kari's uncertain expression and an angry look over to an unsmiling Josh, he had drawn himself up to the fullest height he could muster and declared in carefully pronounced English, "I take my sister to Minnesota. There is where we belong."

It had been Mrs. Hennessey who had decided the matter, finally. After careful scrutiny of the handsome young couple standing stiffly on either side of the parlor sofa, a speculative gleam appeared in her eyes. "Mr. Lyman is absolutely right," she said firmly. "Winter is no time for you young people to be traveling. You never know what you might encounter...blizzards and bears and what all."

Josh refrained from pointing out that if there were blizzards, there would most certainly not be bears. No self-respecting bear would be caught out unprepared in the middle of winter. He was not in the mood to give a nature lesson. It seemed all at once that Kari staying or Kari leaving were equally painful choices. He forced his eyes to meet hers and immediately felt the bolt of attraction that sizzled between them. It had become so palpable that he thought surely the other occupants of the room must see it. Were they all blind that they couldn't see the pull of those sky blue eyes when she looked at him?

And so it was decided. Josh promised to take Kari and Arne to Minnesota himself at the end of the winter when he went to check on the lumber camps. The Olsens were wished well and ushered on their way, somewhat bewildered by the turn of events but too reserved to argue to change anyone's mind.

Kari took Arne to her bedroom for a private talk. She avowed that by the spring thaw they would be on their way to their aunt and uncle's farm. In the meantime, they would be safe and warm and well fed through the cold winter. And he oughtn't worry about Josh making her unhappy. They were in America at last and staying with a wonderful family. She couldn't be happier.

His doubts resolved, Arne's thundercloud expression vanished like a quick summer storm and he ran off cheerfully to find his friends. Kari walked slowly down the narrow stairs. Mrs. Hennessey had gone and the front parlor was empty. The stout door to Josh's office was shut as tight as a miser's purse. Kari hesitated before it. She should thank Josh for his continued hospitality and for his offer to take them west himself. She lifted a hand to knock, but stopped herself in midair. There had been enough emotion spent for one day. Her thanks could wait. She would spend the rest of the evening upstairs with Helen, and talk with Josh tomorrow.

But by the next day Josh was gone. He had left before dawn, announcing his departure only to a sleepy-eyed Daisy as he grabbed a bit of bread and cheese to fortify himself for the cold early-morning ride.

"He said he was riding out to Greenwood camp," Daisy told a surprised Kari, who had come down to breakfast with Josh's mother.

Helen's sweet smile disappeared when she heard Daisy's news, but she did not look surprised. The pattern of Josh's sudden trips had begun shortly after his marriage to Corinne. Evidently, his wife's death had not cured his restlessness. She sighed. "Poor Josh."

Kari looked stricken. "I feel this is my fault," she said in distress. "He had to leave his home because we are still here."

Helen shook her head and placed a gentle hand over Kari's strong fingers. "Josh has his own demons to fight. And they were bedeviling him long before he ever met you. This is his problem, my dear, not yours."

Kari's eyes filled. "It would be easier for him if I were gone."

"Then why did he insist that you stay?" Helen asked softly.

"He feels responsible for me. He saved my life."

The older woman's fragile smile masked a steel conviction. "Joshua needs to find peace with himself. When he does, he will have the strength to be at peace with the rest of the world, starting with you, my lovely girl." She reached a thin, blue-veined hand up to wipe the tear from Kari's cheek. "Give him time...."

Chapter Eight

"Good ye-wel."

"No! Listen better." Arne's high-pitched voice was intent. *"God Jul."*

Davey scowled. "How come Norwegian has so many funny sounds?"

Arne gave him a push and both boys tumbled off the front stoop into the new snow, which had arrived just in time to cover the city of Milwaukee in a bright Christmas blanket. "Is not so funny like English," the Norwegian boy said vehemently, oblivious to the powdery white crystals that clung to him from head to foot. "How about English and all your 'th' sounds?" He stuck his tongue up against his front teeth and blew until his cheeks turned red. "Thhh...thhhh...thhhh. You sound like old men with no more teet'."

Davey grinned. "Tee*thhh*," he corrected his friend.

"Ya." Arne grinned back. "Anyway, *God Jul*—Merry Christmas...my first Christmas in America!"

The front door opened and Kari poked her head out. "What are you doing out there, boys? We're supposed to be leaving for church and here are you two rolling around in the snow."

The boys stood and started brushing themselves off. "We're all ready, Kari. Arne was just giving me another lesson in Norwegian."

Kari shook her head, smiling. "It doesn't look like much of a language lesson to me. Come on now. The carriage is ready out back." She disappeared into the house.

Davey pounded Arne's back, ostensibly ridding his friend of snow. In the process, an ice-cold lump managed to find its way down the Norwegian boy's collar. With a howl Arne turned around and tackled his taller and heavier companion around the knees. Both went down again into the soft mound of snow that had drifted up against the stairs.

"Davey, get a wiggle on! We'll be late for church," Helen Lyman yelled out the door.

Davey looked up in amazement. It had been months since he had heard his mother's voice raised like that. And he couldn't remember the last time she'd used that expression. He grinned to himself. "We're coming, Mama."

He stood and put his hand out to help Arne out of the snow. His friend looked at him suspiciously. "No more tricks, Davey!" he said sternly, his face with that serious look that made him look much older than his thirteen years.

"No more tricks," Davey agreed with a smile. He felt terrific. He had a great new friend to joke with; his mother was yelling at him just like in the old days; and the ground was covered with snow. This was promising to be one of the best Christmases in years.

If only Josh would come out of the doldrums, Davey thought with a brief scowl, as the two boys slogged their way around to the back of the house. His brother was standing impatiently next to the polished black carriage, which would take the whole family to Christmas Eve services.

Josh had arrived home from the camps the night before just as the gently falling snow began tracing sparkling patterns along the streets and sidewalks of the town. He had entered the house to the tantalizing aroma of ginger and cinnamon.

His mother emerged from the parlor, and Josh bent down to give her a distracted kiss on the cheek. His eyes were on the freshly cut pine boughs that framed the big parlor fireplace.

"Kari put them up," his mother told him, her eyes alight as he had not seen them in some time. "She says that back in her country they decorate the whole house that way for Christmas."

"It smells like I'm back at the lumber camp," Josh said without enthusiasm.

His mother refused to let her good spirits be dampened. "If you don't want to smell pine, just go into the kitchen. You've never smelled so many wonderful things in all your life."

The swinging door to the room she was referring to banged open and Davey, Phineas and Arne came toppling out. As a group, the three never seemed to move normally.

"Josh, you're home!" Davey bent over and rammed his head into his brother's flat midsection in a brotherly greeting that had once been standard between them. Though the blow came padded by Josh's heavy wool coat, the surprise nearly knocked him over.

"Hey, little brother!" Josh protested. "You're getting too big to do that."

Davey grinned. "I'm catching up on you, big brother. I'm taller than Mama now, and almost as tall as Kari. Well, not quite—but she's really tall for a girl."

"In Norway all girls are so tall," Arne interrupted, his face solemn. His smile had disappeared the minute he had seen Josh.

"Anyway," Davey continued, ignoring his suddenly sober friend, "you've got to *eat* some of this stuff, Josh. Kari's made..." He turned to Arne for support and the Norwegian boy nodded his head in confirmation as Davey pronounced each item. "... *krum kake* and *sandbaakels* and *fattigmann*. It's better than Schnickelheimer's Bakery! And Mama's made suet pudding!"

Josh looked at his mother in surprise. She was beaming proudly. "I've been plumping the currants for days," she said with a happy smile.

Davey tugged on one sleeve of Josh's massive coat and pulled him through the kitchen door. Kari was standing over the stove holding what looked to Josh like a curling iron. She was in a bright blue frock, which matched exactly the color of her eyes. A much-stained apron covered the front, following the firm curves of her breasts. Her cheeks were flushed from the heat, and moisture showed on her upper lip and along her slender neck. Josh's breath caught in his throat.

He had actually forgotten, these weeks away from home, how extraordinarily beautiful she was. Even here—in the kitchen, in a dirty apron with her sleeves rolled past her elbows—she looked like a vision from another life. He blinked once, hard, and started to unbutton his big coat.

"Welcome home, Josh," she said softly.

Davey was waving a tray under his nose, filled with all manner of delicate confections. "Look, Josh. They're great! You've got to try some."

"Hello, Kari," he answered.

Seeming to regain her composure after a moment's hesitation, she turned her attention to the instrument in her hand.

"What are you doing?" Josh shrugged out of his coat and crossed the room to her side. He asked the question loudly. He wondered if the other occupants of the room couldn't hear his heart thunder as it did in his own ears.

Kari looked up with the smile that had haunted his sleep every single night he was away. "This is *krum kake*. Mrs. Bjornsen at Henrik House has loaned me her iron. I think you will like it. It's very light and sweet."

Josh watched as she poured batter onto a round, flat plate and pressed it down with another so that it cooked to golden brown like a wafer-thin pancake. Then she deftly rolled the fragile pastry around the curling-iron-type instrument so that it cooled into a perfect cylinder, which she carefully rolled in a plate of sugar.

She slipped the last pastry expertly off the metal rod and then reached over to pick out a cooled piece for Josh.

"Here," she said, holding out the offering between sugary fingers.

Josh leaned over and let her put it directly into his mouth. It seemed to melt there of its own accord. He could not say how it made its way to his stomach. She smelled of spices and pine.

"Well?" she asked.

"Well, what?" Josh knew he was staring at her, but he couldn't seem to help it. He wiped his forehead. The kitchen was stifling with steamy warmth after his long ride in the snow.

Kari looked exasperated. "Do you like it? Do you like my *krum kake?*"

"It's very good," he said stiffly. "Thank you." This was ridiculous, he thought to himself. He couldn't even make normal conversation any longer. This was why he had stayed away these past weeks. He should have kept away.

He turned around to leave. He would go call on the Penningtons, he told himself. He had left the city without even saying goodbye to them. It was one of the reasons he had decided to come home for Christmas. The holiday would be difficult for them. But perhaps the visit could wait until tomorrow.

All at once he felt incredibly tired. He looked back at Kari. She had a look of hurt in her eyes that had become too familiar to him. A look which he put there. She never looked that way with anyone else. He took a deep breath and started toward the door.

Helen Lyman stood in his path, her eyes calculating. "You will join us for morning services tomorrow, Joshua?" she asked.

Josh nodded. "Of course. But I think I'll just turn in now for the night. It was a long ride."

Without another word he disappeared through the swinging door. Helen smiled at Kari. "He's just too tired, my dear. You'll see—in the morning everything will be better."

But everything was not better as far as she could see, Kari thought to herself. Josh made a point of touching her as briefly as possible as he helped her into the carriage. And the chattering of Davey and Arne was the only conversation during the drive to church. Josh sat morose and silent in one corner of the vehicle.

Of course, he was undoubtedly thinking about his wife, Kari reasoned. It was only natural at this time of year. She certainly had been full of thoughts about her father as she went through the familiar Christmas rituals of decorating and baking. Josh hadn't had that many years with Corinne, but he must be remembering that this time last year they had been together. Whatever he was thinking, he didn't appear to be about to share it with her. In fact, Josh had never talked with her about his marriage. Kari had come to dread the coldness that shut off all communication whenever the subject came up.

The Lymans and their Norwegian visitors arrived at the First Methodist Church just in time. The large clapboard building would serve another year or two as the home for the church until the imposing stone structure on the edge of town was finished.

Josh found it comforting to be once again inside the old cavernous structure. It wasn't a pretty church. The windows were plain, and didn't have the soaring angles of the Catholic church that had been built downtown. But there was that familiar odor—candle wax and mustiness. The church was not kept heated during the week, and the pew cushions smelled like wet clothes left too long in the basket. They needed a good airing in bright sun, Josh reflected idly. Of course, they'd needed that for years.

The service was about to start and the front left-hand pew, which was informally acknowledged by the other church members as the Penningtons' property, was still empty. Josh shrugged the stiffness out of his shoulders.

Reverend Patterson's homily was mercifully brief, and then came the rest of the traditional Christmas ritual. Davey joined a row of freshly scrubbed youths who took nervous turns reciting the verses that told the age-old Christmas story.

Davey's eyes held a mischievous twinkle as he ended his lines. "...which the Lord ha*thhhh* made known unto us." He stepped back after a quick wink at Arne who was sitting next to Kari trying to keep a properly sober expression.

Finally, the service ended with a curiously pretty blend of young, middle-aged and old voices joining for the familiar Christmas hymns. They stood to leave, and Josh was surprised to find himself smiling, at peace for the first time in weeks.

He ruffled Davey's thick brown hair. "Nice job, little brother," he said affectionately.

Davey grinned his pleasure, then pushed past Josh to catch up with Arne. Josh took his mother's arm, leaving Kari to walk behind them down the narrow church aisle, but as soon as they reached the wide church doors, he reached backward and drew her up to walk beside them, his arm snugly tucked around hers.

The snow had started again and big, wet flakes floated lazily down around them. The children dashed here and there catching them on their tongues. Kari, Josh and his mother stopped at the top of the church steps to watch them.

Josh took a deep breath of the pleasantly cold winter air. "Nothing like being young in a snowfall," he said with a smile.

Kari smiled back at him. The golden crown of her braid was beginning to sparkle with fluffy snow. "It's good for Christmas. There should always be snow for Christmas."

Unconsciously, Josh had released his mother's arm, but not Kari's. He stood with the shoulder of his thick wool coat pressed against her arm and back, enjoying the warmth of her next to him.

Inevitably, a group of the older children had started a snowball fight in the corner of the churchyard. Davey and Arne appeared to be among the leaders. With a swift pang, Josh wished for a moment that he again were fifteen years old, being pelted with icy-cold splatters of snow. He pulled Kari closer to his side and looked down at her. The tip of her nose had reddened with the cold.

"We should get started home," he said, noticing finally that his mother had descended the stairs on her own and was engaged in a surprisingly animated conversation with Theo Pratt who ran the feed mill at the edge of town.

But it was quite some time before they actually loaded back into the big black buggy for the trip home. First, Kari had to be introduced to Mr. Pratt, and then Josh had been called on to settle a dispute among the snowball warriors, and somehow had ended up smack in the middle of the icy fracas, giving as good as he got, which was quite good. By the time the fight had ended, his navy blue coat was mostly a powdery white. His neck was wet from where the most strategic missiles had landed inside his collar. And he was *laughing*. Laughing so hard that the merriment spilled over into the buggy as they all climbed in for the ride home.

"Hey, Josh, you got that Johnny Hofmeier right in the cheek," Davey congratulated his brother. "He looked like he'd swallowed a horny toad."

Josh took a sideways glance at his mother. He ran a finger along the inside of his damp collar. "I think he paid me back for that one," he said, his smile only slightly chagrined.

Helen Lyman's gentle laugh was heartier than usual. "You boys are soaked through. You'll catch your death, I swear."

Kari leaned back against the cold leather of the carriage seat, and listened in quiet contentment as Arne and Davey recounted the epic snow battle blow by blow. Arne looked so happy, she thought to herself. So at peace and comfortable with his new friend, his new home. And Josh... Relaxed and joking with the younger boys, he looked heartbreakingly handsome and suddenly years younger. The smile on his face was genuine and looked much more natural on him than the tension and strain that was all she had seen there for so long. In spite of the cold inside the drafty carriage, it seemed as if a lump of ice around her heart was beginning to melt.

Over Kari's fish chowder at supper, there had been a lively debate about when the gifts would be exchanged. Kari and Arne voted for Christmas Eve, while the Lymans held out staunchly for Christmas morning. Davey had recited an entire passage about democracy and majority rule from his American history textbook, but finally Helen and Josh voted to defer to their foreign guests, and it was decided to bring out the gifts around the fire in the parlor after everyone pitched in to help with the washing up, since Daisy was spending the holiday with her family.

Still without funds to purchase Christmas gifts, Kari had enlisted Helen's help in obtaining the yarn for making identical scarves for Arne and Davey, knit in a tightly woven pattern of white geometric snowflakes on a dark blue background. For Helen herself, Kari had painstakingly written out the words to several of the Norwegian songs that they enjoyed singing together. She'd bound the papers with ribbon and decorated the volume with expertly detailed sketches of songbirds. Painting and drawing had always been easy for her, and her skillful hands wrought the same magic with her designs that her voice did with the old Norwegian melodies.

She'd thought, as she worked on the volume, that it would be something for the older woman to remember her by when Kari was gone. It was the same impulse, she supposed, which prompted her to spend long hours on Josh's gift. She'd found a wooden cigar box and had polished and lacquered it to a brilliant shine. Then she'd painted it in the rosemaling fashion she'd learned back in Stavanger—intricate designs of flowers and brightly colored patterns of spirals and lines. The result was a veritable work of art.

During the weeks Josh was away, she had begun to wonder if she would be brave enough to give it to him. But the day had gone so well, and Josh had been in such a good mood, that she decided it would be all right. Then he, too, would have something to remember her by when she and Arne went off to make their new life in Minnesota.

"Arn' and I made our gifts together," Davey announced loudly as his brother dropped a huge sugar maple log on the fire.

Josh stepped back from the shower of sparks and dusted off his hands. "Well, let's see 'em, then!"

The two boys stood and, sharing their hold on each crudely wrapped package, delivered them with broad smiles, first to Davey's mother, then Kari, then Josh.

Josh had his open first and he gave a low whistle. "You say you boys *made* this?" It was a carved wooden pipe, with the bowl fashioned into the twisted face of an old man or something resembling a dwarf.

"It's a Norwegian troll," Davey explained eagerly. "Arne taught me how to do it. Actually *he* did the hard parts," he added reluctantly.

Josh smiled his thanks to the towheaded boy, but Arne averted his eyes and went over to stand next to his sister. Her gift and Helen's were both wooden combs. Kari's had roses carved all along the spine and Helen's looked like a twisted grapevine.

"These are beautiful, boys," Kari said warmly. She reached over the arm of the sofa to give her brother a hug. The smile, which had briefly left his face, returned.

Josh pulled several packages from behind the corner whatnot. "These are from Mother and me," he said softly, handing Arne the first bundle.

The boy tore into the package eagerly, his customary awkwardness when around Josh forgotten for the moment.

"Oh," he breathed, sitting down on the carpet. The brown paper package held three schoolbooks, duplicating the ones he had been sharing with Davey each day. He looked up, eyes shining. "Now, I *really* will learn the English very, very good," he said happily.

Kari's eyes filled. She looked from Josh to Helen. "Thank you both. You've been so very kind to us."

Josh held out a package. "This one's for you."

He watched as she carefully folded back the paper to reveal three dress lengths. The first was a bright checked green gingham, then a cozily soft gray muslin and finally a shimmering blue silk. Her slender fingers smoothed along them reverently. "It's too much," she said softly, keeping her eyes down and focused on the fresh new fabrics. Bright spots of scarlet had appeared on each cheek. "But it will be wonderful to have something of my own again."

Helen reached across the sofa and gave Kari's hand a gentle squeeze. "It's the least we can do, my dear, after the way you've taken care of all of us these past weeks."

It was just like Helen to know the right thing to say to put her at ease with the gift. Kari raised her eyes to the older woman. "Thank you," she said simply.

"So." Josh cleared his throat. He turned away and handed the last package to Davey, who set himself immediately to untying the cord which held the brown paper around the long box. Inside was a rifle, its sleek wooden stock gleaming in the firelight and reflecting the sparkle in Davey's eyes.

"Oh, Josh," he breathed. "It's my own...really mine?"

Josh grinned and nodded. He remembered when he'd gotten his own rifle at just about Davey's age. He'd been proud as a struttin' rooster and had looked nearly as silly, he imagined, as he remembered dancing around the room with it under his papa's indulgent smile.

Arne dropped his new schoolbooks and knelt beside Davey, his hand outstretched to touch the gun. "In Stavanger I have a...how you say...shotgun," he said softly, running his finger reverently along the polished metal barrel. "But we sell to come to America. I never have a rifle."

Josh took one look at the Norwegian boy's face and resolved that before he and Kari headed off to the wilderness of Minnesota, the boy would have his own rifle.

Kari rose from the sofa and reached for four neatly wrapped packages she had left on the side table. The boys pulled themselves away from admiring the new rifle long enough to open their scarves. They both shouted their thanks and draped the warm garments around their shoulders, but soon the two heads were bent together again over Davey's present. It was Helen who said, "Kari, those are beautifully done."

She was opening her own package and her eyes opened wide when she saw the exquisite sketching. "Oh, my goodness, child! You did these?"

She held the book up for Josh to see and he gave a low whistle. The drawings were truly expert quality, and it delighted Josh to see his mother's enthusiasm as she turned the pages of Kari's painstakingly done book.

"Aren't you going to open yours?" Kari asked him shyly. She couldn't remember ever having given a gift to a man before, except her father. Perhaps Josh would think it was a silly gift. All at once the flowers and swirls seemed entirely too flippant for a serious and successful businessman. She sank down on the sofa again, her expression shuttered.

Josh opened his package slowly. He hadn't expected a gift from Kari. The truth was he had hardly remembered it was Christmas. He had had a vague notion of ignoring Christmas entirely this year, in deference to their mourning, but his mother had protested that it would not be fair to deprive the young boys of their holiday. It was her prompting that had sent him downtown upon his arrival in Milwaukee yesterday to pick up gifts for Davey and their visitors.

He pulled the paper away from his gift and bright colors spiraled out at him from the gleaming black background of the box. Josh had never seen anything quite like it. He looked at Kari in wonder. "You made this, too?" he asked her.

Kari nodded. Her hand, which had clenched the fabric of the sofa arm, relaxed slightly. At least he wasn't laughing. In fact, his strong fingers were tracing lightly over the polished surface of the box with something of the same reverence that Arne and Davey had shown the rifle.

"It's . . . not so much," Kari stammered, her accent becoming suddenly more pronounced. "Just a box . . . to use for things, you know."

Josh felt an unfamiliar heat rising in his cheeks. He imagined Kari laboring over the intricate design and felt as if he was holding a little piece of her vibrant spirit.

His mind shifted suddenly to last Christmas. Corinne had given him an expensive pair of Spanish riding boots. They were exquisite, made of the finest leather and entirely too flimsy and impractical to be of absolutely any use to him. The bill had arrived on his desk a week later. He'd paid it, worn the boots once or twice to try to please his wife and then had tucked them away in the back of his wardrobe.

Corinne had been happy that Christmas, he remembered. He had carefully chosen several gifts for her, hoping, he supposed, to bring back the sunny child he had once known. And he had very nearly succeeded. The day had passed pleasantly. His mother had managed to leave her room long enough to join them at their traditional Christmas dinner with the Penningtons, and Corinne had been all smiles most of the day. It was only after her family had left that the cheerfulness disappeared. With suddenly dull eyes she had shrugged away the sight of the dining room full of dishes and had retired to her room. A newly employed Daisy had left early for her own Christmas celebration, so Davey and Josh had finished the day cleaning up the mess. Josh looked down again at the beautiful box in his hands, forcing the unwanted memories back into a troubled area of his consciousness.

"It's splendid, Kari," he said at last. "Among all your other talents, we now discover that you are an artist."

Kari flushed with pleasure. "Hardly an artist," she said with a laugh. "But I do love to paint and draw. In Stavanger I painted almost everything in our home. Sometimes I would drive our papa crazy."

"Papa loved your designs, Kari." Arne had jumped up and was regarding Josh with a fierce gaze as though daring Josh to disapprove of his sister.

Josh gave him a patient smile. He wished there were something he could do to convince the lad that he meant his sister no harm, but, then again, perhaps Arne was right. By not being able to control his feelings around Kari, he *was* doing her harm. He tucked the thought away, back in the same corner with those memories of Corinne. It was Christmas Eve and he suddenly resolved that, for once, he was going to put aside the recriminations and pain, and enjoy this special time with his family and the beautiful young woman who had come mysteriously into their lives to brighten a household that had seen too much mourning.

"I think it's time for some music," Josh said. The enthusiasm in his voice radiated into the room, and Kari and Helen shared a smile. When Josh was happy, the whole world seemed brighter.

"We've been practicing Christmas songs, these nights you've been gone, Josh," Davey volunteered. "Some in English and some in Norwegian."

Josh placed Kari's box carefully on the table and then settled himself on the floor next to the fire. "Well, let's hear 'em!"

The next hour passed quickly as the group mixed the familiar with the new, blending Christmas sounds and memories from two different sides of the ocean. Finally, Helen stood and announced that it was well past bedtime.

Arne looked up in sudden anxiety. "Kari, we have forgotten to put out porridge for the *nissen!*"

Kari smiled at her brother. "What's a *nissen?*" Davey asked.

Helen settled back into her chair. "I sense that there is another one of your Norwegian tales behind this *nissen,* Kari," she said indulgently.

Kari looked down briefly at her clasped hands. "It's only a custom, it's not important." Then she looked over at Arne's blue eyes watching her intently. "You see, every farm in Norway has a little elf, a *nissen,* who lives in the barn. *Julaften*—Christmas Eve—is when they take stock of everything, decide if the farmer has been doing a good job."

"Like I tell you, Davey." Arne jumped into the tale. "You must to be very good to the animals in the days before Christmas because at midnight on *Julaften* they can *talk*. If they tell the *nissen* bad things, he will go away to another farm."

"It's very bad luck if your *nissen* leaves," Kari agreed, the twinkle in her eye contrasting with a solemn expression. "Some people become so desperate that they emigrate to America."

They all laughed, but Josh said with a serious face matching Kari's, "By all means we must get some porridge out for the poor little fellow. We Americans want to be sure *all* our Norwegian visitors are happy this Christmas."

Kari gave him a brilliant smile. "All right, Arne," she told her brother. "You and Davey go set a bowl out in the stable, and then it's to bed with you."

Arne gathered up his books and Davey the rifle and they dashed off toward the kitchen with the enthusiasm of children who had decided to push impending adulthood aside for a few more magical moments.

Helen gave her son and Kari a last sweet smile before she, too, went up to bed. With just the two of them left, Kari and Josh avoided each other's eyes. Finally Josh said lightly, "What kind of report do you think the *nissen* will get tonight, Kari? Will he want to stay on with us?"

"I think he will get a very good report."

"And he'll want to stay?"

She hesitated then said softly, "Yes."

Josh watched the fire flicker in her incredible blue eyes, then turned away. "I don't know how you had time to make all those things with all the other work you do around here.''

"I'm used to working," Kari said. "And the gifts...this was not work. This was...how do you say it?...from the heart.''

He busied himself banking the fire. "Mother is very appreciative of everything you've done here, Kari.''

She nodded but didn't reply. Helen's feelings weren't the ones she was interested in hearing about.

Josh cleared his throat. "Of course, I am, too. It's wonderful to see her looking so strong, feeling good again. And Davey is a new boy. I swear he's grown a foot since you started feeding him.''

Kari giggled. "He says they're starting to call him shorty-pants at school because all his pants are suddenly way above the ankle.''

Josh frowned. "Why hasn't he bought some new ones?''

"Well, I guess you weren't in town and he didn't exactly know how to go about getting them himself.''

Josh shook his head impatiently. "He should know he can put anything on account at the mercantile. Mother knows that, too." He sighed. "I suppose I should have thought of it before I left.''

"No," Kari said firmly. "You are right. He's old enough to know these things, and your mother is well enough now to see to some of them, too. Not every problem in the family should be on your shoulders, Josh, broad as they are.''

Josh couldn't tell if she flushed as she finished the last phrase or if it was just the way the dying firelight hit the delicate lines of her face. He smiled at the way her full lips had clamped into a stubborn line. It was a new sensation to have somebody standing up for him, and it gave him a warm feeling inside.

He opened his mouth to make a joking remark but, unbidden, the words came out seriously. "After my father died, my mother seemed to fall apart, and it was as if Davey and I had lost both parents at once. He was too young to do much on his own so..." He shrugged, and his smile turned a shade less bright.

Kari walked toward him where he stood by the fire. "So you took over," she finished for him. "You became mother, father, big brother, money-maker, businessman and head of house all in one."

Josh grinned. "From the way you make it sound, I guess it *is* lucky these shoulders of mine are broad."

Kari's eyes swept involuntarily across the strong expanse of his chest, which always looked just a touch too wide when he was in his "city" clothes. She reached out a hand and rested it against his arm. Even through the broadcloth of his jacket, the muscles beneath felt rock hard. "I know a little of how it feels, Josh. Remember, I was the 'mother' of my family, too. You've done a good job. Davey is a fine, happy boy."

Josh nodded thoughtfully. "I managed to do all right by Davey most of the time," he said. "But I couldn't seem to help Mother. You are the first one who's been able to do that."

"I think, perhaps, she was just ready to be helped. I happened to be the one who came along at the right time."

"You underestimate yourself, Kari. You have a tremendous power with people. I can feel it in this household.... Mother, Davey, even Daisy... they're like different people."

He covered her hand with his own, then took it gently to his mouth. His lips brushed gently across her knuckles. She shook her head in silent protest, but he didn't know if it was against his words or his action.

"You are the one, Josh, who...under-estimates," she said softly, stumbling over the word. "You have done so much for your family. More in three years than many men do in their whole lives."

Josh dropped her hand. He had made money, that was true, but he hadn't been able to replace his father. He hadn't been able to make his family happy. He hadn't even been able to make his wife happy. He looked down at Kari. Her blue eyes searched his face intently. But he couldn't get out the words to explain himself to her. It was rare that he had confided as much as he had. He couldn't remember ever being able to talk to someone like he could to her. Except, perhaps, to Grandpapa Lyman, back in Philadelphia. And that had been long enough ago as to seem like a dream.

He shook off the mists of the past. "Good night, Kari...Merry Christmas," he said softly, and leaned over to kiss her satin cheek.

Kari felt the brief warmth of his lips and her eyes fluttered closed. But in the next instant, a draft blew across her face from the opening of the double doors, and when she opened her eyes, he was gone.

Chapter Nine

Davey, Arne and Josh had been up since dawn. The boys had wanted to try out the new rifle, and Josh had insisted that the nearest to town they could use it would be Johnson's Wood. So off they trudged through the new snow just as the late-winter sun was casting its first feeble rays.

They came in stomping the cold out of their bones and all three talking at once about the morning's adventure. Kari encompassed them in one of her most angelic smiles. She loved these rare moments when all at once Josh was indistinguishable from the younger boys. His grin became cockier and his voice brightened a notch.

"So what did the mighty hunters bring home for breakfast?" she asked them, trying to look serious.

"We shoot only a tar-get," Arne volunteered, trying out his newest word.

Kari shook her head. "And here I was all ready for a nice bear steak."

"A little more practice and I'll bag you that bear, Kari," Davey said firmly. He seemed to have grown another inch since yesterday.

Kari let a corner of her smile show through. "Well, while we're waiting for the bear, maybe you'd like to try some of the chokeberry flapjacks I've got waiting."

The boys started to move eagerly toward the dining room but Josh stopped Davey with a firm hand on his shoulder. "That's *after* you put your rifle away, little brother, and after both of you wash up."

The little-boy grin was gone, but Josh still looked relaxed and at ease with himself. The tiny fire that had kindled in Kari's heart when she saw him at the snowball fight yesterday blazed warmer. It was good to see this side of him. The side that could be both a friend and a guardian to his little brother. The side that was not so consumed by self-reproach that no room was left for any enjoyment of life's small pleasures.

She had awakened this morning still feeling the tingle of his kiss on her cheek. Unlike the other times he had kissed her, with the desperation of guilt and thwarted passion, this kiss had been a simple communication of connection between two people. And it had reached down and entwined itself around her heart.

"How about you?" she teased, as Josh turned toward the dining room himself. "The 'big brother' does not have to wash up before breakfast?"

Josh grabbed her hand with a grin and led her toward the table. "Listen, Viking, if those flapjacks of yours are as good as the pie you made yesterday, I'm not waiting until those two stomachs with feet get their chance at them."

Kari laughed and her heart missed a beat at his use of the name he had given her back on the steamer to Milwaukee. That time now seemed very long ago.

Josh looked incredibly handsome seated at the head of the table as Kari came swinging through the dining room door with a plate piled high with the fluffy pancakes. His rugged features were flushed from the morning outing. He was wearing a red wool lumberjack shirt, which brought out the rich chestnut highlights of his unruly dark hair and made him look an entirely different person from the suit-clad businessman he usually appeared.

He smiled at her and her own expression brightened yet another degree as she carefully transferred several of the pancakes to his plate. She set the platter on the table and turned to move to her own place, but Josh caught her hand once more in his and held her there by his side. "It's been a long time since this family has had a cheery Christmas-morning breakfast, Kari," he said. "Thank you again."

"I'm glad that I could..." she began softly, but her words were drowned out by the arrival of their duly washed-up younger brothers, who attacked the platter of flapjacks as if the food had in fact been that bear they had talked about earlier. Kari quietly took her seat and she and Josh watched in amusement as the gigantic stack disappeared in minutes.

For once, Arne seemed to have forgotten his resentment of Josh as the boys took turns telling Kari about the morning's shooting match. It seemed that Arne, though smaller and much more slender than Davey, had, with Josh's coaching, beaten the older boy in the target shooting. Davey had been so delighted by his new rifle that he hadn't minded losing the match. So both boys were full of good humor that infected the entire room.

Even Daisy, who had come in early this morning after spending Christmas Eve with her relatives, was caught up in the mood. She giggled like a little girl when Josh teased her about the new silver necklace hanging prominently on the outside of her apron.

"I don't remember seeing that beautiful necklace on you before, Daisy," he told her with mock severity. "Could it be Charles is finally declaring his intentions?"

Daisy rubbed the smooth pendant lovingly between her fingers. "Christmas seems to bring out the best in men, Mr. Josh," she answered him with a dreamy air that lacked her usual sauciness.

"You just make sure he keeps up that good behavior after the Christmas spirit's over," he told her. His face was serious but he looked over at Kari with a wink.

"Yes, sir," Daisy answered emphatically. "I surely do intend to see to just that very thing." She grabbed the empty pancake platter as if it were her beau's collar and marched off with it to the kitchen. With the food gone, Davey and Arne stood with mumbled thank-yous and dashed away to answer once again the call of the fresh snow.

Kari leaned back in her chair with a contented sigh as she watched them go. "Daisy is right—the Christmas spirit brings out the best in everyone."

"When I was a child, every fall I used to count up the days left until Christmas," Josh said. "Then I'd put that many stones in an old milking pail out in the stable, so each day I could take out one stone and see Christmas getting closer and closer." Josh took a long sip of his coffee. "I remember one year one of the horses kicked the pail over and the stones scattered every which way. I was in a panic—it was as if Christmas wouldn't come if I couldn't count the stones."

"But it came anyway," Kari said softly.

Josh smiled. "Yes, it came anyway."

"You look younger when you smile." The words were out of Kari's mouth before she had thought about them, but Josh didn't seem to mind.

"Well, now, that's not necessarily a good thing," he told her, his smile teasing now and more youthful than ever.

"How do you expect me to order around a whole camp of lumber men twice my size if I look my age?"

"Twice your size?" Kari's eyes widened as she glanced quickly across the broad expanse of red wool covering Josh's chest.

"At least," Josh said firmly. He picked up a stray chokeberry from beside his plate and popped it into his mouth. "Wait until you see Baby Olav. He eats his stew every night out of a washtub."

Kari giggled. "I don't believe you. In Stavanger we have lots of big, big men, but they all eat out of bowls, just like the rest of us."

"Not Baby Olav," Josh said firmly, but his brown eyes twinkled.

"You like to go to the camps, don't you?"

Josh nodded. "Sometimes life seems so basic out there. You work hard, eat hard, laugh hard. There's not much time or energy left for frettin'. It seems like back here in the city, folks spend too much of their time frettin' about one thing or another."

"At least, *you* spend too much time frettin', Josh. It's good to see you laughing with the boys these past two days."

Josh stretched his long legs out under the table. The strong black coffee had filtered out through his limbs. He felt relaxed and pleasantly full of flapjacks. Frettin' was the farthest thing from his mind. He had the sudden thought that he would be happy to stay here like this forever, listening to Kari's musical voice talking and laughing.

He looked at her across the table. Her braid was different again today. How many different ways did she know to weave that golden hair? She was in her yellow dress, the one that made her look like a captured ray of sunlight. Or... "The first buttercup in spring," he said aloud.

"I beg your pardon?" Kari asked.

"You...in that dress. You're like the first flower you see all at once on the side of a hill after a whole bleak winter." His voice grew husky. "Unexpectedly bright. Life-giving."

No slow flush this time, but a sudden flaring red that had her cheeks burning in an instant. "Why, Josh...what a lovely thing to say."

"I can be lovely when I want to be," he said with his little-boy grin. He pushed himself back from the table and stood up, extending a hand to her. "C'mon. Let's go see if buttercups wilt in new snow."

Kari felt pleasantly tired as she sank into the downy cushions of the parlor sofa. It was the first day since she had come to America, she realized, that she could call herself truly happy. And the first day in a much longer time that she had laughed so hard, she felt the pull of it in the muscles around her stomach. Josh was building up the fire and she smiled at the back of his head. He had changed out of his informal wool shirt after a wild romp in the snow that morning with Davey and Arne. But for once, he wore his snowy-white shirt open at the neck without a cravat. And his hair fell in careless waves, minus the grease he often used to slick it back.

They had all laughed so hard at dinner that Daisy had come scowling in from the kitchen to scold them for not paying enough attention to the carefully prepared meal. Of course, she had started the whole thing by bringing in the roast leg of pork with a wicked, significant grin at Davey. "Enjoy your Christmas dinner, young man," she'd said smugly. Which had sent Davey, Arne at his heels, tearing out to the stable to check on the status of Porky, the little piglet of the boys' practical joke, which had now become a member of the household.

Assured that all four of Porky's legs were still firmly attached to his squat little body, the boys trooped sheepishly back into the dining room and resumed their places. But by then, Josh, Kari, Helen and Daisy were sharing a good laugh at their expense.

All in all, it had been a wonderful day, Kari reflected. And the most wonderful part had been seeing Josh enjoy himself. Perhaps, finally, the shroud of mourning and guilt that engulfed him and seeped out from him to spread itself over the whole household would begin to disintegrate. Perhaps the specter of his wife would begin to fade and the two of them could begin to relate as normal, healthy young people who feel a natural attraction for each other.

By now Kari knew that the attraction was certainly strong enough on her side. And every now and then she had the feeling that Josh felt it, too. But then he would pull back into himself. That haunted look would come into his eyes and his face would tighten. She hadn't seen that look all day. And in spite of her fears that Christmas would prove to be a time of painful memories, no one had even mentioned Corinne. Kari had thought a lot about her own father, and she suspected that Helen's thoughts were full of her late husband, but, as if by mutual consent, neither woman broke the mood of gaiety with talk of lost loved ones.

The fresh wood crackled as Josh added it to the fire. Its pungent smoke joined with the smell of Kari's pine-bough decorations to fill the room with the wonderful odor of the forest. Josh took in a deep breath and turned to glance around the parlor at his family.

His mother was in her usual, favorite rocker, which she'd brought with her all the way from Pennsylvania. He could picture her as she had sat there last Christmas, pale and tired. And he'd wondered if by the time the next Christmas rolled around, he would have neither one of his parents to celebrate with. Now, amazingly, after a full day, she was taking her embroidery out of her red lacquered sewing box. She looked up at him and smiled, her cheeks glowing and her hazel eyes dancing in the blazing light of the fire.

Davey and Arne were lying on their stomachs, heads together over a game of cards.

Kari had changed into an old maroon silk dress of his mother's. The dark color heightened the natural rose of her complexion. She looked serious and dignified, not at all as she had pushing him into a snowbank that morning with her hair flying loose and her blue eyes snapping with mischief. Now every hair was in perfect order, piled in gold twists on her head. The maroon dress was edged with a simple strand of ivory lace, cut low enough to just hint at the perfection of her full breasts. She stared into the fire, her silhouette a flawless cameo, and all at once Josh realized that the breath he had taken had gotten stuck somewhere deep in his chest. He exhaled shakily, and moved to the sofa to sit beside her. His mother watched him with a knowing gaze.

Kari came out of her reverie and smiled brightly at Josh as he sat beside her. "Our first Christmas in America...it's been wonderful," she said softly. "Thanks to you." She turned to look at Helen. "Thanks to *all* of you," she amended.

"Well, it's not over yet," Josh said after clearing his throat. "You promised me some Norwegian Christmas songs, and I promised the boys some popcorn."

Kari put a hand on her stomach. "After that meal? I can't believe I will ever eat again. But singing . . . yes, this we can do."

She stood and went to stand by the fire, her hand on the mantelpiece. She wasn't used to such a formal pose for her singing, but decided that it would be easier than trying to find her voice with Josh sitting there so close to her on the sofa, his intense eyes watching her. Here she felt herself again, and without any preliminaries launched into a clear simple song that told of the magic events of that Christmas so long ago. Only Arne could understand the words, but each occupant of the room was nevertheless caught up in the spell of the tale. The boys left their cards untouched, and Helen's hands froze over the sewing hoop.

So engrossed were they all in the enchantment of Kari's music that no one had heard the visitors' arrival in the front hall. As the song ended, Daisy cautiously opened the parlor doors. "The Penningtons are here, Mrs. Lyman," she announced in hushed tones. Josh jerked up straight as if a spark from the fire had jumped out and burned him. His face paled. "The Penningtons are here?"

The Penningtons and the Lymans had spent Christmas together since Josh was a boy. But it had not even occurred to him that they would continue the tradition this year, with their tragedy so recent. They had not appeared in church for the Christmas Eve services yesterday. He berated himself for not having visited them as he had planned as soon as he had come back from the lumber camps. Perhaps if he had spent some time with them, this awkward visit could have been avoided.

Helen bent to put her sewing into the bag at her side. "You know they always come Christmas afternoon, Joshua," she said gently. "They have for years. Show them in, Daisy."

Kari didn't move. Her fingers tightened on the edge of the mantel.

Davey threw his cards onto the pile on the floor. "C'mon, Arne," he said. "Phineas is here. Let's go show him my rifle."

They jumped up and made their way out of the room just as the two older Penningtons appeared at the parlor doors. Mr. Pennington stepped aside to allow the two boys to pass, and then the shouts of three boys filled the sudden silence of the room. After what seemed like an interminable moment to Kari, Josh stood and went to the door to usher them into the room.

"Vernon, Myra," he said quietly. "It was good of you to come."

"We haven't missed a Christmas with you folks since Homer and I went into partnership back in '41," Vernon said brusquely. "Weren't about to miss one now. Regards of the season, Helen, miss...."

This last he addressed to Kari, who stood like a statue next to the mantel. For just a fleeting moment, his faded eyes warmed as they swept down the length of her long, well-formed figure, silhouetted in the maroon dress against the firelight.

Josh took his hand in a hearty shake, then turned to give Myra a heartfelt embrace. Raw emotion, which he had held at bay throughout the day, surged to the surface. "I'm glad you're here," he said to her softly, surprised to discover that he really meant the words.

The older Pennington boys had by now joined the group and, after polite greetings to Mrs. Lyman, were all three focusing on Kari. Emmett and Chester were frankly staring at the statuesque blond beauty, but the oldest, Thaddeus, walked across the room to her and put out his hand.

"We haven't formally met, miss. I'm Thaddeus Pennington."

Kari shook his hand and rewarded his gesture with one of her sweetest smiles. "Pleased to meet you," she said, and all eyes in the room turned toward the musical sound of her voice.

Emmett and Chester bumped into each other trying to maneuver around the long sofa to reach her and follow their brother's lead.

"I'm Emmett."

"I'm Chester."

Both young men spoke their names and extended their hands toward her at the same time, which elicited an enchanting laugh that left all three brothers utterly under her spell.

Recovering from his initial emotion at the Penningtons' arrival, Josh watched the reaction of the brothers with surprise and the slow beginning of a strange feeling at the pit of his stomach.

Myra, too, had seen her sons' reaction to the beautiful foreigner. Though pleased by the sincerity of Josh's greeting, she was not over her resentment at this intruder into her mourning. And she was not about to let her sons forget it.

"My dear Helen," she said with a kind of loud determination, "it's good to see you looking so healthy, especially after the affliction we have all so recently suffered."

All three Pennington sons snapped their heads around toward their mother. By now they knew their roles well in this particular family drama. Their smiles disappeared instantly, and Thaddeus walked over to his mother and put his arm around her. "Now, Mama, you promised you weren't going to go all mushy on us for Christmas."

"I'm not going to go mushy, Thaddy," Myra said, her voice breaking slightly. "I'm just commiserating here with Helen. Corinne was her daughter, too, you know."

So the name was out. Corinne. The spectral presence that seemed to hover below the surface of everything he did nowadays. Josh backed away from Myra and turned to Vernon. "Sit down, sir. Let me go ask Daisy to bring us all something to drink."

With relief he slipped out from the suddenly overly warm parlor to the chilly front hall. He took a deep, cleansing breath of the frigid air. Except for that brief moment when they were opening gifts last night, he had pushed thoughts of Corinne to the back of his mind for two days now as he let himself enjoy the luxury of a real family Christmas—a healthy mother, a happy little brother...and Kari, laughing and serene and bright through all of it. But it was time to let Corinne surface. It wasn't fair to hold her down any longer. She had never come up to the surface of Lake Erie, but she could at least be allowed to surface in his thoughts, be welcomed by him, for this first Christmas separated from her family.

Slowly he walked toward the kitchen to find Daisy. He remembered with pain the scene in Corinne's bedroom last Christmas. After he and Davey had finished cleaning up the kitchen that night, and his brother had gone to bed, Josh had gone to her room, determined to end the day on a note of understanding, or at least of hope.

He had found her in tears in her bed. And when he had taken her gently in his arms and tried to get her to talk about what was disturbing her so, she had only stiffened and pushed him away. He remembered feeling the unshed tears in his own head that day, but he had not let them fall. He had never cried for Corinne...not then, not that night on Lake Erie...not now.

The mood had shifted when he once again entered the parlor. Vernon and Myra had taken chairs next to his mother and were involved in a conversation that evidently had something to do with the deteriorating state of the waterfront establishments as Milwaukee became an ever-more important port. He heard the term "riffraff" several times.

Kari was seated again on the sofa, flanked by Thaddeus on one side, Chester on the other and a kneeling Emmett practically at her feet. Her cheeks were unnaturally pink from the unaccustomed male attention, but Josh could see that she was not at all displeased by it. In fact, there was an almost coquettish sparkle in her eyes, which he didn't recognize.

"Was that you singing as we came in, Miss Kari?" Thaddeus was saying. "You have a most extraordinary voice."

It was a jolt to hear Thaddeus use Kari's first name, though of course Aslaksdatter was a mouthful. Kari must have given them permission to address her so. The Pennington boys were nothing if not polite.

Josh looked around the room. Unless he wanted to join Emmett on the floor, the only place for Josh to sit was the settee at the far end of the parlor. He moved toward it glumly. All the good feelings that had built up over the past couple days had completely disappeared in the past ten minutes.

"Won't you sing something else for us?" Chester asked and Emmett's "Oh, yes, please do" came right on top of it.

Josh settled uncomfortably on the straight-backed silk settee. He felt Kari's big eyes looking over at his with a question, and he reluctantly nodded to her. "Go ahead if you'd like, Kari."

Kari looked at the two strapping young men crowding her in on the sofa and said in a pretty confusion, "I believe I'll have to stand. I don't think I can sing with you two gentlemen so close by me."

Josh rolled his eyes as the two brothers jumped up and each offered a hand to help Kari to her feet. Laughing, she put each of her hands in one of theirs and gracefully stood. If Josh hadn't known better, he would have sworn that Kari's artless innocence was by design.

She went to stand once again by the mantel. "Most of the songs I know are in Norwegian," she said softly, her golden lashes sweeping demurely down against her cheeks. All three Pennington brothers had their eyes fixed on her as if she were some kind of ice-cream treat, Josh thought to himself. He had, he decided, never really been that fond of the Pennington brothers.

"We'd be happy to hear anything," Thaddeus assured her with a warm smile. He was the tallest of the three, who were all well above average height, and his business dealings had given him a self-assurance and polish that the two younger brothers still lacked.

The older Penningtons and Helen had stopped their conversation and had also turned their attention to the Norwegian beauty. Helen was smiling at her; Vernon's expression was noncommittal; but Myra sat stone faced.

Josh worried for just a moment that the woman's animosity would make Kari nervous or affect her singing, but it took only the first few notes to assure him that he had no cause for concern. As usual, when she sang, Kari seemed to enter another world. Her face became transfixed and the clear, perfect tones of her song reached deep into each of the listeners.

As the song ended, Josh tore his gaze away from Kari and surveyed the room. Thaddeus, in particular, was regarding Kari with a look of awed fascination that gave Josh another strange twist in his insides. Vernon looked on with a sad smile, but Myra now sat with her eyes closed, a single tear making its way down her rouged cheek.

This wasn't working, Josh thought violently. How many times had they all sat together in the Pennington music room listening to Corinne's expertly trained, emotionless piano recitals? He should have known better than to let Kari sing for them. She shouldn't be here. Or the Penningtons shouldn't be here. He couldn't quite decide which. At any rate, his head was beginning to feel as if someone had set off Independence Day rockets inside.

Kari could see immediately that her singing had been a disastrous mistake. How could she have been so insensitive? she berated herself. This poor woman had so recently lost a daughter, and now here she was singing and carrying on as if this were not a house of mourning.

She ignored the admiring congratulations of the three brothers and went directly over to Mrs. Pennington. Taking one of the woman's plump, soft hands in hers, she sank down next to her. "In my country we say that music is the language of the soul," she said to her gently. "So perhaps your beautiful daughter, whose soul is now freed for eternity, will hear us. Perhaps she's here with us now and knows that the tears you shed are for love of her."

Myra's tears were now falling in earnest, but she pulled her hand away from Kari's without answering and sat straighter in her chair. It was Vernon who reached over to pat Kari on the shoulder. "You have the voice of an angel, child," he said.

Josh stood and cleared his throat. He could see that his mother-in-law was one person who simply was not going to fall under Kari's spell. This meeting was a mistake, and the sooner he brought it to an end, the better. "It was good of you folks to stop by, Vernon,'' he said, calling the visit firmly to a close.

With varying degrees of relief, everyone except Helen arose and the customary goodbyes began. Myra had regained her composure. She leaned over to give Helen a little hug and allowed Josh a tepid embrace, but ignored Kari. Her rebuff went unnoticed amidst the attentive goodbyes given the beautiful Norwegian by the three Pennington boys. Thaddeus bent over her hand and brought it to his lips in a sophisticated gesture that left his two brothers gaping.

"Perhaps we will see you again soon, Miss Kari," he told her. His light brown eyes kindled for a moment, then became more reserved as he saw his mother glaring at him reproachfully. He dropped Kari's hand and turned to extend his own to Josh. "Thank you for having us," he said briskly, his voice a younger version of Vernon's.

Thaddeus and Josh had gone through school together. They shook hands now with that peculiar sense of adulthood that only comes between those who have once shared boyhood. "Anytime, Thaddeus," Josh said sincerely. "You all are always welcome in this house."

After a brief interlude while Phineas was summoned to take his leave, the Penningtons filed solemnly out the big front door, and it seemed to Kari as if the joy of the holiday followed right out with them.

There was a brief silence after they left, then Kari turned to Josh. His face was closed like a shutter. "We could finish our singing now," she said hopefully.

Josh shook his head. "I've heard enough singing for one day," he said curtly. "I've work to do." And without another word he turned and disappeared down the hall, heading for his office.

Kari turned to Helen with a look of exasperation on her face, and the older woman pursed her lips in distress. Davey and Arne, who had come down the stairs with Phineas as the Penningtons left, looked on in confusion. "What happened?" Davey asked.

Kari didn't answer him. What had happened, indeed? One minute the family was enjoying a happy Christmas day, and now all at once the air had become chillier than a winter morning with no firewood.

"The Penningtons still have a lot of hurt to get over about losing Corinne," Helen explained gently to her son. "It was just hard to be all together on Christmas without her. That's all."

Davey sent a worried look down the hall in the direction Josh had gone. "Did Josh get all sad, too?"

"Of course Josh is sad when he thinks about her, dear," Helen continued. "She was his wife."

"Yeah, but..." Davey stopped whatever he was going to say. He was beginning to learn that it was not always the wisest course to say everything one was thinking right out loud. He gave a half-disgusted sigh. "Well, that's it, then. Looks like Christmas is over with. C'mon, Arne."

He started to tug the younger boy back up the stairs with him, and Arne, after a quick troubled look back at his sister, went along.

"It's still all very recent, Kari," Helen said softly.

Kari nodded, her throat full. "I know. It's all right. At least we had a good Christmas... for a while."

"That we did." Helen put her arm around Kari and gave her a surprisingly forceful hug. "We had a very good Christmas. And now I'm going to go study that beautiful book you gave me. I'm going to have every one of those songs learned by the time you leave for Minnesota."

Kari gave her a wavery smile. "Thank you for everything, Helen. I'll never forget my first Christmas in America, and I'll never forget you...any of you."

A few tears began to fall as Kari wandered slowly back to her bedroom. They were tears for her father, for Christmas, for the Penningtons, and most especially...for Josh. But after a few moments, she wiped them away with an angry hand.

It had all been so perfect. Since the church service yesterday, it had seemed as if they were actually a family. Josh had been happy, playful, tender, all the things she had once thought she'd seen in him before he had become so distant and brooding. And his kiss last night. That, too, had been tender, a gentle side of him he seemed to want to keep from surfacing.

Now it was as if the events of the past two days hadn't happened. That cold look had slammed down over his face and he'd run away, just like before, to the bleak security of his chilly office. Well, she'd be darned if she'd let him spoil her first Christmas in America, Kari decided all at once. *She,* at least, had had a good time. The dinner had been wonderful...and the gifts. Arne had been so happy all day, he hadn't even brought up the subject of their father...or of Minnesota, either. If Josh wanted to wallow in grief or...or...whatever it was he was wallowing in, that was his problem!

She sat up in her bed and smoothed out her crumpled maroon gown. She hadn't needed to see the frank admiration in the Pennington brothers' faces to know that the dress suited her perfectly. Both the graceful lines and the color complemented her long, trim body. She bit her lip. There were, after all, a lot of interesting men in America.

She didn't have to rely for her happiness on a widower who shifted moods like a candle in the wind.

In fact, she thought to herself, her indignation building, she might just tell Mr. Josh Lyman that very thing.

Chapter Ten

Josh added the column of figures for the fourth time and got the fourth different result. Obviously, his concentration was not what it should be, he decided, to be working on the books. He was badly behind in his accounting after spending the extra time in the camps, and he needed to get back to it. But the past two days of holiday and family made it difficult to think about work.

He supposed he should have returned with them all to the parlor after the Penningtons left. He had seen the disappointment in Kari's face and the resignation in his mother's. But the Penningtons' visit had made him realize how close he had come to forgetting about Corinne and his responsibilities to her and to them; it had been almost as if he had put the past behind him for good and was starting over again with a new family. Which, of course, was not true. Kari and Arne were not his family. And soon they would be heading out to make their own lives in Minnesota.

He yawned. He'd been up with the boys before dawn, but rather than feel tired throughout the day, he'd felt exhilarated, full of energy. Until now. Now all at once he felt exhausted.

Without warning the office door opened and Kari came walking in. No, stalking in was more like it. Josh sat up in his chair, his fatigue all at once gone.

Two bright spots on Kari's cheeks almost matched the maroon of her gown. Her eyes flared a brilliant and angry blue. His guilt and unhappiness suddenly forgotten, Josh leaned back in his chair and enjoyed the sight. The serene, waxen beauty who had taken over the running of his house with such calm efficiency had all at once turned back into his Viking, full of spit and spirit.

He smiled and asked mildly, "Can I help you?"

"Yes!" Kari snapped and plunked herself down in the chair across from him. "You can stop making your family miserable."

Josh's smile disappeared. He regarded Kari's heaving chest for a moment and then said directly, "I wasn't aware that I was making anyone miserable but myself."

Kari jumped up, too upset to be still. In all her experience of caring for her father and raising Arne, she had always relied on logic and good common sense to deal with problems. She wasn't used to confrontation...or the churning kinds of emotions she was feeling now as she watched the shadows from the oil lamp play across the strong features of Josh's face.

She took a deep breath and made an effort to keep her voice low. "Now, there! That's just the problem. You think that you can shut yourself off from everyone, lock yourself away in here night after night, or run away to the woods, and that no one will be hurt but yourself. You're not thinking about your mother...or your brother..."

Or me, she wanted to say. But there she stopped. She had no right to expect that he would think about her. There was no reason for him to do so. The fact that *she* had fallen in love with him didn't mean that he...

Kari felt as if someone had hit her with a solid fist in the middle of the chest. She clutched the side of Josh's desk for support. It was true, she realized. She *had* fallen in love with him. And heaven help her. Because Josh had his own demons to fight before he could ever even think about loving again.

She turned slowly to face him once again and spoke slowly. "You've been thinking only of your own pain, Josh. Others hurt, too. They hurt with you…and *for* you. But you shut them out. You shut the world out. I thought with the nice Christmas we had that maybe you were beginning to realize that you have to be part of this family, not just provide for it, but when the Penningtons came, you changed. Everything changed."

She ended with a helpless wave of her hand that seemed to encompass all the good and all the painful feelings that had engulfed them in such quick succession that day.

Josh had seen Kari confused and struggling to find her memory. He had seen her indignant. But he had never seen her this way, this mixture of anger and emotion that seemed to have her long limbs literally atremble. He rose from his chair and went to her.

"I haven't meant to hurt anyone, Kari, least of all you."

His voice sounded bereft. He stood within inches of her, and all at once she felt an overwhelming urge to take him in her arms and tell him that everything would be all right. But she steeled herself. She had come to this room with the intention of shaking Josh out of his self-pity, and she wouldn't weaken now.

"Sometimes, Josh, I think if you could have buried Corinne—really *buried* her, I mean—" she paused and let the words fall cruelly into the shadowy room "—it would have been easier for you to bury this guilt and wretchedness along with her."

Josh winced. The swift, haunting image of his dreams flashed across his wide-awake eyes—Corinne's white body floating aimlessly in dark, troubled waters. Endlessly. "I couldn't find her," he said in a cracking whisper. His eyes were glazed.

Kari took a strong grip on each one of his arms and turned him to face her. "*You* couldn't find her, and nobody else could. Any more than they could find three hundred other people that night. It was horrible." She paused and gave a little shudder, the nightmare memories pulling at her, too. "It was horrible, Josh, but *it wasn't your fault*. There was nothing more you could have done that night. There's nothing more you can do for Corinne now. She has her tomb. It's called the SS *Atlantic* and it's at the bottom of the lake."

Kari's voice was shaking now. It was no longer clear who was steadying whom as she kept her fierce grip on his strong arms. They stood like that for a long moment, then without conscious effort on either part, Josh's arms slid up around her and hers moved behind him in an embrace that left their bodies pressed tightly together. Through the thin muslin of her gown she felt his heat along her entire length. Her breasts stiffened and, though covered, it seemed as if she could feel on them the rasp of his wool waistcoat.

"Oh, Kari," he said in a breath, and then his mouth was on hers, demanding and firm, asking for succor and, perhaps, forgiveness, perhaps oblivion.

Kari felt a swift, almost painful, wave surge through her, starting at the base of her groin and radiating to where the taut tips of her breasts crushed against the ungiving hardness of his chest. His tongue swept greedily along the sensitive areas just inside her lips, then mated with her own in a desperate tangle. Without losing an inch of contact, he turned her against the edge of the desk where he could steady her as he made her aware of the hard ridge of his manhood.

It seemed to Josh as if he had waited for this moment since he had first seen Kari on the docks in Montreal. Nothing in his experience—the fumbling experiments of boyhood, the practiced lovemaking of the shantyboy "ladies," his rejected attempts to apply the art he had learned from these generous experts to his own marriage—none of it seemed to have any relation to the swift, absolute hunger he felt for this Nordic goddess. It pulsed through him now and left him shaking with need.

"Kari," he groaned and ground the lower part of his body once more against her. "I want you. Let me..." His hands began pushing at her dress, finding her strong, smooth thighs beneath bunched-up petticoats.

She was, by now, half sitting on Josh's desk, her back pushed uncomfortably against the hammered brass corner of an old record book. With his mouth off hers and his body pulled away, Kari felt her blood slow. A sob of frustration rose in her throat. "Josh!" she said and pushed against him forcefully with the heels of both hands.

For a moment her protest had no effect, but when she said his name again, more sharply, he let go of her abruptly and took a step back. He was breathing deeply, and his chestnut hair fell in waves across his forehead. "I'm sorry," he said softly. The desire faded from his eyes, replaced by the same troubled look Kari had seen so often these past weeks.

He straightened and averted his eyes as Kari stood and rearranged her rumpled skirts. "I'm sorry, I don't know what happened.... I acted..." His face got that closed look and he said stiffly, "Forgive me, Kari. I don't know what came over me."

Kari finished shaking out her skirts with a little stamp of her foot. "Sorry... always sorry!" she said angrily. "I'm not asking for you to be sorry, Josh. That's the problem, you're too much sorry!"

As usual, when Kari became flustered, her accent deepened a bit and Josh felt himself relax as the charming inflection forced an inner smile. She looked so beautiful standing there, her face flushed with indignation. Her braids had tumbled out of their neat twists and hung down to her shoulders like a little girl's.

"All we did was make a kiss," she continued. "Nothing to be sorry for. A kiss is nothing.... I kiss lots of boys." She couldn't believe that such a lie had crossed her lips. Josh certainly did bring out the bad in her. But she had been so very angry with his endless self-recriminations, and then had gotten even angrier as she had seen the beginnings of a smile turn up the corners of those full lips, which had so recently wreaked havoc to her insides. Was the man trying to drive her crazy?

"I kiss... lots of times." She repeated the lie firmly.

Josh's eyebrow shot up. Was she telling the truth? he wondered. She seemed to have the innocence of a babe, yet he remembered all at once how the three Penningtons had crowded around her like alley cats at full moon.

"Well, then," he said smoothly, suppressing a swift surge of irritation. "Since you're so... experienced, I withdraw my apology. Now are you happy?"

His aggravation rose as she returned a smile that in his mind could only be described as smug. And it wasn't helped any by the fact that his body was issuing a screeching protest at the abrupt withdrawal of attention at an almost unbearable pitch of excitement.

"Yes, I'm very happy!" she snapped, and turned with an uncharacteristically dramatic flounce toward the door.

"Well, good!" he snapped back.

Kari was more than happy; she was exultant. She had roused Josh from his lethargy, and when it looked as though he would sink right back into it, she had managed instead to make him angry. Instinctively she knew that anger was healthier than the constant guilt, the withdrawal, the denial. She didn't know exactly what the next step would be, but perhaps from the anger would grow something more positive. Perhaps even something that could mean a future for the two of them.

She stopped at the door and turned back to him. "That felt like *akevitt*," she said with a smile.

Josh looked up from an intense examination of his shoe. "Excuse me?"

"You remember my *Onkel* Einar and the *akevitt?*" She made a weaving circular motion with her head.

Josh nodded with a slight frown of confusion.

"The kiss...it made me feel like too much *akevitt*." She grinned. "Very nice."

And then she was gone, leaving Josh staring in amazement at the closed office door.

"I want to go right now." Arne spoke the words in Norwegian and looking at his tear-stained face, Kari didn't have the heart to scold. In a gesture from their childhood that was becoming increasingly infrequent these days, she put her arms around his bony shoulders and her forehead up against his.

"C'mon, *lille bror*," she murmured gently. "You're just upset because Davey and Phineas ganged up on you."

Arne shrugged out of his sister's embrace and wiped away a sniffle. Traces of flour from Kari's apron clung to the front of his shirt. "What is 'ganged up'?" he asked with a glower.

"Well, I mean you three were arguing and it ended up with you against the two of them. That always makes the odd one feel bad."

"They are sonofabitches."

"Arne! Shame on you. Where did you learn that expression?"

He looked up at her with a glint of triumph in his eye. "From Josh. That's where I learn this word. The man at the pier yesterday told him he couldn't have his old docking space and when the man leaves, Josh calls him 'sonofabitch.'" Arne smiled smugly, his tears almost forgotten with this sudden opportunity to discredit their American host in his sister's eyes.

"Mmm. Well, it's not a nice thing to say, Arne. Don't use it again."

"Josh used it three times. 'Sonofabitch, sonofabitch, sonofabitch.'" His cracking thirteen-year-old voice spewed out the words with relish.

"That's enough, Arne." She gave her brother a shrewd look. He had continued his unrelenting hostility toward their American host. It was only when Josh took the two boys out to the woods for target practice that Arne became the agreeable boy she was used to. And once or twice after these sessions, she had caught her brother looking at Josh with a glimmer of respect in his eyes. "I didn't know that you had become so fond of Josh as to want to model everything you do on his behavior."

Arne pulled his head up sharply. "I model *nothing* on him," he said vehemently.

Kari sighed and shook her head. "Josh has been very good to us, Arne."

"Then why does he make you sad? He makes you cry. . . I've heard you in your room."

Kari wished she could hug him again. It was easier, somehow, when comforting could be done with a warm touch rather than words. "I can't explain to you what's between Josh and me," she said at last. "But whatever it is, you don't have to worry. I'm not unhappy. In a few weeks we'll be on our way to Minnesota, and neither one of us will have to concern ourselves about Josh."

Arne looked skeptical. "Do you promise?"

Kari gave in to the impulse and put one arm around him for a brief moment. "I promise, little brother. Now why don't you go see if you can show those two friends of yours that we Norwegians don't put up with any bullying."

"What is 'bullying'?"

"It's when big people pick on little people."

Arne drew himself up to his fullest height, which was still only a little above Kari's shoulder. "I will show them."

"Good for you," she said with a carefully serious face.

He slammed back out the back door where he had come in so forlornly just a few minutes before, and Kari shook her head as she smiled after him.

"Do I make you cry, Kari?" a soft voice asked from behind her.

She whirled around. Josh was standing quietly on the kitchen side of the swinging door. "The boy said that I make you cry," he repeated. His compelling brown eyes searched her face.

Kari sighed. Another male to comfort. "Why should you make me cry? Didn't you just hear me tell Arne that we Norwegians are not to be bullied?" She turned back to her *lefse,* feeling much shakier inside than she was willing to let on.

Since their encounter on Christmas night, she had scarcely seen Josh all week. He claimed he had a lot of work to catch up on at his offices downtown and the shipping company down by the waterfront. And it was probably true, she reasoned. Before Christmas, he had been gone for several weeks. But in her heart she knew that he was once again avoiding her, and the little bit of hope which had begun to grow that night in his library had shriveled up like a flower under the snow. Fiercely she kneaded the dough back and forth against the wooden table.

Josh watched the rippling movement of her back, then moved his eyes up to the back of her white neck and the curly wisps of hair that had escaped from her braids. For just a moment he felt once again the surge of... lust, he supposed was the word, he had felt Christmas night in the library. It had terrified him then, and still did. Never in his life had he felt so out of control of his own body, his own head.

"When I asked you to stay here," he said finally, "the last thing I wanted was to see you unhappy."

"I'm not unhappy."

"Then what was Arne talking about?"

He watched the shrug of her slender shoulders. "Who knows? He feels that he is my—how would you say?—my protector."

Josh nodded to her back. "And he's anxious to get you away from here and off to Minnesota." Watching her working there in his kitchen did something to his insides. And he was quite sure that the feeling went beyond lust. It was a feeling of wholeness, of completion, the pieces of the world falling into their preordained places.

She gave the dough one last pummel, then turned to face him. "We *both* are very anxious to get to Minnesota," she said, her chin tipped up slightly and her eyes staring straight into his.

Josh crossed his arms in front of him. "You are, too?"

"Yes."

He took a step back. "Well, it's been a mild winter. The roads are in good shape. We should be able to head out west in about a month."

One month. Kari couldn't remember a month ever sounding so short to her before. "Good," she said.

"My mother will miss your company when you leave."

"Yes, well, I'll miss her, too. She's been very kind to me."

Josh seemed to be about to say something else, but in the end he just unfolded his long arms, nodded to her and left the kitchen. Kari turned slowly back to her dinner preparations, but her mind was on Minnesota, and winter roads, and potent brown eyes under chestnut hair.

Folks were calling it "the year without a winter." Except for the spell of snow around Christmas, the weather had been extremely mild. By the beginning of February, grass was beginning to show green in spots, and in Miss Throckton's class the windows were kept open a crack to relieve the steamy heat of the stove. The air outside already had that moist, fecund smell of spring.

Much to Arne's relief, the date had been set for their departure for the logging camps, barring any late winter storms. He had hovered over Kari like a brooding hen for the past month, and became uncommunicative any time Josh was around, which was not often. Their host had managed once again to spend most of the month at his offices, leaving before the boys were off for school in the morning and coming home after the supper dishes had been washed and put away.

Without fail, Josh took noon meal twice a week at the Penningtons and paid a Saturday-afternoon call, as he had each week before his marriage to Corinne. On the last

Saturday before his scheduled departure, he sat with Vernon and Thaddeus in their formal front parlor. Chester and Emmett were off making Saturday-afternoon courting calls of their own, and Myra had retired to her room with a case of the megrims.

Perhaps it was an unfair assumption, but Josh had the impression that Myra's megrims would continue to get more and more severe until "that Norwegian girl" was out of his house.

"So if the yield isn't any better this year, we're going to have to think about shutting 'er down," the older Pennington was saying. Though Vernon's rumbly voice was calm, Josh could tell that he was more upset than he let on about the diminishing returns from the lead mines. It had been a business that had brought incredible profits, but no one had expected that after only a couple decades, the rich Wisconsin lead deposits would already be playing out.

"It's what I've been trying to tell you for the past three years, Vernon." Josh leaned forward in the uncomfortable dainty parlor chair. "Lumber's the wave of the future. If I had more capital available, I'd be opening more tracts, but I've already put everything I have into it."

They'd had this discussion before. Vernon had so far turned down all Josh's attempts to draw him into partnership in the logging business.

"Josh showed me his books the other day, and the returns he's getting are amazing," Thaddeus told his father. An uncharacteristic excitement simmered just below the surface of the young Pennington's light brown eyes.

"It's hard to imagine that much money in the cutting down of a bunch of trees," Vernon said, shaking his head. "Now *lead*—there's something substantial, something that's worth something."

Josh answered patiently. "But the lead is almost gone, Vernon. While the entire West is full of trees just ripe for the taking."

"I think we need to look into it, Papa." As the oldest, Thaddeus was the one Pennington brother who didn't hesitate about speaking his mind.

Josh nodded his agreement and both younger men waited while Vernon pulled his gold watch from his pocket and consulted it as if it were some kind of oracle. "Gettin' on toward suppertime. You staying, Josh?"

Josh stood and shook his head. "No, I've a lot to do if we're to be off by midweek."

Josh watched as Vernon pushed himself up from his chair. The old man moved more slowly each year now. It suddenly occurred to Josh that, as much as he missed his own father, at least he would never have to watch him grow weak with age. He waited a moment to give Vernon a chance to steady himself, then put out his hand. "Thanks for having me."

Vernon shook his son-in-law's hand and held it a moment in a grip that was still firm. "What would you say to an extra traveling companion on your trip out to the camp?"

Josh looked at Vernon doubtfully. The roads should be fine after the mild winter, but you never knew for sure what you would encounter. He wasn't certain the older man was quite up to the rigors of a late-winter trip.

Vernon smiled, crinkling the aging skin around his mouth. "Not me. I was thinking about Thaddeus here. It sounds like he's interested in your proposal, and maybe it's time we give the thing a look-see."

Josh was taken aback for just a moment. Normally he'd have no problem traveling with Thaddeus, but on this particular trip...

"You know I'm taking the Norwegians with me?"

The smile dropped off the old man's face. "Yes. Is that a problem?"

A quick image of Thaddeus bent over Kari's hand on Christmas day flashed through Josh's mind. "No, I guess not." He turned to Thaddeus. "Feel like leaving behind all your account books for a spell in the woods?"

Thaddeus grinned. "Just try to stop me."

"So it's settled, then. We hope to leave by Wednesday. Will that suit you?"

With the excitement now plain in his face, Thaddeus became quite a good-looking fellow, Josh decided. He had the long, even features of aristocratic Eastern breeding, and when his light eyes sparkled that way, he could almost be described as handsome. Josh's forehead furrowed unconsciously as he thought of the long trip ahead.

"Wednesday's fine, Josh. That is—" he turned to his father "—if you can take over for me at the office."

Vernon chuckled and put his hand on his son's shoulder. "It appears to me that I don't have much choice in the matter."

Thaddeus accompanied Josh down the brick walkway to the low white fence that set the Pennington house off from the rest of the neighborhood. For the first time since either of them could remember, Thaddeus shook Josh's hand with real enthusiasm.

"By the way," Thaddeus said with a wink, reaching for the latch on the side of the gate, "I'll be happy to entertain your Norwegian guest for you all those tedious miles on the road." He swung the gate open for Josh to pass, oblivious to the flush that crept over his friend's face.

"Miss Aslaksdatter doesn't need to be entertained," Josh said stiffly. "She's very anxious to be traveling on to her relatives in Minnesota."

Thaddeus looked up sharply at the tone of Josh's voice. His smile dimmed and a speculative look came into his eyes. "I see," he said simply.

Josh cleared his throat. "So...we'll see you Wednesday, then."

"Fine, yes. Wednesday." Thaddeus watched his former schoolmate walk down the road toward his home. The smile returned to his face, and as he turned back toward the house, he began whistling a high-spirited tune.

Kari had resolutely refused to think about the moment when she would have to say goodbye to Josh, but her goodbyes to Helen couldn't be put off any longer. It was time. Tomorrow at dawn they would set off, and she and Arne would be leaving Milwaukee behind forever.

She had hurried to finish sewing the dress lengths the Lymans had given her for Christmas, and the results were packed along with the other few possessions she had collected during her stay with them. Arne had an equally meager bundle of belongings, which had been stuffed along with hers into a canvas bag Helen had supplied. It wasn't much with which to start a new life. For just a moment she thought back on the carefully packed trunks that now rested somewhere at the bottom of Lake Erie. Well, there wasn't anything to be done about that, Kari said to herself resolutely. They were starting anew. This was what they had come to America for. This was what her father had dreamed for them for so many years. It was up to her and Arne to make it a success.

But first came the goodbyes. She had given Daisy a tearful hug after helping her clean up after supper. Although, knowing Daisy, the girl would probably be up before dawn to wish them Godspeed as they left tomorrow. But Josh had told his mother that they would not awaken her so early, which meant the farewells must be said to-night.

Helen was looking out the dark bay window toward her spreading oak tree as Kari entered the room. She turned with her uniquely sweet smile. "Kari, my dear. I've just been sitting here thinking that I don't know how I'm going to stand this house with you gone."

She held out her hand to draw Kari to her side. "It was so big and empty, you know, after my Homer passed." She turned her face out to the darkness once again and said slowly, "Sometimes I used to shut myself up in here just because I couldn't stand how empty those rooms seemed. Then you came and filled them with life again."

Kari sank down by Helen's chair, her eyes already filling. "Rooms don't have life, Helen, people do. Now that you are feeling healthier, you'll feel that life in yourself. You won't need me for that."

"Ah, but I will miss you sorely, child."

Kari nodded and put her cheek against Helen's soft hand. "I will miss you, too. I can hardly remember my own mother, you know, and spending all these weeks with you, I feel—" a tear slid down her cheek "—as if I had found a piece of myself that was always missing."

Helen reached over to enfold Kari against her and two wet cheeks pressed against each other. "If I had had a daughter, I would have wanted her to be just like you," Helen said brokenly.

Kari nodded again, her throat too swollen to speak, the tears falling now in earnest. They held each other for several moments, but at last Helen pulled away with a shaky laugh. "La, what ninnies we are, my dear, ruining your last evening here with tears. What I really wanted was to sing with you. I've learned all the beautiful songs you wrote down for me, and they'll be with me always."

Kari took the delicate hankies Helen held out to her and wiped her eyes. They shone a brilliant blue through the remnants of the tears, and a bittersweet smile transformed her face. "I'm so glad," she said, her voice barely above a whisper. "Because you'll be with me always, too."

As the tears threatened to roll down Kari's cheeks once again, Helen straightened up. "So, are we going to keep on wasting time frettin' or are you going to give me my last Norwegian singing lesson?"

Kari wiped her eyes one more time with Helen's hankie, then pushed herself up and went to sit in the chair opposite the older woman. "What would you like to sing tonight?"

Helen turned to the first page of the book in her lap. "Let's just start at the beginning and go right on through," she said with a kind of false brightness.

Kari didn't know how she could manage to make music with her tear-tortured throat, but somehow the sounds came, and after the first few notes, she felt her body relax with the serenity her singing always brought to her.

Before long the music had lifted both their spirits, and they laughed together as they had many evenings over Helen's difficulty with some of the difficult Norwegian words. It wasn't until they had sung the very last song in the book and Helen had closed it reverently, that their smiles again became forced.

"You know," Helen said after a moment's silence, "it's Josh who will miss you the most sorely."

Kari shook her head. "I can't believe that. I think it's Josh who will be the happiest to see me gone. I only seem to disturb him, and goodness knows, he has enough with handling his own grief."

"That's just the point. He's not handling it. He's as efficient as always at the office. He's making more money than Homer ever did, but the boy hasn't been happy since the day he brought that poor, spoiled child into this house."

A loud crack from one of the logs in the bedroom fireplace startled them both. "I'm talking about Corinne," Helen went on in response to Kari's puzzled look. "Joshua hasn't had a truly happy day since they got married."

"But, surely . . . I mean, he *did* love her."

Helen hesitated a moment, deep in thought. Finally, she said, "Josh is a person who has always done what was expected of him. Correct, competent, sensible, in control. I guess none of us ever even questioned if he was doing the right thing by marrying the only Pennington daughter. It seemed the most natural thing in the world. It made perfect sense."

"But he *did* love her," Kari said once again, trying to understand what was to her the only really important issue.

Helen shrugged. "I don't really know. I thought he did. He certainly was devastated when she was so obviously unhappy living here."

She carefully placed the songbook on a side table and shook out her skirts. "Anyway, as I say, Joshua doesn't seem to be dealing with Corinne's death any better than he dealt with his marriage. I wish I could help him . . . or that someone could. I had hoped these past few weeks . . ."

She stopped and looked up at Kari, who was watching her with troubled eyes, then she shook her head. "Well, they say there's nothing more foolish than a mother's hope." She smiled and reached out to take Kari's hand in hers.

"My child, I wish you happiness in Minnesota. May your days be filled with sunshine and may your beautiful spirit thrive."

This time, Kari, in a valiant effort, held back the tears. She said a last goodbye and held the older woman in a long embrace. Then she left Helen staring into the darkness out her window and retired to her own bedroom. It was only then that she let the hot tears flow, thoroughly soaking the pillow of Josh's dead wife.

Chapter Eleven

It had been decided that the buckboard was too fragile for the rough winter roads, and Josh had secured a farm wagon for the trip. He and Davey had been busy modifying it for the past week. They now had it rigged up to look almost like one of the Conestogas that were crossing the Great Plains in numbers that multiplied daily. The entire back of the wagon was draped with a tarpaulin that provided a cozy shelter against the late-winter winds.

The size of the traveling party had increased yet again. With annoying persistence, Phineas Pennington had begged his father to let him accompany Thaddeus to see the logging operations. Since Josh had already given permission for Davey to miss school and travel with Arne, Phineas's father had given in, on the condition that Josh was willing to take on another passenger.

In spite of his increasing misgivings over the presence of Thaddeus on the trip, Josh saw no harm in Phineas's company, and so it had been decided to let the younger Pennington brother join the expedition.

The three boys had been out at the wagon before dawn, rearranging, loading, unloading, and in general showing off high spirits that Josh surmised would diminish substantially after a few hours of plodding along the road.

Thaddeus arrived precisely at the appointed hour of seven o'clock, carrying a wine-colored carpetbag that looked brand-new. Josh took it from him without comment and threw it carelessly up into the wagon.

Kari stepped out of the kitchen, one arm around Daisy and the other clutching a book of printed etchings that Helen had given her as a farewell gift. She was wearing Helen's old blue wool pelisse. The hood was lined with rabbit fur that framed her face in luxurious softness.

Before Josh could say a word, Thaddeus had crossed the carriageway to where she stood and was doffing his hat, bowing slightly in front of her. As if they were at a cotillion instead of about to take off into the wilderness, Josh thought with irritation.

"Good morning, Miss Kari. May I help you with this heavy volume?" Thaddeus reached for the big square book in her hand, and Kari relinquished it before she had a chance to think. The way he kept his eyes on her made her flush pink within her fluffy rabbit-fur halo.

"Thank you, Mr. Pennington," she murmured. Actually, she would rather have held on to the precious tome herself, but over the edge of Thaddeus's heavy brown greatcoat she had had a quick glimpse of Josh's eyebrows drawing together in a frown, and the gesture had given her a perverse little twinge of pleasure. It was quite satisfying, she was discovering, to have such ready male attention, especially after being made to feel guilty every time she and Josh grew close.

"C'mon, you two," Josh was saying. "It's time we got started." His voice was uncharacteristically harsh. He couldn't believe how the mere sight of Thaddeus's gloved hands touching Kari as he took the book from her had set the blood to pounding in his ears. This was ridiculous, he thought, thoroughly vexed with himself. Kari and Thaddeus were two handsome young people without compromises. There was no reason why a little flirting was out of order.

It was just that Kari was from another country, he fumed as he checked the harness on one of the two sturdy farm horses hitched up to the wagon. She might not be used to the fast ways of courting in this new land. Out here on the edge of the frontier, young people sometimes fell in love and got married in just a few short weeks. Not that he could imagine Kari would be attracted to a pantywaist like Thaddeus Pennington. He gave a snort of disgust which made the horse jerk its head up in protest.

Having worked himself into a thoroughly disagreeable humor, Josh turned to his traveling companions. "Someone can ride up front with me."

"Why, there's plenty of room up there," Thaddeus said heartily. "Boys, you scramble on up so's you can see the scenery. Let Josh teach you how to drive this thing."

The three boys followed his suggestion with alacrity, and Thaddeus turned to offer a hand to Kari, who was giving Daisy a final embrace. "Miss Kari and I will take the rear. It will give us a chance to get better acquainted."

This last was said with a smile that lent charm to the aristocratic lines of Thaddeus's face. Kari returned his smile, and Josh could see that her blue eyes warmed until they were a match to the bright blue wool of her cloak. He turned away without a word and climbed up onto the wagon seat.

"I can't believe I'm finally going to get to see a real logging camp," Davey said excitedly. "Do you think they'll let me chop down a tree, Josh? And can I get spikes on my boots? Hey, can we really drive the wagon with you?"

Josh gave a tug to the reins and turned the hitch slightly to set the big horses off in the right direction. "Mmm. We'll see, Davey."

Thaddeus's deep bass voice came out from the rear, muffled by the makeshift wagon cover. "So, Miss Kari, I want you to tell me all about Norway. You know, of all the emigrants that have come here, I've always thought Norwegians to be among the most intelligent . . . and you're certainly a handsome-looking people, as well, if I'm not being too forward in saying so."

Josh bit his lip and gave an impatient flip to the reins, but the big animals kept to their lumbering gait. It was going to be a long trip.

Elizabeth Stanley was a handsome woman. Three toddlers and the harsh winters of the Wisconsin frontier had only just begun to wear away the edge on her good looks. She had resigned herself to a lot of things settling into life on the farm she and her husband, Tom, had carved out of the wilderness. But she still had enough pride to want to spruce herself up a bit knowing that Josh Lyman would be paying a visit any day now.

Josh had been Tom's friend, really, when they were all growing up together back in Milwaukee. But Elizabeth had always had a secret interest in the tall, attractive Lyman boy. Her heart had chosen Tom in the end, but the Lord had given her two good eyes for lookin', and she felt no guilt about letting them do their duty every time Josh came to stay. My, but the man's looks could turn a woman's heart to cornmeal mush.

Josh had been different the last couple visits. He seemed less able to get into his normal rambunctious play with the children. His usual high spirits were dimmed. Of course, there was the tragedy about Corinne. Though Elizabeth had frankly never understood that marriage in the first place. When Elizabeth had known her, Corinne Pennington had been a spoiled girl in her midteens who showed very little promise of maturing.

But of course it was a terrible thing to lose a wife, and Elizabeth supposed it was only normal that it would take Josh time to recover his accustomed energy and good humor.

Thoughts of Josh had filled her head all morning. With some sort of sixth sense developed through long months of isolation, she felt that today would be the day. She was glad she had used the last of her store-bought soap with real coconut oil on her hair last night. And sure enough, just as she finished the washing up after the noon meal, she could hear sounds of a wagon way down the trail.

Both Elizabeth and Tom were waiting outside with big welcoming smiles by the time the wagon pulled up to their comfortable four-room farmhouse. Around them tumbled three golden-haired sprites who were indistinguishable from one another at first glance.

"Hallo, Stanleys! Civilization has arrived," Josh shouted, jumping down from the wagon almost before the big horses had pulled to a stop.

"That'll be the day, Josh Lyman, that you bring along civilization," Elizabeth said with a smile as she watched Josh lift her good-size husband completely off the ground in a bear hug. "I swear the only time Tom ever acts like a wild man is when you two get together."

Josh and Tom grinned at each other without bothering to refute her charges. Then Josh turned to Elizabeth. "I knew you missed me, Bethy," he said, and bent over to give her a resounding kiss right on the lips.

Elizabeth colored brighter than Tom's neckerchief. "Josh!" she protested.

But Josh had turned back to the wagon and was lifting down a young woman. Upon closer inspection Elizabeth saw, with a tickle of envy, that the woman was beautiful ... with skin the color of lily petals and the most extraordinary white-gold hair.

"This is Kari." Josh had taken the girl's hand and pulled her eagerly forward, ignoring the other members of his party. He looked into his friends' faces as though awaiting a sign of approval.

Tom's mouth fell open as he looked at the unexpected visitor, but Elizabeth stepped forward and offered the girl her hand and a warm smile. "Welcome to our home, Kari," she said.

Josh had briefly mentioned his Norwegian visitor during his stop with them before Christmas, but Elizabeth quickly concluded that he had guarded his comments carefully. It was obvious that the young woman meant much more to him than he had led them to believe.

"It's beautiful here," Kari was saying, looking around at the tall pines that formed a semicircle around the Stanley farmhouse. The house itself was of planed boards, not logs, with real glass windows, and was large for a place on the edge of the frontier. "It reminds me a little of my home in Norway."

By now a recovered Tom had come forward to meet Kari and to shake hands warmly with Thaddeus. "Last time I saw you boys, you were knee-high to a grasshopper," he said to Davey and Phineas. Then he nodded and smiled at Arne, who had stayed back by the wagon and was watching the greetings with big, solemn eyes.

Elizabeth was now trying to identify her lively offspring for Kari. "This one's Thomas Joshua," she said, pointing to a tousled head that was slightly higher than the other two. "Named for his pa and his pa's best friend. And then comes Mary Elizabeth, but her pa's name for her is Marigold, and it looks like it's gonna stick.''

"Mari-gold," the middle-size golden pixie agreed, looking up at Kari with big, solemn eyes.

"And this here's my baby, Jonathan." She beamed at her youngsters and Kari felt a surge of empathy with Elizabeth's maternal pride.

"What a wonderful family," Kari said warmly, losing track instantly of which child was which. They were dressed in identical cotton smocks that skimmed just above tiny ankles and grimy feet, which were bare in spite of the early-spring chill. "But surely they're not triplets?"

Elizabeth laughed. "Ten months apart, as regular as the chimes of a clock. Tommy's almost five, Marigold four and Jonny three."

"So what's happened now?" Josh asked, giving big Tom a punch on the shoulder. "You slowin' up, old man?"

"You're one to talk about slow," Tom answered his friend indignantly. "I don't see you showing up here with any young'uns."

Tom realized his error even before the words were fully out of his mouth. "Jeez, I'm sorry, Josh. I didn't mean..."

Josh's smile faded, but he said good-naturedly, "Don't worry about it, Tom."

"Well, let's get you folks some refreshment," Elizabeth said loudly.

Though the house was spacious, it seemed to Kari to be overflowing with people by the time the Stanleys and all the visitors had situated themselves in the parlor to drink the hot apple cider Elizabeth Stanley was passing around. But the crowding had a warmth to it that settled into her, relaxing the stiffness out of travel-weary muscles. She could tell that this was a happy household. It was as if yesterday's laughter had floated up to the rafters and hung there gently, assured of more of the same today.

The lively conversation was occasionally punctuated by a shriek from one of the toddlers, but the cries were never desperate. They were simply the impatient protests of youngsters who knew with confidence that a loving parent would soon see to their needs.

The little girl, Marigold, seemed fascinated by Kari, and stopped her play every now and then to turn great round eyes to stare in her direction. Finally, she walked cautiously over to the Norwegian visitor and lifted a chubby hand toward Kari's braided hair. "So pretty," she said with a sweet lisp. Kari bent over slightly and the little girl gave the braids a gossamer pat. "You are beautiful," she said shyly.

Kari was enchanted. This is the kind of family she would like to have, she realized. She compared it to the Lyman household back in Milwaukee. Even when Davey and Phineas had been at their most exuberant, the house lacked a certain zest. And that, she knew, was directly related to the withdrawal of the head of the household. Had things been different when Corinne was there? she wondered. Had Josh been different?

He certainly didn't look withdrawn now, she thought, watching him in animated discussion with Tom. His eyes sparkled in that way she had only seen a few times. It made her throat ache just looking at him.

"Your men are still out decking their logs, Josh," Tom was saying. "You'll have another couple weeks at least before you can start down the river. Plenty of time to stay for the sap run."

"I must admit the thought of fresh maple syrup with some of Bethy's flapjacks is mighty tempting," Josh answered with a grin. He turned to the three boys who, in an uncharacteristic display of good manners, were sitting up straight and quiet on a wood trestle bench. Josh could see a flicker of excitement in his brother's eyes. "How about it, boys? You want to stay and help with the maple sugaring?"

He got two decisive nods from Davey and Phineas, but Arne shook his head. "Kari and I go to Minn-e-sota," he said firmly.

In spite of Kari's admonitions, Arne had been more openly hostile toward Josh since they had started their journey. He answered the boy slowly. "We know you and Kari are going to Minnesota, Arne. But we agreed that you would wait until the log drive was started so that I could take you there. If the drive won't be ready for another couple weeks, we can wait here at the Stanleys or we can wait at the lumber camp. That's what we're trying to decide."

"We want to stay here!" Davey shouted. He banged his friend on the shoulder. "C'mon, Arn'. Maple syrup! Don't be a dimwit."

Arne rubbed his shoulder and shifted his eyes to Kari, who gave him a reassuring smile. "All right, we stay here for maple syrup time . . . *then* we go to Minn-e-sota."

The boys' enthusiasm for the maple sugaring had dimmed by the time they had trudged up and down the hill behind the Stanley farmhouse for what they claimed was the hundredth time, carrying the heavy pails of sap. Josh laughed at their groans and sent them back for yet another trip. "It takes fifty gallons of sap for each one gallon of syrup," he told them. "And you boys practically drink the stuff. So if we're going to leave the Stanleys with anything for themselves this next year, we need to keep busy.''

He, Kari and Thaddeus had been taking turns watching the big sap boiler, which stood several yards beyond the farmhouse. The fire beneath it would be stoked continuously for the next several days. The distinct, sweet odor of boiling maple permeated the entire area.

"Can we have some yet, Josh?" Davey asked, emptying a pail of the clear sap into the boiler. All three boys had already tried sampling the sap itself, and had been disappointed to find that it had only a tantalizing hint of the rich maple flavor that would develop as it boiled down into dark, sticky syrup.

"Not yet, Davey. It has to boil for many hours." He gave a stir to the gently bubbling mixture with a long wooden paddle. It really was tedious work, he thought. But he knew that Tom took many jars of the finished product into Milwaukee when he went to buy seeds in the spring and the extra money enabled the Stanleys to purchase such luxuries as Elizabeth's new iron cookstove.

Tom came up the path, his arms loaded with wood—seasoned ash and oak to keep the fire good and hot. "Hey, Josh! Why don't you pass the paddle over to that pretty lady you brought along and give me a hand with this wood? That city life is making you soft as a baby's bottom."

Josh grinned at his friend and turned to find Kari, but as she took the wooden stick from him, Thaddeus stepped forward and placed his hands right alongside Kari's. "We'll handle it, Josh. You go on ahead with Tom."

Josh looked at the two of them standing with shoulders touching, moving the big wooden paddle up and down the length of the long cylindrical boiler. They made a handsome couple...Kari with her fair hair and skin and

Thaddeus with his dark hair and intent light brown eyes. Josh's grin died.

Tom rolled the heavy load of wood onto the fire underneath the big boiler. "Are ya comin'?" he asked Josh.

Josh nodded. "Sure." Without a backward glance at the two people at the boiler, he followed Tom into the woods with long, angry strides.

"It smells wonderful, no?" Kari said, looking up at Thaddeus with one of her intoxicating smiles.

Thaddeus moved a step closer to her and tightened his hold on the wooden paddle. "Hmm," he agreed, his eyes on the golden hair wisping down along her neck. "Wonderful."

"I think it's very beautiful here in Wisconsin," Kari said, moving her gaze to take in the tall stands of pines surrounding the Stanley farm.

"I don't know why you think you have to go all the way to Minnesota, Kari. You could have a wonderful life right here . . . back in Milwaukee."

All at once aware that Thaddeus had moved so that the entire length of his body was up against hers, Kari gave a nervous laugh. "We promised my papa that we would go to Minnesota, Thaddeus. It was all he dreamed of for so many years." She released her hold on the wooden paddle and took a step back, separating herself from him.

"Your papa's gone now," he said gently. "You have to do what's best for you."

Kari nodded and relaxed. She liked Thaddeus, and he was becoming a good friend. "I know, but I have Arne to think of, too. His dream of Minnesota is almost as strong as Papa's."

"He gets along really well with Phineas and Davey."

"Yes, we've been very lucky to find such good friends as the Lymans—" she hesitated a moment before adding a bit shyly "—and you and your brother."

It was rare, Kari realized, that Thaddeus's smile reached his light eyes, but it did so now, and she smiled again in response.

"We're the ones who are lucky, Kari." Thaddeus stopped moving the big paddle and reached for her hand. Before he could clasp it in his, the three boys appeared at the top of the hill. This time, instead of pails, they were each carrying a wooden bowl.

"Hey, Thad, Kari!" Phineas came running down the hill toward them. "We've found some snow."

Most of the snow had long since disappeared, but the boys had managed to find the melting remains of a drift deep in the woods.

Davey ran down beside his friend. "Mrs. Stanley gave us the bowls and said we could give it a try even if the syrup's still thin."

Thaddeus had dropped Kari's hand. "Have you ever had snow with maple syrup?" he asked her.

Kari shook her head. Arne stood next to her, carefully balancing his heaping bowl of snow.

"Well, you're about to sample one of Wisconsin's tastiest treats," Thaddeus continued. His grin was almost boyish, and there was little to recognize of the serious accountant she had first met in the Lyman's parlor. He unhooked the big ladle from where it was hanging along the metal frame that held the boiler in place and dipped it into the steamy sap. The boys held out their bowls as Thaddeus carefully poured a ladleful on each snowy mound.

"We'll need spoons," he said to Phineas. But the boys had had enough of waiting. Three sets of grimy fingers dipped into the sugary, frosty treat. He turned to Kari. "Well, at least *we'll* need spoons."

He handed her the stirring paddle and took off toward the farmhouse. In moments he was back with two big serving spoons. "They were all I could find," he said.

Kari laughed at the size of them, but imitated his actions, taking a great big bite of the flavored snow from Arne's dish as he took one from Phineas's.

"It's delicious," she said. The confection felt smooth and icy cold all the way down her throat.

"It's better if the syrup's thicker," Davey told Arne with the voice of a connoisseur. But Kari noticed that thick syrup or no, the heaps of snow were disappearing at an amazing speed.

She lifted another huge spoonful to her mouth and laughed when chilly drips of it fell off the side to run down her chin. "It certainly is cold!"

Thaddeus had ignored his own spoon and was watching Kari enjoy the new treat. As the sticky crystals of snow melted on her face, he reached out and wiped them away with his thumb. Kari's laughter faded at the gentle contact of Thaddeus's hand. His fingers were soft, not at all like Josh's, came the instant comparison.

Josh heard her laughter even before he emerged from the trees with his heavy load of logs. As he approached, he could see her standing with Thaddeus, who appeared to be touching her face in a tender caress. Josh gripped his bundle of logs more tightly in an attempt to drive the hollow feeling out of his middle. Instead, the movement just seemed to drive the hollowness to all parts of his body. He watched bleakly as Thaddeus fed Kari another huge spoonful of maple snow against her laughing protests.

"I can't eat so much, Thaddeus," she said, shaking her head with a smile. "It's making my forehead go cold."

"That's part of the experience, Kari," he said, continuing to press the spoon to her lips.

Josh came up to them just in time to hear Thaddeus call Kari by her first name. He felt his blood roiling in accompaniment to the bubbling sap in the boiler.

"Josh, you must have some of this," Kari called to him from the other side of the fire. "It's delicious."

"I thought I said the syrup wasn't ready yet."

The smile left Kari's voice. "Well, I know, but Elizabeth told the boys..."

"Tastes great to me," Thaddeus interrupted. He looked deliberately into Kari's face. "I can't remember when I've had anything so sweet."

Josh dumped his load roughly down on the fire. Sparks and cinders flew and several logs rolled off the pile and came to a stop against Thaddeus's legs. "Hey! Watch what you're doing," Thaddeus said angrily, jumping back from the glowing wood. His fine broadcloth pants were smeared with soot and his right boot looked singed.

"Sorry," Josh said calmly, feeling immensely better all at once. He plucked Thaddeus's spoon out of his hand. "You'd better go see about cleaning that black stuff off those nice pants you got there."

Thaddeus stalked away toward the house, and Josh turned to Kari. The waning afternoon sun had almost reached the tips of the pine trees on the hill behind the farmhouse. Its rays turned Kari's braids into a rich, burnished gold. She was wearing the green gingham dress she had made from the cloth he had given her at Christmas. As usual, her talented hands had wrought wonders, and the dress fit her long, trim figure like a silken glove. "So, you like our maple snow, Viking?" he asked her softly.

Kari had been watching Thaddeus's retreating form with a little frown of concern on her face, but at Josh's warm tone she forgot all about the other man. Josh's brown eyes were looking at her with an intensity she had seen only that one time on Christmas night.

The three boys had finally gotten their fill of the sweet maple snow and had run off into the woods to collect more sap. Josh bent over to pick up one of the bowls they had left on the ground. He dug out a spoonful of the remaining brownish slush and slowly brought it up to Kari's lips. It felt icy cold against her suddenly heated lips.

"It's very good," she said, her voice barely above a whisper. "I think Thaddeus was upset about his clothes."

Josh gave a sardonic laugh. "I'm not about to lose any sleep over it."

"I thought you and Thaddeus were friends."

Josh hesitated a moment before answering. "We never were friends like I was with Tom. The Penningtons were always just one notch above everyone else in town. It was hard to be friends with them. And then there was always Corinne. . . ."

Josh took an absentminded bite of maple snow. It had been impossible, really, to have a normal relationship with any of the Penningtons from the time it became evident that Corinne had wanted him for a husband. From that moment on, in their minds he had been Corinne's property. How ironic that she had staked a claim to him for so many years, and then when she finally had him as her own, she hadn't wanted him.

"Thaddeus and I were never the best of friends, Kari," he concluded. "And it certainly doesn't help our friendship any to see him fawning over you . . . putting his hands on you."

Kari was taken aback by the harshness of his voice. "He has not put his hands on me," she said indignantly.

"No? What was that he was doing when I came out of the woods?"

Suddenly, Kari recognized the source of his anger. She remembered once when Per, the minister's son in Stavanger, had seen Ole Halstensen walking her home from school and carrying her books. Per had had a look in his eyes similar to the one she saw now in Josh's. It gave her a curious, feminine pleasure. She smiled at him sweetly. "Thaddeus was just showing me how you Americans eat the maple snow."

Josh stuffed another frosty bite into his mouth, scarcely noticing the cold or the sweet taste. "It appears that Thaddeus wants to show you how we Americans do a lot of things."

Kari's voice was a touch more melodic than usual. "A girl likes to have a man pay attention to her, Josh Lyman."

Her eyes were incredibly blue in the dying red rays of the sun. She took a shaky breath that drew Josh's gaze to the tight fit of her dress across her breasts. The blood seemed to stop moving in his veins, and all at once Josh felt that if he didn't do something, his entire body might explode right there in the middle of the Stanleys' farmyard.

He dropped the wooden bowl and spoon to the ground and took a firm hold of Kari's hand. "Come," he said simply. With deadly purpose, he led her across the yard to one of the log outbuildings. It appeared to be a shed of some sort, full of farm tools waiting in idleness for the Stanleys' rich, fertile fields to thaw.

Without a word, Josh pulled Kari into the cool, dark interior of the tiny building and shut the door behind them. Still holding her hand, he spun her around. His free arm went behind her back and held her against him as his mouth met hers in an openmouthed kiss that blended passion with skill and left Kari's head swirling.

"If anyone's going to teach you American customs," Josh growled, "it'll be me."

Kari felt the rough-hewn logs of the shed against her back as Josh trapped her there with his body, leaving his hands free to tug at the twists of her hair, freeing the braids and sending hairpins flying in every direction. Meanwhile, his mouth continued its persistent, expert assault on hers and his tongue began to dance velvety magic.

Kari gave an involuntary little whimper that seemed to freeze the action for just a moment, only to have it renewed with fresh energy. Her body felt hot and hard against him, and his, down below, felt even hotter. The shawl she had worn against the early-spring chill fell unheeded to the dirt floor of the shed.

Her hair was free now, and Josh wove his strong fingers through its silkiness, emitting his own groan of pleasure. "I have dreams about your hair, Viking," he murmured. With one big hand he scooped the heavy tresses from behind her neck and brought them around to the front to fall over her chest like a golden blanket.

The top log had been left off under the roof on two sides of the shed to let in air and ventilation. The weakening red rays of sun lit the flat log ceiling, but died before reaching the cool, moist darkness of the room below. Still, Kari could see Josh's face, his eyes, as he smoothed her hair across her breasts with a slow hand.

He cupped her left breast in a silken nest. "I've dreamed of doing this, Kari," he said.

Chapter Twelve

Josh's head was spinning as if the snow they'd eaten had been spiked with his foreman's home-brewed liquor instead of half-boiled maple syrup. In the cool darkness of the shed, the only warmth came from the connection of their bodies, and that felt as hot as burning coals. The confusion in his head would lead him to believe that he was in the middle of another of those night-sweating dreams, but the heat was real—the heat and the firm rise of her nipple against the pressure of his hand.

"Josh," he heard her say. Her eyes closed and her head went back against the rough wall as her breast seemed to swell into his touch. He pushed aside the veil of hair and homed in on the tiny hard bud at the center, caressing it through the thin cloth of her dress. He ran his other hand the length of her trim body and settled it just behind her hip, nestling the lower portion of her body around the thickly aroused portion of his.

By now her lips had joined his in a maple-flavored mating that had his stomach churning. One of her slender hands cooled the back of his neck. The other rested gently against his chest, directly over the spot where his heart thundered.

Josh tried to clear his head. In spite of the primeval urgings of his body, he knew that what he had embarked upon here was impossible. The girl in his arms was not a shantyboy's doxie eager for a tumble after the spring run. This was Kari. Kari, whose life he had saved when he couldn't save Corinne's. Kari, who was on her way to a new life in Minnesota, and would no doubt be glad to see the last of the brooding, contradictory American whom she had wanted to be her savior. He may not know what he was doing, but he knew what he could not do. He could not allow himself to make love to her in the dirt of the increasingly black toolshed where at any moment they might be joined by the brother of his dead wife. If he didn't stop this instant, he would be doing just that.

He pulled his body away from Kari's, and the cool darkness engulfed them both. He was glad for once that he couldn't see her luminous eyes. "We can't be doing this here, Kari," he said in a voice that he knew sounded too cold, too detached.

Kari felt the chill the moment he backed away. Within seconds she was shaking with cold, trembling with uncontrollable shivers. The coldness settled itself around her heart. She reached down to feel along the floor for her shawl.

She'd been rebuffed for the last time, she said to herself bitterly. It seemed that all Josh had to do was crook a finger and she was melting into his embrace, returning his kisses with an abandon she never even suspected she had, but no more. He turned to her when he was lonely, as on Christmas, or now, out of misguided jealousy of Thaddeus. But each time he was able to stop before he could get too involved, too committed. Even through a passion that left Kari as helpless as a leaf in a maelstrom, Josh was able to pull back, to control, to withdraw once again into his self-contained world of reproach and recrimination.

Her fingers touched the light wool of the shawl and she straightened. Josh's form was now no more than a shadow. His face was entirely in darkness. Kari took a deep, cleansing breath. "Josh Lyman, if you *ever* try to kiss me again, I am leaving, even if Arne and I have to walk to Minnesota." She pushed past him and let herself out the shed door.

Josh let her go without a word. He understood her anger with him, shared it, in fact. But it left him with an ache in his heart, not to mention the spectacular aching in various other parts of his body.

It was now nearly black inside the shed. As he turned to leave, he knocked his shin hard against the metal shaft of what was probably a plowshare. The pain made a welcome counterpoint to his mounting frustration.

"You're a damn fool, Lyman," he said aloud to himself.

The steamy maple mixture still bubbled away relentlessly in the backyard, but by now the three boys had tired of the process, and the call to make another round to collect pails elicited groans of protest. They had built a fort for themselves in the woods just beyond the big hill in back of the house. They took off to it first thing in the morning, followed faithfully by their new shadow, little Thomas. Marigold had joined them the first day, but she had come home crying at midmorning, saying they had made her the Indian princess and tied her up to a tree. From that time on, she devoted her attention to the beautiful lady with the sweet voice and angel hair.

They sat outside under a large maple tree, Marigold in Kari's lap with Kari's skirts billowing up around her.

Marigold's eyes grew wide as she listened to the end of Kari's story about a wicked troll with two heads and one eye and the spell he had put on an entire village. Of course, the boy Askeladden had once again outsmarted the troll, who exploded when he was hit by sunlight. Norway sounded like a magical place.

"Snipp, snapp, snute . . . så er eventyret ute! And that is the end of the tale!" Kari concluded.

Marigold's cherubic face lit up with giggles at the funny-sounding language. Her tiny soft hands pressed on each side of Kari's face and she pulled herself up on her knees to give her a wet brush with her little mouth. "More story," she said with pint-size insistence.

Kari hugged the little girl. "I should go see if your mama needs some help."

"Another story!" Marigold repeated her demand.

"You're going to tire Miss Kari out, button." The deep male voice startled them both. They looked up to see Thaddeus leaning against a tree a few yards away. He pushed himself away from the trunk and automatically brushed any clinging bark from the sleeve of his coat. He could be walking into his accounting office instead of out on a wilderness farm miles from civilization, Kari thought to herself.

After a brief glance around to pick a spot that was more grass than dirt, he sat down beside them and reached over to transfer the child from Kari's lap to his own. "You can't hear all of Miss Kari's stories this morning," he told Marigold solemnly, "because then you'll use them all up and there won't be any left to tell at the party we're having tonight."

"Party?" Big blue eyes sparkled in the tiny face.

"Your mama told me that we're going to have a party tonight with johnnycakes and fresh maple syrup, but that we could only have the party if she got some help from her best helper. Now, I wonder who that could be?''

"Marigold is Mama's best helper," the little girl answered quickly.

"Are you sure about that?" Thaddeus looked puzzled. "I thought she was looking around for Thomas Joshua."

The girl jumped off his lap. "*Marigold* is Mama's best helper," she repeated indignantly, and took off in a toddling run toward the farmhouse.

Thaddeus watched her tiny receding form with an amused smile. "She's a handful," he said.

"You seem to know how to manage her." Kari's voice held surprise and admiration.

Thaddeus hesitated a moment before answering. "She reminds me a little of Corinne. I was the only one in the family who could handle her. It was because I knew enough to always make things seem like her idea." A bittersweet smile softened the words.

Kari reached over to touch his sleeve. "I'm so sorry, Thaddeus. You must miss her terribly."

Thaddeus nodded. "We all do." He leaned back against the maple tree, paying no attention now to the bark smudging his coat. "But, you know, sometimes I think to myself that it was perhaps meant to be this way. Corinne was such a pretty child—spoiled and pretty—and it was as if she wanted to stay a child forever. Somewhere along the line she forgot to grow up. I can't see her with a family of her own, for example. I don't know how she managed the Lyman house after she married Josh. It seemed that she was never there—she was always over at our place."

Kari watched him in silence. He appeared to be speaking more to himself than to her.

"Maybe Corinne never grew up because destiny or God—" Thaddeus waved a vague hand in the air "—or whoever it is that controls these things knew that she would never have to. She'll be that pretty little girl forever.''

"But she did grow up," Kari protested gently. "She was Josh's wife."

"Mmm," Thaddeus replied noncommittally. He jumped to his feet and reached a hand toward Kari. "Let's go collect some sap pails. I have a feeling our brothers have slowed up on the job."

She took his hand, though she did not need the help as she gracefully stood and shook out her skirts.

From inside the farmhouse Elizabeth looked out her front window and watched the two young people move off together into the woods. She shook her head. This was certainly a coil. What in the world possessed Josh to bring a dapper, eligible man like Thaddeus Pennington along on this trip when he so obviously was head over heels about the Norwegian girl himself? And why in heaven's name was he so determined to take her off and leave her in Minnesota? Why couldn't he just come out and tell her how he felt about her? The two had been as prickly as two porcupines in a patch of nettles since coming in for supper last night.

Maybe time alone was what they needed, Elizabeth thought with a sigh. With three young ones constantly underfoot, she could hardly remember the luxury of solitude. As if echoing her thoughts, the front door banged open and Tom came in bellowing, "I'm hungry as a bear!" On his heels came the three older boys, followed by little Tom. Their shouts woke baby Jonathan, who immediately began to howl, upon which Marigold added to the din by chirruping repeatedly, "They woke the baby, Mama! They woke the baby!"

Elizabeth put cool fingertips to her temples for just a moment, then laid a soothing hand on the top of Marigold's tousled golden head. "Never mind, sweetheart, it's almost dinnertime anyway."

By the time Josh, Kari and Thaddeus had been rounded up and everyone fed, the afternoon sun was high in the sky. The older boys had consented to play with the three little ones outside when Josh had given them the choice of that duty or cleaning up the dishes. Tom had taken Kari and Thaddeus off in the wagon to show them the back acreage of the farm, which he was planning to begin clearing next year. Josh had declined his friend's suggestion that he accompany them.

"Someone has to help Elizabeth with this mess," he'd said, surveying the debris left after the hearty noon meal.

It was one thing Elizabeth had always liked about Josh. He seemed ready to pitch in and do whatever had to be done, even if it was considered woman's work. She couldn't imagine Tom so much as lifting a dirty plate from the table.

They worked in silence for a while, but finally she said, "So when are you going to talk to me about this Norwegian of yours?"

"She's not my Norwegian."

Elizabeth arched an eyebrow and waited.

"She's not," Josh repeated.

"All right, all right. She's not yours. Are you ready to let her be Thaddeus's?"

Josh shrugged. "It's not up to me."

She plunged her hands furiously into the sudsy water of the washtub. "I'd given you credit for being smarter than some men, Josh Lyman. I guess I was wrong."

"I don't think Kari's interested in Thaddeus, Bethy. She and her brother want to get to Minnesota."

"Her brother does, maybe. But that girl would turn around and skedaddle back to Milwaukee in an instant if you told her you wanted her there." She slammed a wet dish into the towel in his outstretched hands.

"I don't think so."

"Did you ever ask her?"

"Ask her what?" He sounded irritated.

"Don't you get huffy with me, Josh. We've known each other too long." She turned to face him and put two soapy hands on her hips. "Did you ever ask this Kari of yours if she wanted to stay in Milwaukee?"

Josh shook his head and the belligerence in his expression was replaced with a look of pain that made Elizabeth's heart twist. "How could I ask her to stay, Bethy, with Corinne gone not yet half a year?"

"Six months or six years...gone is gone, Josh. Out here you can't afford to wait around for things to progress in their own natural time. A new land like this, you've got to make things happen, or you lose out. Life passes you by."

Josh gave an absentminded swipe to the dish. He knew exactly what Elizabeth was saying, and up to now he had felt the same way. It was just what he had told Vernon about opening up the land to lumber instead of waiting around for the death throes of the played-out lead mines. But in this case, he was uncharacteristically reluctant to take action. When it came right down to it, who was to say he would make a better husband to Kari than he had to Corinne?

"I think things are best left be," he said finally.

"Funny thing," Elizabeth said breezily, going back to her suds. "All these years we've been friends, I've never known you to be a coward."

Josh bristled for just a moment, then let his face settle into a grin. "Anyway, Bethy, you know my heart was broken in two when you went and picked old Tom over me. I can't very well offer some girl only half a heart, now, can I?"

Elizabeth laughed. "Oooh...go save your grease for another pig, Josh Lyman. You never even knew I was alive until Tom had me roped and lassoed."

"Now, see, that's part of my problem. Where women are concerned, it seems I've spent a great part of my life being a danged fool."

"Well, maybe you'll wise up for the rest of it, my friend," Elizabeth said gently. "You could start by having a serious conversation with that beautiful Norwegian...whose life I understand you saved."

Josh scowled and placed the last dry dish on the stack. "If I do, will it stop you from yammering at me?"

"I only want you to be happy, Josh," Elizabeth said, looking up at him.

"I know you do, Bethy." He gave her a playful flick of the wet dish towel. "Now get away from me before I forget about that lug of a husband of yours and give you a kiss."

Elizabeth blushed, grabbed a basket full of laundry and turned toward the door. In the winter she boiled the clothes to ward off the winter sicknesses and the bed chiggers that settled in so persistently with the first cold snap in the fall. But now the creek had melted and the air smelled of spring. She was going to let the brisk rush of water over the smooth stones do her work for her. Josh would figure things out, she decided. The man had a good head on his shoulders. The shoulders weren't bad themselves, she thought with a little giggle. She headed out the door with a decidedly lighter step.

Two of the partygoers had already fallen into exhausted sleep and had been tucked carefully into their beds by their papa. Thomas Joshua was doing his best not to follow the example of his brother and sister, but his little eyes had the exaggerated blink of a gray owl, and every now and then he snapped his head out of a nod.

"Does anyone want anything more to eat?" Elizabeth asked.

The three older boys, who were lying on the floor by the fireplace with their hands covering their stomachs, chorused a groan.

"It's a lucky thing we're heading out of here, Bethy," Josh said, nodding at the three prone figures. "These three can eat in a week your provisions for the next year."

"I enjoy seeing people eat what I cook," Elizabeth said firmly. "You're welcome to stay as long as you like."

"It's been a wonderful evening," Kari said warmly.

It had been. They had eaten Elizabeth's corn johnnycakes smothered with the new maple syrup until they all felt that they would burst. Then Kari had led the singing, impressing the Stanleys with her marvelous voice. Now they were all feeling a bit sleepy, so Tom had gotten out his harmonica.

"If these three dishrags would get out of the way, we could have some dancin'," he announced to the group.

Thaddeus, who had been sitting next to Kari on the straight trestle bench, stood and pulled her up alongside him. "An excellent idea," he said, giving his brother a gentle nudge with his foot. "Get up, Phineas. Give us some room here."

The three boys got reluctantly to their feet, but when Tom started tapping out a lively reel, they seemed to come to life and started their own version of the dance, letting little Thomas weave in and out among them. Thaddeus wasted no time in putting his arms around Kari and sweeping her into a sort of Western version of the schottische. That left Josh to invite Elizabeth, which he did with a smile, though his eyes slanted over to where Thaddeus's hand was settling just below Kari's waist.

"It's like I said earlier," Elizabeth whispered to him with a telling grin. "You can't afford to let life pass you by."

Josh gave her an exasperated shake of the head. "Let it go, Bethy," he said, but his gaze drifted regularly over to the young couple across the room.

Tom's first song ended and he picked up the tempo for a second thumping melody of his own design. The boys and Thomas turned it into a melee, which ended on the floor in a tangle of arms and legs, but Thaddeus managed to keep to some semblance of a dance, and he now held Kari more tightly as he swung her in perfect rhythm with the fast-paced tune.

Josh and Elizabeth maintained a more circumspect distance from each other, but both were breathless as they tried to keep pace. "Enough, Tom," Elizabeth said, laughing as he finished up one tune and prepared to launch into another. "Give us a chance to breathe."

Thaddeus still held Kari in a close embrace. For the party she had donned the dress she had fashioned from the Christmas blue silk. It brought out the deep tint of her eyes, especially now as they sparkled with laughter in her flushed face. The dress billowed out in a graceful bell skirt, but as she stood clasped in Thaddeus's arms, Josh could see the outline of her long legs.

Josh dropped his hand from Elizabeth's shoulder. He made an effort to keep the stiffness from his voice. "Listen to the lady, Tom. One more of those numbers and you'll have to carry us all to bed like you did Marigold and Jonny."

Tom grinned and set his silver harmonica on the mantel. "I remember the days when you could dance all night without breaking a sweat, old man," he said to his friend.

"Yeah, well, life has a way of catching up with us, I guess," Josh answered a bit distractedly. Thaddeus had still not released Kari, and she didn't seem the least bit disturbed to be standing there so close to him.

Josh cleared his throat. "I think it's time for all of us to turn in," he said loudly.

Finally, Thaddeus dropped his arms and took a step back from Kari. His eyes scanned quickly and discreetly down the length of the blue dress. The predatory male look in his eyes was only a quick flash, but Josh could see it all the way across the room, and it made the muscles across his stomach tighten.

Elizabeth saw Josh's eyes narrow. "Come on, boys," she said to the disheveled group on the floor. "Time for bed."

With the innate efficiency of a mother, in minutes she had all four boys making their last trip out to the jakes and trooping off into the children's bedroom along with Thaddeus. The latter shut the door behind them with a good-humored "good night," oblivious to his former schoolmate's dark looks. Josh had been bedding down on the sofa in the parlor, and they had set up a makeshift cot each night for Kari next to the stove in the kitchen.

Tom echoed Thaddeus's good-night and headed toward his own room, but Elizabeth lingered a moment longer. "I wonder if you two might do me a favor," she said with a studied air of innocence.

Josh shot her a suspicious glance, but Kari answered immediately, "Of course, Elizabeth. What can we help you with?"

Elizabeth pulled a shawl off a hook by the door. "Last night one of the horses got out of the barn and we had to chase clear over to the Farringtons' place looking for it this morning. I meant to check the latches, but forgot about it until just now. Would you two go out with me?"

"Shall I call Tom?" Josh asked, a bit bewildered by Elizabeth's sudden late-night energy.

"No, I think we three can handle it," she said carelessly. She lit the wick of a lantern, which stood ready on the parlor hutch, and started out the door. Kari and Josh followed behind her, sharing their puzzlement with a quick glance.

The Stanleys' spacious barn looked eerie as the lantern light cast giant shadows on the far side wall. The animals appeared to have settled into their nighttime cycle and barely raised their heads as the three walked in through the big raw wood door. "Everything looks fine," Josh said.

"If you could just check along the stalls, Josh. Be sure they're fastened up tight."

"Sure." Kari moved along at his side as Josh deftly checked each metal latch for firmness.

"In Norway, we have no gates to the animal stalls. But they don't run away," she said.

"Maybe Norwegian animals aren't as independent as American animals," Josh said jokingly. He pulled on the last gate. "Well, these certainly all are working just fine."

He turned back to reassure Elizabeth, then stiffened as he saw the dark expanse of the barn. The lantern Elizabeth had been carrying sat by itself in the dirt in front of the closed door. "Bethy?"

"Where is she?" Kari asked.

Josh took Kari's arm and stalked toward the barn door. "Bethy!" he called angrily. "This isn't funny."

There was no answer, only the silent glow of the lantern. Just before they reached the door, they heard a noise like the sound of a crossbar falling into place. Josh grasped the rope handle of the door and gave it a forceful tug, but it didn't budge.

"Damn you, Bethy," Josh whispered under his breath.

"What is it, Josh?" Kari sounded confused.

He turned around and looked at her vivid blue eyes, then let his eyes drift downward to where the matching blue silk sheathed her long bodice. "It appears, Viking, that we are locked in."

"This is an American joke?" Kari sounded more puzzled than annoyed.

"I'm not laughing," Josh said grimly.

"Why would Elizabeth do such a thing?"

Josh ran his hand back through the thick wave of chestnut hair that had become disheveled with the evening's vigorous dancing. "She thinks we need to talk," he said with a heavy sigh.

Kari gave a little shiver. "It would be easier to talk someplace not so cold, don't you think?"

Josh gave a disgusted kick at a pile of hay, sending dust and broken stalks whirling into the air. He picked up the lantern from the floor and lifted it high to give the barn a quick survey. As the widening circle of lamplight fell on the wall opposite the stalls, Josh saw that a pile of blankets was thrown over what looked like a freshly stacked mound of hay. Next to the blankets was one of Elizabeth's earthenware jugs where she kept the hard cider.

"Bethy's been busy," Josh said, nodding toward the items. He gave another tug to the door. It was definitely barred. Kari stood next to him, shivering in the thin silk dress. He shifted the lantern to his left hand and reached out his right for hers. "Come on. There's no point in your freezing to death."

He pulled her toward the blankets, then dropped her hand while he spread the two thickest ones out to make a sort of mattress over the fresh hay. "Sit down," he said, doing so himself and indicating a place next to him for her.

Kari sank into the soft wool bed and felt her trembling increase as Josh draped one of the cold wool blankets around her shoulders. Funny, she thought to herself. She'd been able to stand on the edge of an icy fjord in the middle of winter back in Norway without feeling the cold. But now the nighttime chill of a barn had her shaking like an aspen leaf.

"I'm sorry," she said softly. "I don't know why I'm so cold."

"These blankets are cold, but they'll warm up soon enough with the heat of our bodies." Josh most definitely felt the heat building already. Damn Bethy, he said to himself for the tenth time. He reached around Kari and rubbed briskly up and down her shoulders and arms. Slowly he felt her trembling subside and her long body relax under his hands.

"What did she want us to talk about?"

"Excuse me?" Josh was concentrating on keeping the feeling of his hands on Kari from running riot throughout the rest of his body.

"You said Elizabeth thought we needed to talk about something."

"Hmm. Yes." He took a deep breath. He withdrew his hands from her and picked an idle piece of hay off the blanket. Finally, he blurted out, "Are you sure you want to go to Minnesota?"

She looked at him, her sky blue eyes snapping with annoyance. "What kind of a question is that? Getting to

Minnesota is all my family has planned and struggled for
these past few years.''

Josh nodded. "I know. I guess what I meant to
say...um... Bethy said..." Criminy! Josh bit hard into
the side of his lip. What was wrong with him? He'd always been one of the smoothest talkers in Milwaukee, and
now he couldn't seem to get out a simple sentence. Trying
to organize his thoughts, he pushed himself back a ways on
the blankets and started again. "Did you ever think you
might be happy staying here in Wisconsin?"

The expression in Kari's eyes changed from annoyance
to wariness. "Just what are you asking me, Josh Lyman?" she said slowly.

Josh felt suddenly that he would give half he owned to
erase the doubt from those beautiful eyes and see in its
place one of her bewitching smiles. He reached out a hand
to touch her cheek. "These past few months have been
hard on both of us, Kari. You know my situation. I've
been in mourning for Corinne, but beyond that...well,
someday, perhaps, you'll understand some of the guilt I'm
carrying. Perhaps someday I'll understand it myself. All I
know is that when I think of leaving you in Minnesota, I
feel like my world is being torn away from me again, as
surely as it was that night on the *Atlantic.*"

Kari gave another involuntary shiver.

"You're still cold." Josh's voice held the tender concern of a lover. He reached for the jar of cider and pulled
out the cork. "Here, drink some of this. It'll put warmth
in your veins."

Kari felt as if she had gone to sleep and was in the middle of a dream. How many times had she thought about
hearing these words from Josh? How often had she imagined his voice with that mellow tone meant only for her?

She took a drink of the cider and welcomed the burning sensation down the length of her throat. It helped her focus. This wasn't a dream, after all. They were in the Stanleys' barn in the middle of the night and Josh was looking at her as if she were a sweetmeat he couldn't wait to devour.

They had come near to this before, she reminded herself. They had let the lure of their bodies bring them together, only to have Josh pull away each time and retreat into his aloofness and guilt. Kari took another drink of the cider. "Speak plainly, Josh," she said bluntly, not letting the softening of her heart reach her voice. "Are you saying that you *want* me to stay in Wisconsin?"

Josh took the cider jug from her and tipped it back for a long, long swallow. Then he deliberately replaced the cork and stretched his long arm to set the bottle well out of their way. "I'm saying, Kari Aslaksdatter, that Bethy was right . . . I've been a damn fool."

With no noticeable effort, he lifted her, blankets and all, and settled her in his lap. "I'm saying that if Thaddeus had put his hand one inch lower on you during that dance tonight, I would have torn his head off." He brushed a feather-light kiss along her lips, then over each eye.

"I'm saying—" his voice was husky "—that what we're about to do has been—" he searched for the words "—*preordained* by your thundering Nordic gods since the first moment I set eyes on you. They won't be denied anymore, those ancient ones." He moved his lips back to hers and opened her mouth in a still-gentle kiss. "And neither will we, Viking."

Chapter Thirteen

Josh deepened the kiss, and Kari felt the insistent penetration all the way down into her stomach. The apple liquor was spreading itself languidly through her limbs, and, Josh was right, the heat began to build in slow, liquid waves.

She shrugged the blanket away from her shoulders. Josh pulled it out from under her and threw it aside with sudden impatience. His mouth continued its erotic massage, but his hands were now on her dress, his big fingers struggling with the neck-to-waist row of tiny buttons. She leaned back against the rock-solid biceps of his left arm and let his movements stoke the fires inside her.

"Help me, Kari," he said finally, hoarsely, and the plea clanged inside her head and cleared away all the remaining shrouds of apprehension. She lifted her hands to his and together they shed her delicate silk covering.

Josh pulled away from her mouth and looked down at the creamy expanse of her chest. She watched his eyes flare darkly before he asked, "Do you want me to blow out the lantern?"

She shook her head, and then . . . there it was. The smile Josh had been waiting for . . . that bewitching, fascinating, heartrending smile. He closed his eyes for an instant from pure elation. His heart swelled to match that other, more carnal part of his body...which had become aroused the instant he had heard the soft thud of the crossbar closing him in with her.

For several moments he just looked at her...the softly moist lips, the perfect rose-accented cheeks, the blue eyes shining as he had never before seen them. Tender and... *loving*. But the call of his body was unrelenting and so he moved to stretch them both out on their wool bed and let his legs entangle themselves, still clothed, with hers.

He had loosened her undergarments to release her trim, firm breasts. He caressed them first gently with his roughened hands, but soon replaced his fingers with the soft laving of his tongue, and then, as they began to tremble at her shaky intake of breath, he pulled one of the pink tips into his mouth and sucked in sensual, age-old rhythm.

Kari's fingertips were in his hair, massaging, then gripping tighter as the first newly awakened surges of passion radiated through her. Josh turned his attention to her other breast, and she felt the pulling there and lower where his body pressed hotly against hers. Her senses seemed about to detonate...like the gunpowder in her father's old musket. For a moment, she felt an overwhelming panic. "What do I do, Josh?" she asked, her voice stretched with tension.

Josh reluctantly pulled himself away from her. He was trying to go slowly, to remember her inexperience, but it had been a long time since his body had sought relief inside a woman. He had been faithful to Corinne in spite of her refusal to accept him as a true husband. And besides everything else, this was Kari, his Viking, and now he could admit that he had wanted this moment from the very beginning. His other feelings for her had developed slowly, but the wanting, this overwhelming, almost savage *desire* such as he had never known for another woman had been instantaneous and inescapable. Still, he had waited this long, he could wait . . . he could make it good.

He pulled them both up to their knees so that they touched as equals from knee to shoulder. Then he put his arms around her to steady her and proceeded to devastate her mouth with long, slow, endless kisses. When Kari would have drawn them back down to the blankets, he continued holding her there against him with an iron grip, and didn't take his mouth from hers until they both were shaking with need. Only then did he strip away the remainder of his clothes and hers and ease himself on top of her.

Her body was lean and well toned, and she flinched for only a moment as he made the first thrust into her. They fit together well, but by now neither one was capable of the coherent thought to appreciate the fact. Josh had lost the grip he'd had on his resolution to go slowly. A more primeval force drove him now to fill her relentlessly again and again. His eyes closed on a blinding light, and then all the power of his body converged in a mighty convulsion followed by . . . blessed relief. And darkness, relaxation, weakness, wetness, peace.

Kari had stiffened in his arms, but it took a few moments for him to realize that the male compulsion he had succumbed to at the end had not allowed her unpracticed body any ultimate satisfaction. Instantly, the guilt that had become so familiar during his attempts at lovemaking with Corinne washed back through him, making him want to retch. Maybe it *had* been his fault that Corinne had never reconciled herself to the physical part of their marriage. As soon as the thought entered his head, he discounted it. Nothing about his relationship with Corinne compared to what he felt for Kari. Kari's response to his attentions had been warm and passionate. It was only the ending that needed some adjustment, and he intended to take care of that right away.

"You made me lose my head, Viking," he told her, his voice soft and teasing. "And everything else along with it," he added with a rueful chuckle.

Kari's bright eyes were glazed with unshed tears. He kissed them shut. "Don't worry about it. We've got all the time in the world."

Her eyes fluttered open. "Did I not do it right, Josh?" she asked shyly.

He kissed her closed mouth with hot, dry lips. "You did everything just right, love. I was the one who messed up a bit, but we're going to work on that right now."

Kari's agitated stomach did another turn at the endearment. Was she truly his love? she wondered. The idea was so amazing that for a moment she forgot about the continued clamoring of her aroused senses. But soon the clamoring became more incessant than ever as Josh began a slow discovery of her body with hands and lips and tongue.

He stopped midway down and looked up at her. She could feel the rasp of his whiskers against the sensitive skin of her belly. "There's more than one way to handle these things, Viking," he said with a sensual smile.

Kari forgot to breathe as his erotic exploration continued down into the core of her private woman's body. First with gentle fingers, then with the silky tenderness of his tongue he opened and tasted and loved. Her back went rigid and his hands moved around to cup her firm buttocks as she pressed herself up against the exquisite assault of his mouth. Suddenly her body was flooded with incredible swells of pleasure, intense almost to the point of pain. They washed through her again and again like great breakers in an angry sea, and she cried out and clutched the wool blanket on either side of her, until the tide subsided, leaving only gentle waves that lapped gently at the edge of her consciousness.

Then she was again in Josh's arms. He held her close against him for several minutes without words, allowing her to recover her senses, to gain her shore legs after the remarkable thing that had happened to her.

"Was that better?" Josh asked. He sounded sleepy and amused.

"Mmm." Kari didn't think she could move her jaw to answer, or any other part of her body for that matter.

Josh nestled her more comfortably in his arms and pulled a blanket over them. "Rest now. Go to sleep if you like."

She closed her eyes and drifted for several moments. Little by little the delicious lethargy began disappearing, and it started to dawn on her exactly what had transpired between them. She opened her eyes, pulled out of his arms and sat up. "But, Josh, we can't stay out here. We have to get back to the house. What will they say? My brother..."

Josh took hold of her slender wrist and in one strong movement had tumbled her back down into his arms. "Don't worry about it. I'll have you back in the house before dawn...even if I have to break the door down." He didn't tell her that he had heard the crossbar being slid out from the other side of the door some time back.

Kari looked up at him, her eyes doubtful. "Are you sure?"

"I promise," he said firmly. He kissed her softly. "Of course, we don't have to go to sleep if you're not tired." His voice grew husky and he nipped gently at her chin. "Now you know what this is all about...I intend that next time we do it together."

"Next time?" Her eyes flared blue fire in the shadowy barn.

"And the next...and the next," he whispered in her ear.

Spring seemed to have arrived overnight. The bitter nip in the air had been replaced by a mild breeze and the fecund smell of thawed earth. At first Kari thought the change was in herself rather than the weather, but it was Elizabeth who first made the comment as the two stood side by side hanging out the wash. "It's so warm, I do believe the trees are budding," she said.

"It's a beautiful day," Kari agreed, taking a deep breath of fresh air.

Elizabeth peeked at her smugly from behind a pair of long muslin drawers. "I'm glad to hear you say so. I thought you might be a trifle ornery today after sleeping in the barn."

Kari could feel the flush start from the top of her breasts. She and Josh had stumbled back to the house in the predawn darkness, afraid to use the lantern. The night had turned icy cold, but neither felt it. After a night of only brief moments of sleep, and long, drugging interludes of loving, they had both felt invigorated.

"I'll never be able to sleep," Kari had whispered just before they reached the door.

"Yes, you will." Josh had pulled her into his arms for one last hungry kiss before he had let her go in front of him, tiptoeing into the quiet farmhouse.

"Josh was very angry with you at first, Elizabeth."

"Only at first?"

Kari concentrated fiercely on the garment she was clipping to the clothesline, though she couldn't for the life of her have told anyone what it was. "I think...I don't think..." She stopped, faced Elizabeth squarely and said forthrightly, "He didn't appear to be angry at anyone by the time we came back to the house." She could feel the heat radiating from her red face.

Elizabeth gave a gentle laugh and reached into the basket for another piece of damp clothing. "Don't you go getting embarrassed with me, Kari. If I didn't have a pretty good idea what might go on between the two of you alone out there together, I wouldn't have risked getting my Tom's dander up—not to mention Josh's—by shutting you in. Tom always says one of my worst faults is being a meddler."

Kari recognized the finesse with which Elizabeth had cooled her embarrassment by focusing on her own supposed shortcomings. Kari reached a hand out to her. "Josh is lucky to have a friend like you, Elizabeth."

"Josh has been an unhappy man these past few months, Kari. Tom and I were both mighty glad to see that satisfied grin on his face this morning. He looked like a pussycat in a creamery."

The blush deepened again on Kari's face, but she laughed. "I was afraid everyone would—" she hesitated and her voice dropped to a whisper "—know."

Elizabeth smiled with understanding. "I know. You feel so wonderful, so *exploding* inside, that it's hard to imagine that everyone can't see it."

Without a mother or older sister to talk to, Kari had never had the experience of confiding in another female. She found it immensely comforting, even though she had trouble forming the words. "I only hope that Josh doesn't come to have...regrets. Several times before he has seemed to be more...friendly, and then the next day he's cold again. It's like he doesn't want to allow himself to be happy."

"Well, he certainly didn't look cold this morning. The looks he was giving you were melting the butter on my flapjacks."

Kari beamed. "What kind of looks was I giving him?"

Elizabeth folded a length of linen and looked down her nose at Kari. "Come to think of it...that butter didn't stand a chance."

The last two days with the Stanleys were busy for everyone. Tom had come up with a number of two- and three-man jobs that he wanted Josh and Thaddeus to help him with, and Kari and Elizabeth worked hard bottling syrup from morning to night. There was no time for stolen moments in the barn or anywhere else, and if it weren't for the sensual smile Josh bestowed on her every time their paths crossed, she would almost think she had dreamed that long, erotic night.

Much to Kari's relief, and in spite of Elizabeth's observations, the younger boys and Thaddeus seemed oblivious to any change in her relationship with Josh. Thaddeus still was quick at hand to pull out her chair at the noon meal, and his light brown eyes rested on her more often than not. Arne continued to be truculent around Josh, but not any more so than he had been in Milwaukee. All in all, the incredible transformation in her world seemed to have gone unremarked by all but Elizabeth.

Late afternoon of the day before they were to leave, Kari and the three boys loaded the wagon. "Are you quite sure *all* this stuff was in this wagon when we left Milwaukee, Davey?" Kari asked, tiredly wiping the fallen wisps of hair from in front of her eyes. She was perched on top of a pile of packing crates that threatened to spill out of the back lip of the wagon.

Davey surveyed the several boxes which remained on the ground. "It all fit somehow, Kari."

"What seems to be the problem?" Kari's heart gave the little skip it had given every time she had heard Josh's voice for the past two days.

"What is all this stuff, Josh?" Davey asked his brother with disgust. "There's no way it's all gonna go in that wagon."

Josh grinned. The way he'd been feeling lately, moving an entire mountain might cause him some problem, but he doubted it. Especially not when Kari was there watching him with that special smile, the brand-new one that had been born in a chilly barn two days ago.

"Supplies for the camp," Josh answered absently, watching the brightness of Kari's blue eyes above the green gingham dress she was wearing. "Why don't you boys run along and batten down your fort so's it'll be here next time. I'll finish up the loading with Kari."

His suggestion was met with three whoops and a flying of heels as Davey and Phineas took off into the woods with Arne close behind. Josh approached the wagon. "Alone at last," he said softly, his voice suggestive and warm.

Kari laughed. Elizabeth was sitting not ten yards away on the front stoop peeling the last of the winter's store of potatoes. The three little ones pecked happily in the dirt at her feet like chicks around a mama hen. Thaddeus and big Tom were out in front of the barn loudly disputing the mechanics of a new hayrack they were constructing from boards the men had planed yesterday.

"Not alone exactly."

Josh jumped nimbly into the wagon beside her, and before she knew what was happening, he lifted her easily in his long arms and moved to the front part of the wagon, out of sight of the yard. Half sitting on a big flour barrel, he pulled her between his legs and took her mouth in a thirsty kiss.

Kari's heart did an instant plunge from throat to abdomen, and it was several moments before she pulled away in protest. "Josh! We can't...everyone will know."

Josh's reply was to put his hand firmly on her posterior and situate the lower portion of her body directly between his powerful thighs. "To hell with them."

His kiss became less focused, and more of Kari's attention was drawn to the hard heat below. His arousal threatened to defy the confines of his shiny wool work pants. She put a slender hand on each of his thighs and felt the muscles contract at her touch.

"You see what a state you have me in, Viking?" Josh said irritably. "How's a man supposed to get his work done?"

"I've had a bit of a problem concentrating myself," she admitted ruefully, her voice catching on a little gasp as the solid ridge of him rubbed directly along the most needy part of her.

Her obvious response to him, the sudden stiffening of her nipples against his cotton shirt, roughened Josh's voice. "At camp I'll have the foreman's cabin to myself. Holstein bunks with the boys when I'm there."

"Mmm." Kari's hands made their way up the long muscles of his thigh and caressed him now through the wool of his trousers. "They're going to wonder what we're doing in here," she whispered.

"If you don't move your hands soon, there will no longer be any doubt what we're doing in here."

"Move them...like this?" Her voice was wicked with feigned innocence.

Josh made a sound somewhere between a growl and a purr. Suddenly Kari's skirts and petticoats were up around her waist and Josh's warm fingers had unerringly found the split in her drawers. "You were warned, Viking."

He put his mouth back on hers and, this time, suckled it with unrelenting expertise until Kari's entire body seemed to dissolve. At the precise moment when she felt she could no longer stand, Josh lifted her completely in the air and set her down carefully on his now-freed staff. Kari felt it slide hard into her liquefied body. With his hands grasping her firmly at the waist, Josh showed her how to move to stoke the pressure deep inside. Following two days of wanting, it didn't take long for either of them. After not more than a dozen slow, thick strokes, Kari gave half a sob, trembled and clutched at Josh's shoulders. Instantly he stiffened and experienced a glorious release.

The flour barrel wobbled crazily underneath them. "Whew," Josh said.

Kari came crashing down to earth. "Oh, Josh," she said, her accent suddenly heavy. "What if they heard? Oh, my goodness, what you must think of me!" She pulled away from him and began to frantically rearrange her clothing.

Josh watched her with a lazy grin and nonchalantly buttoned up his pants. "I gave fair warning, Viking."

Kari's face was scarlet. "Do you think they heard?"

Josh's grin widened. "Some people say there were Norwegians in these woods long before the first Englishmen ever came here. Maybe they'll think it was just the echo of one of those ancient Viking warriors."

Kari's face registered dismay. "Oh, dear."

Josh chuckled and pulled her into his arms. "Don't fret, love. No one is paying us any attention. In fact, if you like, we could try that last part one more time...."

"Oh, no, you don't, Josh Lyman." Kari backed away from him and scrambled over the tops of the boxes to the rear of the wagon. "You don't come near me again, you...you...*geit!*"

"What's *geit?*"

"It's a—" her golden eyelashes fluttered down "—a goat!"

"A goat, am I?" Josh advanced toward her on all fours like a sleek predator and spoke with deadly softness. "I didn't notice you complaining a few minutes ago."

"Now, Josh..."

"Uncle Josh!" Marigold's tiny head barely reached over the tailgate of the wagon.

Josh looked startled, but recovered immediately. "What is it, sweetie?" he said to the child.

"Are you finished with your nap yet?"

Josh stretched his long legs and jumped out of the wagon. "What's that, hon?"

"Papa says to tell you if you're finished with your nap, he needs help."

"Oh, he does, does he?" He shot a look around the side of the wagon to where Tom was standing over by the barn, his wide-brimmed hat pushed way back on his head and a mischievous grin on his face. Josh snatched his own hat from where it had fallen to the ground. He shot a wink at Kari, who was sitting with a flaming face in the middle of the wagon, then headed across the yard toward his friend with long, angry strides.

"Did you take a nap, too, Kari?" Marigold asked.

"Sort of."

"I didn't know big people took naps."

Kari sat on the edge of the wagon and scooped the child into her lap. "They do sometimes, sweetheart," she said, giving the girl a hug. "When they're very tired."

Their first view of Horseshoe Camp 3 was not promising. The shanties from which the logging men got their shantyboy nickname were hastily constructed of rough-hewn logs. The roofs were flat, made of split hollow bass-wood. After the relative luxury of the Stanley farm, both Kari and Thaddeus viewed the motley collection of build-ings with disappointment. But at least they had finally ar-rived, Kari thought wearily. They had traveled the last mile into the camp on a corduroy skid road built to move the logs down to the river's edge where they would be decked into great piles by the cant-hook men until time for the spring drive.

Kari accepted Thaddeus's offer of his arm to help her jump from the wagon. She was quite certain that several of her bones had been jolted loose from their sockets dur-ing the trip.

The appearance of the camp had in no way dampened the enthusiasm of the three younger boys. "Can I ride a skidder, Josh?" Davey hollered, jumping down from the wagon and turning around to take in a view of everything at once. "Phineas and me want to learn to roll logs. Someday we're gonna be jam crackers, Josh. Can we put calks on our boots, Josh?"

Josh had climbed down from the front of the wagon and was making his way back toward Kari. "Hold on there, little brother. We just got here."

Kari stretched to assure herself that all her body parts were still in working order. "You all right, Viking?" Josh asked gently, ignoring Thaddeus, who had kept his arm lightly supporting hers. "It was kind of a rough ride to-ward the end there."

"I'm fine," she told him with a smile. She took a deep breath of air and found it sharp with the scent of cut pine. The majestic trees towered over the tiny buildings of the camp, leaving them in shadow in the midst of a cloudless day.

Josh directed his eyes pointedly first to Thaddeus's hand gripping Kari's arm, then to his face. The look that passed between them was not cordial. Thaddeus was of a much slighter build, but the two men equaled each other in height, and though Kari was tall, both reached several inches above her. For a moment, standing between them, she felt as if they had cast her into shadow in the same way the lofty pines did to the camp. She gently withdrew her arm from Thaddeus's hold and took a step away from them both.

"Shall we unload the wagon?" she asked quietly.

Josh and Thaddeus continued their staring match.

"Hey there, Josh, welcome back!" A burly, barrel-chested man was coming toward them with one hand outstretched and a grin on his face. Everything about him seemed red, from his plaid wool shirt to the rosy tinge of his skin to the bright red hair that sprouted from his head in unruly curls.

Josh turned away from Thaddeus and a smile lit his face. "Holstein!" He shook the man's hand with obvious pleasure. "Kari, this is Holstein Ericssen," he said, turning to her. "The best loggin' man west of the Alleghenies."

"Ain't no more loggin' worth a spit east of the Alleghenies," the big man said, laughing. "Guess that makes me the best in the country!" He gave Kari an outrageous wink.

For the first time since arriving at the camp, Kari felt her heart lift. She smiled at Holstein and his blue eyes danced with pleasure. "Pleased to meet *you*, ma'am," he said, engulfing her hand in his massive fingers.

"This here is Thaddeus Pennington," Josh interrupted, his smile a touch dimmed.

Thaddeus held his own in a strong handshake, though the lumberman's hand was twice the size of his. "Pleased to meet you, Mr. Ericssen," Thaddeus said solemnly, as if he were greeting the president of a bank.

By now some of the other loggers had come up and Josh was greeting them all by name and presenting them to the newcomers. They were big men, good-humored and loud, and obviously impressed with the statuesque blond beauty who had suddenly appeared in their midst. Kari felt as if she had been transported back to one of the marketfair days in Stavanger when strapping young Norsemen engaged in spirited male rivalry to impress the eligible young girls of the town.

Several of the men were Norwegians, and were delighted to learn that she spoke their native tongue. Arne, too, received his share of attention. Kari looked on in amusement as he puffed up like a gull in the wind, speaking Norwegian with the men. He seemed pleased that for once he had the edge over Davey and Phineas.

Through the din of big bass voices, Kari heard Josh ask, "Where's Olav?"

"The Babe's a mite under the weather," Holstein answered.

Josh looked concerned. "Nothing serious, I hope." Sickness was no laughing matter at the camps. On the edge of civilization, far from any medical care, an illness could often lead to death.

Gradually Josh became aware of the stifled chuckles of his men. Holstein cleared his throat to ward off a grin. "Baby Olav and Cookie had a *dis*-pute here two, three days back. Seems Cookie didn't take kindly to Olav comin' into the cookshed and finishing off an entire barrel of apples." He rubbed a hand over the bright red sideburns that ran down each cheek and shot an uneasy glance at Kari before he continued with his story. "So yesterday, Cookie fed Olav his 'special recipe' fish chowder. 'Pears he made it with a whole bottle of cod-liver oil."

Josh grimaced. "Is Olav going to be all right?"

Holstein finally broke down and hooted out a laugh. "Oh, he'll be fine…he's just been busy back in the woods all day long airin' his hindquarters. Beggin' your pardon, ma'am," he said with another wink at Kari.

Josh gave a reluctant smile. "Poor Olav."

"Knowing the Babe, he'll be the first one lined up for supper tonight," Holstein said, still chuckling, and the men around him nodded their agreement.

Olav's recuperative powers did not quite measure up to the men's expectations, so it was at breakfast the next morning in the dining shanty that Kari finally got a look at the huge logger. He moved with such easy grace that it wasn't until it came right up to meet her that Kari could appreciate his size. His lower arms were the size of small tree trunks and each hand as big as a loaf of bread.

"How d'ye do, ma'am," he said to her in a reverberating bass voice. She looked up to see his head nearly scrape the rough log ceiling as he inclined it politely toward her.

Kari answered him in Norwegian, and was rewarded with a wide smile, which revealed the biggest, shiniest teeth she had ever seen. "I hope you're feeling better," she ended, switching to English so that Josh would not be left out.

Olav ducked his head and, for all his tremendous size, reminded Kari very much of Arne when he was chagrined over something. "I'm fine, thank you kindly, ma'am." Then his little-boy expression disappeared, and he shot a dark glance across the shanty to where Cookie was serving up huge wooden bowls of oatmeal for the men. His bright eyes had clouded and to Kari he all at once resembled nothing so much as the thunder god of the ancients, Thor. "Baby" Olav did not appear to be a man to take for granted.

Breakfast was Kari's first chance to meet all the men at once, and she found the meal exhilarating. Most of them had not seen a female for six long months of winter, and none of them had seen one so pretty for much longer than that. Her health was inquired after more times and she heard more "ma'am's" than she had in her entire life.

At first Josh seemed to be taking his men's attentions to her with good grace, but when Thaddeus sat down on one side of her and Holstein slid in on the other, leaving him no choice but to take a seat at the very end of one of the long tables, Josh appeared a bit irritated. His humor didn't improve as the meal progressed. Kari was passed the maple syrup for her oatmeal at least ten times. She could not get more than a sip taken from her tin cup of coffee before the cup was filled again to the top. So many pieces of Cookie's dense brown bread were buttered and set in front of her, so many thick slabs of bacon were piled on her plate, that she would be eating from now until sundown if she were to finish her breakfast. With each new offering, Kari gave one of her dazzling smiles, and by the end of the meal the hearts of the entire camp were conquered.

The veritable mountains of food that had covered the long tables disappeared in an amazingly short time, and Holstein made a great show of reluctance when he turned from Kari and shouted for the men to head back to work. They had already put in two to three hard hours since dawn and would work until sunset.

Holstein gave a hand to Kari to help her from the bench. "Ah, Miss Kari, it's a real pleasure to have a lady like you in camp," he told her, his blue eyes sparkling in his shiny red face. "Makes a man kinda long for the finer things. It surely do."

Kari laughed. Perhaps it was the Norwegian heritage of so many of these men that made her feel comfortable with them. She could almost be back at home, teasing with the boys on the green at Stavanger. These transplanted Norsemen made her feel welcome and beautiful and just a little homesick.

On the other hand, Thaddeus appeared to be uncomfortably out of his element among the robust loggers. Kari had seen his eyes widen in horror as he watched Olav consume an entire one-pound slab of bacon in two bites and wash it down by taking a big mug of scalding coffee in an incredible gulp that one would swear had gone directly from mouth to stomach without ever touching his throat.

Kari reached out a hand to touch Thaddeus gently on the arm as they prepared to leave the shanty. "First I have to get used to a new world in America," she whispered to him, "and now I have to get used to a new world of *logging*. It's not exactly like home, is it?"

Thaddeus smiled, grateful for her obvious attempt at putting him at ease. "This meal would have fed us for the next three years at *home*," he said wryly.

Kari giggled. "*Olav's* meal would have fed us for the next three years."

Thaddeus shook his head, still bemused by this new experience. "I've never seen a man so big."

Josh interrupted them and asked without a smile if they were ready for their promised tour of the camp. He appeared to still be smarting from being done out of a place at her side at breakfast, but Kari's smiles soon restored his good humor.

It had turned cold again overnight, and the group of newcomers had to bundle up as Josh and Holstein led

them around the camp. The loggers seemed impervious to
the cold. They worked without coats in colorful plaid wool
shirts and stagged trousers, cut off above the boots to keep
them out of the snow.

Holstein explained the strictly organized assignment of
duties. First were the scalers, who chose the next set of
trees to be harvested from among the magnificent white
pines.

"Some of these here beauties have been around all of
three, four hundred years," Holstein told them with a
professional's respect for his craft. He pointed to one that
soared out of sight above them. "Look at this 'un ... near
eight feet across at the base."

Thaddeus, Kari and the three boys craned their necks up
at the splendid specimen, but Josh and Holstein were already moving on to the next station. Here the sawyers were
systematically denuding the land of each tree the scalers
had marked. Olav, effortlessly sliding one end of a huge
double saw back and forth across the four-foot trunk of a
huge pine, waved to them with one free hand. His companion on the other end of the saw was another big Norwegian logger, but unlike Olav, he had his back bent into
the sawing, and sweat rolled down his face in spite of the
rise of a wintry wind.

"We're in for a spring snowfall," Holstein said with a
practiced look at sky. Kari pulled up the hood of Helen's
blue pelisse.

The group moved on quickly toward the river, passing
the swampers, who cut and bundled the branches from the
fallen trees, and then the bark peelers, who stripped the
huge trunks with admirable speed using a strange-looking
tool called a spudder. A good peeler could peel a cord of
bark a day, Holstein told them.

By the time they reached the water, snow was beginning to fall in big, wet flakes. The men there were decking logs into huge piles, while keeping an eye on the snow.

"If this gets much heavier, we'll stop work here," Holstein told them, looking up at the gray sky. "Decking's one of the most dangerous jobs in camp. Our toploader there—" he pointed up to a man standing on top of the pile with a cant hook "—he earns his two dollars a day, let me tell you. If those logs start to roll..." He ended with a shrug of his shoulders.

The heavy snow was beginning to paint a coat of white over the logs, the surrounding trees and the people. It fell faster and faster, and the three boys pounded one another with delight. "You're an old man, Phin," Davey joked with his friend. "Your hair's pure white."

Holstein told Josh he was glad to see this last blast of winter. The warm season had ruined their ice skid roads, and this new coating would mean they could move more logs down to the river. But he suggested they return to camp before the storm became worse. "Could get nasty on us...ya never know."

So they ended up spending most of their first day at Horseshoe Camp 3 back at the cook shanty listening to the men's tales while outside the heavy, wet, spring snow bent the trees into frosty white arches.

The snow stopped around midafternoon and most of the workers headed back outside. The three boys, who had been champing at the close confinement, followed them.

"Stay out of the men's way," Josh yelled after them. He, Thaddeus and Kari chose to stay inside, relaxing next to the potbellied stove with great mugs of apple cider. The comforting smells of steam and wet, woolen clothing had Kari thinking of home, her papa and brother coming in after a hard day working in the snow.... She had almost dozed off when she was awakened by a shout of rage coming from just outside the shanty. The log door opened and Cookie stomped into the room.

"Wherrre's that thievin' Norsky?" he bellowed. Cookie was a husky Irishman who had retained both the brogue and the quick temper of his homeland.

Holstein, who had joined the group by the stove for a late-afternoon drink of cider, got to his feet. "Simmer down there, Cookie. What's the problem?"

"Where's Olav?" the cook asked again. "I swear, this time I'll grease my griddle with his lard..." His listeners never got to hear the exact nature of his threat as the Irishman caught sight of Kari and stopped in midsentence. "Where is he?" he finished in a more subdued tone.

"Exactly what are you accusing Olav of, Cookie?" Holstein asked in a conciliatory tone. "He hasn't even come in from the woods yet."

"Well, *someone* has stolen my last barrel of butter," Cookie huffed.

"What would Olav want with a barrel of butter?" Holstein looked puzzled. "What would *anyone* want with a barrel of butter?"

As if in answer to his question, the door behind Cookie opened and three snow-covered bodies tumbled in. "Wow, Josh, you should come out with us!" Davey's cheeks were bright red with cold. "Arne has shown us the greatest thing."

"Just a minute, boys," Josh interrupted, wanting to deal with Cookie's problem first.

But Phineas continued telling of their adventure. "You take barrel staves and put them on your *feet*. Then you can go gliding along the snow like... like a human sleigh. You should've seen us, Thad. We slid down that road to the river smooth as butter across a griddle."

Josh looked over at Kari, who had gotten a sick feeling in the middle of her stomach. "It's what the children do back home," she said weakly. "We call it *skiløping*."

Josh turned to Davey. "Just where did you get these barrel staves, little brother?"

The broad smiles died on the three boys' faces as they suddenly became aware of the cook watching them with an irate expression.

"Uh..." Davey looked nervously from Phineas to Arne, then back to Josh. "We found them."

"Found them where?"

"Uh...on a barrel."

Josh shook his head. "I told you boys to keep out of trouble. Now Cookie here is without butter for the rest of the season."

"There wasn't more than a handful left, Josh, honest."

Cookie's scowl was a shade less deep as he turned to look over the three boys, standing with their heads bent, their enthusiasm of just moments ago replaced by abject discomfort. He waited a few moments before speaking, but finally said, "Bejesus, but if it isn't enough to deal with this camp full of lugheads...now I got children to watch out for."

The boys bowed their heads even lower at the insult. The last thing they wanted to be considered among this camp full of brawny men was "children."

"Sorry, sir," Davey mumbled, then he lifted his head to look directly over to Holstein. "Sorry, Mr. Ericssen. I guess we didn't think it through."

Josh felt bad that their joy over their new sport had been so thoroughly quashed, but he knew that provisions in a lumber camp were precious commodities. He couldn't blame Cookie for his anger. "All right, boys. You have just been officially appointed as Cookie's new dishwashing crew. You can start after supper tonight. Maybe that'll keep you busy enough to stay out of trouble.''

"Yes, sir," Davey and Phineas answered at once, relieved to find their punishment a tolerable one. Arne kept silent, but the glance he turned on Josh was sullen.

Cookie nodded with satisfaction and disappeared out the door, and Josh invited the boys to join them around the stove. But by then the men were starting to come in for the evening meal and confusion reigned for the next couple of hours. The supper was a hearty one of corned beef, "red horse" the men called it, rutabagas and Cookie's ever-present brown bread.

The boys had soon forgotten their disgrace, and delighted in being the center of attention, explaining their afternoon's escapade to the men.

"You boys better watch what you eat tomorrow," big Olav advised them with a grin. "That Cookie's a vengeful fellow."

When the heaping platters of food had been wiped clean, the men retired to the bunkhouse, inviting the boys along to learn shantyboys' poker. Reluctantly, Thaddeus got up to accompany them, since he was to bed down there, too.

"You'll be all right, Kari?" he asked before leaving. "Would you like me to see you to your cabin?" A bed and side table had been moved for her into Cookie's storehouse. Josh would sleep in Holstein's cabin, which also served as the camp office.

"I'll be fine," she said, smiling. She could feel Josh bristling at her side at Thaddeus's proprietary tone.

Thaddeus nodded his head and murmured a somewhat less cordial good-night to Josh, then left them alone.

Kari took a last sip of her coffee. "I like your camp, Josh," she said softly.

Josh chuckled ruefully. "Snow in the spring, a cook who tries to poison my best sawyer, a randy foreman who can't seem to take his eyes off you . . ."

Kari blushed. "Now, that's not true, Josh. Mr. Ericssen has been a perfect gentleman."

Josh grunted. "When it wasn't Holstein's wolf's eyes devouring you, it was Pennington's sheep's eyes. It made me feel like I was in a damn barnyard."

Kari laughed quietly and shook her head. "Your eyes are the only ones I was noticing, Josh."

His body reacted immediately to her soft-spoken declaration. "Come here, Viking," he said, pulling her up from the bench and into his lap. "I need a kiss."

Chapter Fourteen

The snow of the previous day had given way to a blustery March wind that had even the seasoned loggers complaining of chill. Josh and Holstein had plans to view some of the land upriver that they were considering opening up next season. They shrugged off warnings from several of the men to stay off the swollen river and set out in one of the flat-ended little boats that the men called bateaux.

When they didn't come back for the noon meal, Kari began to worry. It was a terribly rough day to be out on the water. She pushed back her tin plate and looked at Thaddeus, fear apparent in her eyes. "Where do you suppose they are, Thaddeus?"

Thaddeus gave a snort of disgust. "Even that behemoth Olav told them not to go out this morning, but Josh always has been too much of a daredevil for his own good."

Kari stood. They were almost alone in the cook shanty. Most of the men had had their noon meal taken out to them on the sleighs. "Do you think we should do something?"

"What can we do? They're out on the river like a couple of goldanged fools."

Out on the river. Kari closed her eyes on a sudden, deadly vision of swirling water and helpless bodies. "I have to go, Thaddeus," she said dizzily. "I'll see you later."

She was out the door before Thaddeus could disentangle himself from the long bench. "Wait, Kari! Where are you going?" he called after her, but the wind banged the heavy door shut behind her and she was gone.

The fear built in her throat and spread in numbing waves along her limbs as Kari made her way down to the river. "Josh," she whispered as a silent plea. "Come back to me, Josh."

She reached the edge. The river waters were nearly black under the slate gray sky. She watched the fast-moving current surge by as her stomach rolled with acute nausea. The sound of the rushing water was replaced by a dreadful humming in her ears. Her eyes were fixed on the inexorable movement of the water at her feet. She weaved unsteadily, then grabbed desperately at a nearby branch to help regain her balance. Her icy fingers closed on it for an instant, then slipped along the rough wood as she lost her footing and tumbled wildly down the bank and into the water. The icy-cold wetness hit like a sharp slap against her face. Breathing deeply in panic, she choked as water filled her throat. The river pulled on her like a relentless monster... until she surrendered consciousness to its icy darkness.

"Kari!" Thaddeus had never yelled so loud in his life. He had rushed after her along the snowy path to the river, but when he reached the shore, there was no sign of her anywhere. His shouts brought the nearby loggers.

"What's the matter?" It was Olav's booming voice.

"It's Kari. I think she came down here to search for Josh and Mr. Ericssen. I don't know what happened to her." He looked down at the wild water with alarm.

Olav stood up straight, reaching more than a head above Thaddeus, and carefully scanned the river. "There!" he said. He pointed to a mass of logs some way downriver from the clearing where they were standing.

At first Thaddeus could only see piled-up logs and a jumble of the accumulated debris of the winter freeze, but after a few moments he could distinguish a lump of blue the color of Kari's coat. "God Almighty!" he breathed.

Before Thaddeus could even think what to do, Olav had taken a giant stride from the bank right into the rushing water. The powerful current didn't seem to affect his massive body. The water reached above his waist, but he walked with strong even steps downriver to the jam of logs and rubble. Thaddeus watched as he reached it and bent down to pick up Kari's seemingly lifeless body. She looked like a doll in his big arms and just as inert. Her head bounced crazily as Olav fought his way back upriver to the clearing on the bank. As they approached, Thaddeus could see that Kari's face was whiter than milk.

"Is she alive?" he hollered to Olav, his voice tight with strain.

Olav didn't answer. It was obvious that even for the big man the fight upriver was taking its toll. He stumbled once, but kept on coming until, after what seemed to Thaddeus an eternity, he reached the bank and climbed out, his great chest heaving with the exertion.

Thaddeus and the other men who had gathered hastened to help him up the steep bank and together they eased Kari to the ground. Knud Knudsen, one of the Norwegians who had been so taken by this lovely new arrival from their former country, knelt beside her and placed a hand alongside her throat. "She's a breathin'," he said.

Thaddeus closed his eyes in relief. "Thank God. We've got to get her up to the camp, get her warm."

Olav, who had collapsed next to Kari on the bank, tried to struggle to his feet, but Thaddeus motioned him down. "Not you, Olav. You've done your part." The initial scare over with, Thaddeus's voice assumed its natural authority. "You men... help Olav back to camp and see he gets a warm bath. You two... go tell Cookie we need hot coffee, lots of it."

Kari was still unconscious. Thaddeus started to lean over to pick her up when his attention was drawn to shouts from upriver. Coming swiftly toward them on the raging current was the small boat with Holstein in back and Josh standing toward the front. "What's going on?" Josh yelled.

Holstein gave a strong push to his pole and the bateau rammed up against the riverbank just below where the group of men were huddled around Kari. Josh jumped from the boat without waiting for Holstein to secure it to the shore. "Kari!" he cried, and scrambled up the bank toward her prone form.

Thaddeus pushed him out of the way and picked her up in his arms. "Leave her alone," he snapped at Josh. "This wouldn't have happened if you hadn't been so foolhardy as to go out on that river today."

Josh acted as if he didn't hear. His expression anguished, he reached his arms for her. "Let me take her."

Thaddeus settled her more firmly in his arms and shoved against Josh with his shoulder. "I said leave her alone, Lyman," he shouted angrily. He looked his rival squarely in the eyes. "Wasn't *one* woman enough for you to kill?"

Josh fell back as if he had been shot. The blood drained from his face. Thaddeus ignored him and started walking toward camp with Kari in his arms.

Holstein tied up the boat. The other men had all followed Thaddeus and Kari up the path, but Josh stood as though frozen to the spot. Holstein walked up the bank and put a heavy hand on Josh's back. "He didn't mean it, my friend," he said.

Josh turned to look at his foreman. His eyes were glazed. Holstein took his arm and led him like a blind man up the path.

Kari felt as if she had swallowed half an ocean. Her head pounded and she wanted to throw up. But, mercifully, there was no return of the spinning, the haze. Her mind was clear, and she remembered immediately that she had fallen into the river. She'd gone to look for Josh when he hadn't returned from upriver. She opened her eyes, squinting against the sudden lamplight. Thaddeus was sitting next to her cot. "Did Josh get back?" she asked weakly.

Thaddeus's mouth tightened. "He's fine. He and Holstein are both back safely."

Kari gave a little sigh and closed her eyes again. "What happened to me?"

She felt Thaddeus take one of her hands. "You went into the river. Olav spotted you and went in himself to rescue you. If it hadn't been for him..."

Kari could hear the uncharacteristic emotion in Thaddeus's voice. She mustered the strength to give his hand a squeeze. She couldn't open her eyes again. Her eyelids were simply too heavy. Perhaps they had gotten waterlogged, she thought crazily. "Where is he?" she whispered.

"The men have taken him for a hot bath in the bunkhouse and are filling him up with coffee. But you know Olav, he'll..."

"No, not Olav...Josh. Where is he?"

When Thaddeus didn't answer, Kari finally opened her eyes again. Her voice filled with panic. "What is it, Thaddeus? Are you telling me the truth? Is Josh all right?"

Thaddeus spoke stiffly. "I swear, Kari, both men came back unharmed."

She struggled to sit up. "Then why isn't he here? Something's wrong...he's hurt...."

Thaddeus tried to gently push her back down on the bed, but she wouldn't let him. "Where is he, Thaddeus?"

He didn't meet her eyes. "He's probably upset over something I said down at the river. I shouldn't have said it. I was just so worried about you...I guess it all came out as anger at Josh."

Kari moved her legs over the side of the bed and sat up. Someone in this all-male camp had removed her wet clothes and dressed her in her heavy cotton nightshift, but at the moment she was more concerned with Josh than with female modesty. "What did you say to him?"

Thaddeus looked ashamed. "I accused him of being responsible for Corinne's death."

Kari groaned. "Oh, Thaddeus, how could you?"

"I'm sorry, Kari."

"Well...I've got to find him, to talk to him." She resolutely got to her feet, only to sway backward as she discovered that her dizziness was not completely gone.

Thaddeus took her arm and eased her back on the bed. "You might as well rest, Kari. You're not in any shape to get up yet, and Holstein says that as soon as Josh found out you were going to be all right, he took off into the woods. He told Holstein that he needed to do some thinking by himself."

Kari felt the prickle of tears in her throat. "Poor Josh," she said under her breath. She settled down against her pillow. She was, after all, incredibly tired. She would get up and find Josh as soon as he came back. She would talk to him and make everything right again. All she had to do was talk to him.... Her eyes closed.

She was alone in her makeshift bedroom in the little storage cabin, and Kari knew immediately that she had slept for many hours. Her first thoughts were of Josh. Though her body didn't feel much like cooperating, she would have to get up and go looking for him.

Cautiously, she sat up, and little by little, strength came back into her arms and legs. Her normal bodily functions seemed to be returning, and she realized that there were also physical urges requiring her to rise. She put on Helen's old yellow dress that had become her favorite. Her wool coat was nowhere in sight. Someone must have taken it away to dry. So she bundled a blanket around her shoulders like a shawl and went outside.

The sun was shining again, turning the fast-melting patches of snow into glistening ribbons decorating the landscape. The gusty winds of yesterday still blew, but their effect was more benevolent with the warmer temperature.

Kari found Josh in Holstein's cabin working at the rough pine table that served as a desk. It gave Kari a queasy feeling to see him sitting there. She could see the tenseness in his shoulders as he hunched over one of his wretched books of numbers. It was as if they had suddenly been transported back to his office in Milwaukee. His hiding place, where he had escaped from her and his family for all those endless hours and days. Were they back where they had started? she wondered helplessly. Did everything that had happened between them now mean nothing?

He looked up when she entered and gave her a bleak smile. "Thank God you're better," he said, but his voice lacked the enthusiasm she had been hoping to hear.

"I'm more worried about you," she said directly, walking across the room to stand in front of him. "I was surprised you didn't come to see me yesterday."

"Thaddeus was taking good care of you."

"Thaddeus wasn't the one I wanted there."

Josh sighed and pushed back his chair. "He'd be a better choice, Kari."

Kari felt a flush of anger. How *dare* he do this to her again! How dare he retreat as he had so often into his self-pitying guilt. "I made my choice back at the Stanleys' farm, if you'll remember, Josh."

"I remember," he said very softly.

"A woman can only make that choice once. She makes it for love...*I* made it for love. I don't regret it, and I haven't changed my mind." Indignation had heightened her tone and she made an effort to bring it down to a normal level. "If you have changed yours...I'd appreciate it if you would tell me directly instead of hiding away in your cabin like a ... *reddhare* ... a ..."

"A fraidy-rabbit," Josh finished for her.

"Ya, like a fraidy-rabbit!" she repeated with an angry nod of her head. Then she turned and stomped out of the cabin.

Josh watched the flash of yellow disappear out the door, and for the first time in twenty-four hours, his lips turned up in a smile.

* * *

Kari was still fuming as she stalked up the path toward the cook shanty after leaving Josh in Holstein's cabin. She couldn't believe that Josh would once again withdraw from her as he had so often in Milwaukee. Of course, except for his few words at the beginning about her staying in Wisconsin, neither one had brought up the subject of commitment. Kari had felt that perhaps it had been too soon for Josh to talk about marriage, with Corinne so recently gone. She had decided that she would be content to wait until he thought the time was right. But now she wondered if he ever really thought about marrying her. Even without having a mother to tell her about such things, she knew that men took lovemaking more casually than women.

Deep in thought, she paid no attention to her surroundings until suddenly she was grabbed fiercely around the waist by two spindly arms. "Kari, are you truly all right now?" She looked down to see Arne's eyes wide with distress and returned his embrace warmly.

"I'm just fine, *lille bror.*"

"They told me that you almost drowned, and Thaddeus said it was Josh's fault. Then Davey got mad at Thaddeus and told Phineas his brother was stupid, so now everybody's mad at everybody."

Kari gave an exasperated shake of her head. "Nothing was Josh's fault," she said. "I got dizzy and fell in the river. Now, how could that be anyone's fault but my own?"

Arne dropped his arms from around her and stepped back. He looked at her closely. "But Josh has made you unhappy again." His voice was bitter with accusation.

"Arne, I promise you, I'm just fine."

"I *hate* him."

Kari was alarmed at his vehemence, but attributed it to the scare he had received in hearing that she had had another brush with death. "Arne," she chided gently, "you know that's not true. You don't hate Josh."

His face was flushed and he looked all at once younger, like the little boy she remembered from Stavanger. "I do. He makes you angry and he makes you cry..." He took a great gulp of air and finished with a rush of words. "And you want to stay with him so we won't go to Minnesota like Papa wanted us to."

Kari tried to grasp his thin shoulders to pull him back into her arms, but he twisted away from her and ran headlong down the path. She thought about going after him. Obviously he was hurting, and they needed to have a talk. But she was still feeling the effects of her bout in the river and didn't think she could possibly catch up to him. She would talk to him later when he had had a chance to cool off a bit, she decided. Right now she wanted nothing more than to have some peace and quiet away from all the men in her life. She turned up the path to make her way back to her room.

Josh had decided not to follow Kari immediately. It had been enough to see her there, healthy and beautiful, her blue eyes sparkling with anger. He smiled again, remembering. Since Thaddeus's cruel words by the river yesterday, he had spent long hours reliving the times he had spent with Kari, the frustrations of trying to keep away from her in Milwaukee and the amazing fulfillment he had felt when they had finally come together after Elizabeth's machinations at the Stanleys' farm.

They hadn't talked about the future. Josh had still been carrying his guilt over his failure with Corinne. But with Kari he had been able to see that he *was* capable of a loving relationship. He had tried to offer the same kind of love to Corinne, but something in her had made her unable to accept. He would never be able to go back and remedy that part of his life. But he could take this gift of love that had come to him out of the terrible night of tragedy on Lake Erie and build a new life for himself.

He had begun to feel ready to share these feelings with Kari, to ask her to sacrifice the completion of her father's dream for a reality of their own, here in Wisconsin. Then came the near disaster on the river...and Thaddeus's words as a bitter reminder of the grief that would be a part of the Pennington family forever.

He had walked into the woods until after dark, pondering all these things, but he had returned with his mind as much a muddle as ever. It had only been when he had looked up this morning to see Kari in front of him, her eyes snapping as she declared her love for him, that all at once things had seemed remarkably clear. For the first time in his life, he was *in love*, and after that awing realization, everything else seemed to fall into place.

He got up from the table feeling more lighthearted than he had since before his engagement to Corinne. He wanted to shout out his news to the entire camp. He would not, of course. Two of his dead wife's brothers were out there, and he would try to do everything possible not to add to their grief. But there was one person with whom he had to share his newfound insight. He had waited long enough to tell her. With a cheerful step he headed out the door.

Kari had to admit that she had expected him to come. She had gone back to her room and, instead of taking the nap she had promised herself, had taken great pains at combing out her long hair until it was smooth and shiny as sunlight. Still, she started at the light knock on her door, and her heart quickened in irregular rhythm.

"Who is it?"

"The *reddhare*."

Josh's self-conscious pronunciation of Norwegian words always made her laugh. But when she answered, she forced her voice to be serious. "What do you want?"

"Can I come in?"

She crossed the room and pulled open the door. Josh's big frame almost filled the doorway. In his hand he held a half-wilted blue crocus. "For you," he said, thrusting it at her. "The first one of spring. I found the poor thing almost covered with snow." He pushed into the room and very deliberately closed the door behind him. "Maybe it's a sign, Viking. Winter's over and it's time to welcome the spring together."

Was this her Josh? Kari wondered. Josh Lyman... bringing her flowers and waxing poetic? She could hardly believe her ears.

Josh took her arms and pushed her gently into the middle of the room. Then he turned back to the door and was evidently looking for some kind of lock. There was no such thing in the rough shed, so he shoved a huge flour barrel firmly in front of the door.

"What are you doing?" Kari's voice was dazed.

Josh turned and lifted her off her feet, the limp blue flower still dangling from her fingers. "I'm barring the door, Viking, because I don't want us to be interrupted."

"Why?" Kari asked weakly as he began teasing her neck with excruciatingly soft kisses.

"Because I'm going to make love to you, Viking. And this time when I do, I'm going to tell you with every kiss..." He put her down on the bed and touched her lips briefly with his. "And every touch..." He knelt beside the bed and ran his fingers up her legs underneath her petticoats. "...that I love you...."

"We have to get up, Josh."

"Mmm."

Kari gave his bare shoulder a shove. "Wake up. I think we've missed supper."

"I'm not hungry," Josh mumbled.

"But what will they be saying? We've been in here all afternoon."

Josh gave a flick of his head as if to clear his senses, then turned to pull her into his arms. "What will who say, Viking? Didn't you know that you and I are the only ones in the world right now?"

Kari laughed at his absurdity. "No, really, Josh. All your men...and Thaddeus...and, oh, dear, what about my brother?" Suddenly she thought about Arne as she had last seen him, angry and confused. "He still is upset with you. He thinks you make me unhappy."

Josh shifted his leg to rub it against her nakedness. "Do I make you unhappy, love?" he asked softly.

"I was angry this morning when I saw you avoiding me with your account books again," she admitted. "But I would say that this afternoon—" she gave a little gasp as his knee brushed against a sensitive spot "—more or less makes up for it."

"More or less?"

His hand was there now, replacing the knee, and she was finding it hard to talk. "More...not less," she said shakily.

"That's good," he said huskily, and then they forgot to talk.

By the time they roused a second time, it was long past suppertime, and the camp had settled down for the night.

Rising before dawn and long hours of hard, backbreaking work made for early bedtimes in the winter camp.

Kari felt like a fugitive as Josh led her along the moon-lit path toward the cook shanty. She shivered in the blanket that was again serving as her only wrap. "What will Cookie do if he finds his kitchen has been raided in the middle of the night?" Kari asked, remembering the Irishman's quick temper.

"I'll handle it," Josh said lightly. He squeezed her hand. "Funny thing, but after this afternoon I feel like I could handle a whole army of irate Irishmen."

Kari gave a silvery giggle of sheer happiness. "You certainly handled one Norwegian well enough."

Josh stopped in the middle of the path to give her a hard kiss. "And I intend to keep on handling her every day of my life," he said firmly.

They reached the cook shanty and feasted on dry brown bread and the cold remains of a stew of dubious origin, washing it all down with cider. It was the best meal Kari had ever eaten.

The embers in the stove were still warm, and Josh added a bucket of coal to stoke it up again. He pulled Kari down beside him on the circular bench. The glow through the iron curlicues of the stove was the only illumination in the darkened shanty.

For over an hour they talked, sharing their contentment and their dreams for a future together. "I promise you that we'll visit your aunt and uncle in Minnesota," Josh told her. "It's not as if you won't ever see the land your father dreamed about."

"I think his dream was the *idea* that America represented, more than any particular place," Kari answered softly. "He wanted us to start a new life in a land where there was still a spirit of adventure and opportunity." She touched his face. "And people like you to tame it."

Josh grasped her hand and pressed a kiss into her palm. Then he stood and pulled her up with him. "Come on," he said with a hint of mischief in his voice. "You need a bath."

"A bath!"

Josh shook his head and motioned for her to be quiet as he led her out of the shanty into the chilly night. Behind the main camp buildings was a narrow path that Kari had not been on before. It led up into the woods for several yards, then stopped at a small log building, less than half the size of the storage cabin where she slept.

"What is this place, Josh?" she asked in a half whisper.

"You should know, Viking. I understand it's an old custom of your people."

He pulled open the log door and at once Kari recognized the distinctive odor of steamed wood. "It's a *bad-stue!*" she exclaimed. "What do you call it here?"

"Mostly just a sweat bath, but *bad-stu-eh* sounds more romantic." He pulled her inside and closed the door, then groped his way in the dark. "There should be a lantern here, and matches."

Within moments the little shed was filled with cheery lantern light and was beginning to heat from a small fire Josh lit in a square metal oven topped with big round stones that stood in the middle of the floor. A wide platform of wood that smelled like cedar ran the length of one wall. Josh sat down on it and motioned for Kari to join him.

She removed the blanket from her shoulders and set it down on one end of the platform. It was amazing how quickly the room had grown hot. Josh reached for the tiny mother-of-pearl buttons running down the front of her yellow dress, but she pulled back, embarrassed. "What are you doing?"

"You don't take a bath with clothes on, do you?"

Kari looked around the room. Back in Stavanger she had known about these steam baths, but it was only the men who took them. A decent woman would never consider such a thing. "There's no lock on the door," she said shyly.

"My love, it's the middle of the night. The only possible other customer for the bath tonight would be a stray black bear too sleepy from its winter's nap to know where it's going."

"There are bears here?" Kari cast an uneasy glance at the door.

"Sweetheart, I'm just teasing you." As they were talking, his fingers had deftly completed the task of freeing her from the yellow organdy. Kari still hesitated. "Are *you* going to take your clothes off?" she asked warily.

"No." Josh grinned. "*You're* going to take them off for me."

He slipped her dress over her head, then sat back to let her reciprocate by removing his shirt. A tiny drop of perspiration was already running from under his collar, down his broad chest. Kari watched as it made its way through the silky forest of mahogany hair, which was just a shade darker than the hair on his head. On a wicked impulse, she leaned over and put her tongue to the drop, just as it reached his erect nipple.

Josh jumped back as if he had been bitten instead of gently touched by her soft tongue. "So that's the way it's going to be, is it?" he drawled. With no apparent effort he lifted her onto his lap, and as his hands worked to free her from her undergarments, his mouth worked hot wizardry on her face and neck and breasts.

Their nakedness now had a light sheen of moisture, and they moved slickly against each other. Kari's breasts felt swollen and ripe as Josh laid her back against the hardwood planking and treated them to a steamy massage with hands and mouth. Then he rolled over, and she was on top of him, his hard arousal cradled between their slippery bodies.

"Do you take these baths often?" Kari asked, sounding out of breath.

Josh groaned and twisted himself against her. "Viking . . . I've *never* taken a bath like this one."

"Back home they say . . ." Kari drew in a quick breath as she felt him plunge deep inside her, then she continued, her voice shaky. "They say these baths are very good for one's health."

"Lord, sweetheart, I've never felt so healthy in my life." He lay back against the platform with his eyes closed, giving Kari a chance to watch the ripples along his magnificent body as it gleamed in the lantern light. His hands were on her hips, gently coaxing her into the circular motion that was building a fire at the joining of their bodies hotter than the one in the sauna oven. Suddenly his eyes opened, he pulled her down hard and tightened his hands on her hips. His deep pulsations reverberated through her and instantly she was over the edge, crying out as waves of pleasure rocked her.

They lay quietly for several minutes, the steamy heat sealing their bodies together. "Are you sure this custom came from the old country?" Kari asked finally.

Josh took her mouth in a sweaty kiss that tasted of salt. "I think we've improved a bit on the technique."

Kari chuckled and sleepily dropped her head once again to Josh's chest.

"Hey," Josh said after a few moments, reaching to give her round bottom a gentle slap. "Time to get up, love, and finish our bath."

"I think we finished it very well," Kari said with a blush.

Josh rolled her off him and stood up. "Nope. We've missed the best part." He let his eyes rove once more over the shiny curves of her body. "Well...*almost* the best part," he amended.

He grabbed her hand and before she knew what was happening, he had half dragged her, still naked, out into the snowy woods. "What are you doing?" Kari asked in dismay.

He filled his hands with snow and walked toward her. She could see his roguish grin in the moonlight. "Don't you dare, Josh Lyman!"

He shrugged. "It's part of the treatment, Viking. Your people invented this, not mine." And suddenly, slushy spring snow was sliding down the length of her sweaty, satiated body.

For a moment she stood still, her outrage giving way to an incredible icy, tingling sensation. "Josh!" she said in wonder.

He nodded and slathered a handful over his own chest. "Pretty amazing, isn't it?"

"It's startling, but..." Josh dumped another load down her back. "Quite wonderful, really."

"It'll be wonderful for about another two minutes." He hugged her to him and let an armful of snow slither down between their still-heated bodies. "Then that beautiful hide of yours will start to turn blue." He rubbed his hands along her back, and, sure enough, the delicious tingles were beginning to give way to an uncomfortable chill. She shivered. "Come on," Josh said. "Let's grab our clothes and get back to your room."

He opened the door to a welcome blast of heat from the sauna. Carelessly he bunched their clothes in a pile in his arms.

"We can't just go running naked through the woods, Josh. We'll freeze our feet, for one thing." Kari felt exhilarated. The truth was, she would probably be willing to run naked all the way back to Milwaukee if Josh asked her to.

Josh took a quick survey of the situation. He sat down in the doorway and pulled on his big boots. Then he wrapped Kari's blanket around her, plopped the bundle of clothes in her arms and picked her up. "Faster this way," he said, planting a kiss on her nose, and he headed down the path to her cabin.

Chapter Fifteen

Kari awoke the next morning to an instant sense of joy. Before she even opened her eyes, she was remembering yesterday's events. She stretched her body against the rough linen sheets, reliving the various sensations she had experienced for the first time.

Her little cot was cozily warm, and Josh hadn't wanted to leave it last night, but she had insisted.

"The first thing I'm going to do at breakfast is announce our engagement, Viking," he'd argued. "So I don't see what difference it makes."

"You'll do no such thing, Josh." She'd given him a kiss to soften the words. "You know very well that first we need to talk to Davey and Arne, especially Arne. He's been so difficult when it comes to you."

Josh had frowned then. "I may have something that will help win him over." He was thinking of the brand-new flintlock rifle he had packed away in the back of the wagon. He had wanted to give it to Arne back in Milwaukee, but the boy's resentment had become so fierce, he had decided to wait and use it as a parting gift when they reached Minnesota. Now it would be a peace offering from a prospective brother-in-law.

"He's usually so good-natured, but these months since Papa's death have been hard on him."

"Just remember this, love. A lumber camp is too small a place for secrets. You'd better find Arne and explain things to him right away, or he's going to find out from someone else."

She nodded, her eyes reflecting unhappiness for the first time in several hours. "I know. I'll see to it first thing in the morning." She took a playful nip of his chin. He smelled like cedar and pine.

At her gesture he reached to take her in his arms, but she pushed him away and let her voice assume a haughty tone. "In the meantime, Mr. Lyman, I'd appreciate it if you would vacate my bedroom."

Josh's eyebrows rose. "I'm not sure I like my Vikings so civilized," he had grumbled. But in the end he had gone, leaving her alone to fall into a deep, untroubled sleep.

She had slept well past dawn, and feared she would almost be too late to join the men for breakfast. She hurried down the path to the cook shanty, praying that Josh had kept his word to delay announcing their plans until she had had time to talk to Arne. Now in the hard light of day she realized that she would need to do some major convincing to persuade her brother to give up his goal of reaching Minnesota.

Just as she had thought, the men were already attacking the big platters of Cookie's deer sausage when she arrived. She scanned the room for Josh, but he wasn't seated at the table. Perhaps he, too, had needed a little extra sleep this morning, she thought to herself smugly.

Thaddeus and Holstein also seemed to be missing, and there was no sign of the boys. Olav was seated at one end of the nearest table. "Have you seen Josh?" she asked him.

His mouth full of food, he motioned with his big head toward the back door of the shanty, and just then the door opened and Josh looked in.

All the way across the room she could see that something was very wrong. She rushed over to him and he pulled her outside the shanty where Holstein, Thaddeus and two of the loggers were standing in a circle, their faces taut with worry.

"What is it?" she asked, keeping her voice calm.

"The boys are missing," Thaddeus answered.

Josh reached to take hold of her hand. "Knud here says he heard them talking yesterday afternoon. Something about heading off to Minnesota."

The blond-haired logger looked up at Kari apologetically. "Your brother, ma'am, sounded het up about somethin'. I didn't pay much never mind, knowing how boys can be at that age."

Yesterday afternoon? Kari closed her eyes. She felt sick to her stomach. Why hadn't she gone to talk to him yesterday when she'd known he had been upset? Instead, she had spent the afternoon and most of the night in Josh's arms. Her eyes met his and she saw her own guilt reflected there.

"But they couldn't have just taken off by themselves...."

"It appears that's exactly what they did, the scamps." Holstein was the only one of the group who appeared to be retaining his equanimity. "Cookie says two of his packs are missing along with a mess of trail provisions. All their stuff is cleaned out of their bunks. Davey's rifle's gone, too."

The other logger standing with the blond shuffled his big boots nervously. "I didn't know they was planning anything like this, I swear. But they was askin'...."

Josh interrupted impatiently. "Asking what, man?"

"It was the tallest one. Your brother, sir," he said, looking at Josh. "He wanted to know how you would go about gettin' to Minnesota from here." The logger dropped his head to watch his boots make patterns in the mud.

"What did you tell them, Jackson?" Holstein's voice held no censure.

"I just said if they was to follow the river, it would take them straight west to the Mississippi."

Josh groaned. "Those damn little fools."

Kari's face was pale. "When do you think they left?"

Holstein pulled open the door to the cook shanty. "Any of you men see those three youngsters at supper last night?" he yelled.

The buzz of conversation in the room stopped. The men looked questioningly over at the door. Some of them shook their heads.

"No one saw them?" Holstein repeated. With the continued negative response, he turned back to Josh and Kari. "Looks like they have more than half a day on us."

Kari felt a lump in her throat and angrily swallowed it away. It was time for action, not tears. Surely it was just a matter of following the boys and bringing them safely back. But she was distressed to see that Josh had that bleak, hard look in his eyes again. She had hoped it had disappeared forever.

"Well, let's go find them," she said briskly. The men looked at her as if she had taken leave of her senses.

"That'll be a task, ma'am," the blond logger commented. "There's not much but wilderness west of here . . . countless thousands of acres of it."

Kari looked at Josh, but he wouldn't meet her eyes. "If they're on foot, the fastest way to catch up to them will be by the river," he said. "We'll take two boats. Holstein, I want your best wilderness man in the boat with me, and I want you to send a party of men by land downriver in case we miss them from the water."

Holstein nodded. "The best wilderness man...now, that would be me," he said matter-of-factly. "And I'll send Knud with the group by land. He's a born tracker."

"I'm going with you, Josh," Thaddeus said.

Josh looked up and down Thaddeus's fine wool suit. "We'll be traveling hard and fast, Pennington."

Thaddeus's lips were pressed into a tight line. "Phineas is out there. I'm not about to go home from this trip to tell my parents that they've lost another child."

Josh paled, but kept his gaze steady on Thaddeus. "All right. You and I will take the front boat. Holstein, you and one of your men will be the rear guard."

"I'm going, too." To her dismay, Kari's voice sounded feeble. The mere thought of going near that river again had her head spinning. But if they found Arne... Not *if,* she corrected herself firmly, *when* they found Arne, she had to be there.

Josh put an arm around her shoulders. "Not this time, Viking," he said gently. "Water travel isn't exactly your strong suit these days, remember. Don't worry, we'll bring them back for you. I promise."

Kari shook her head, a stubborn look in her eyes. "I'm going, Josh. Let's not waste time arguing."

"I'm sorry, Kari. What if you get one of your spells again? We can't afford to have a fainting female on our hands. I'd tell you to go along with the land group, but they'll be traveling right alongside the river, too."

"You said traveling by boat was the fastest way to find them, right?"

"Yes, but..."

"Then I'm going to be in the boat. No spells, no faint
ing. I promise."

He looked down at the unyielding set of her jaw and a
smile flickered briefly across his face before the steely ex
pression returned. "You win, Viking. Let's get going
then."

In the next few minutes, Josh was too busy organizing
the two-pronged expedition to think any more about Kari.
The next time he saw her, she was seated on the floor in the
middle of a bateau, tucked in between bundles of sup
plies. "Are you going to be all right?" he asked her. He
didn't smile, and his strained face reminded Kari of the
days just following the shipwreck.

Worry over the boys and over Josh was helping Kari
fight her own battle. Please don't let us have to face an
other tragedy so soon, she prayed. And *please* give me the
strength to be there for Arne...and for Josh. She grasped
the sides of the boat and rocked it gently, willing her body
to sense the harmony between vessel and water. She stared
over the side at the water rushing by beneath the gun
wales. The river appeared more benevolent today than it
had the windy day she had fallen in.

She reached a hand over the side and let the running
water slide through her fingers. Then she closed her eyes
and let it come...the engulfing waves, the whirling, the
dizziness... She accepted it, let it fill her, and then...very
gently, began to replace the vision piece by piece with the
green cliffs of Stavanger plunging down to the fjord...and
the peace of the pine-covered hills of her homeland....

"Kari! I asked if you're going to be all right?" Josh's
voice was sharp.

She opened her eyes. The rocking motion of the boat
slowed, and she looked over to Josh with an expression of

determination. "I'm going to be fine, Josh. Let's get started."

Josh climbed in the back and they were ready to push off when Thaddeus came up alongside their boat. "Before we leave, Lyman," he said stiffly, "I just wanted to... apologize for my words yesterday. They were unfair."

Josh looked directly at his brother-in-law. In spite of a difference in coloring, the family resemblance was there. Corinne would never be really gone from his life, he realized. But somehow the revelation didn't make him ache inside as it once would have. "We all say crazy things when we're upset, Thaddeus. But I just want to be sure you know one thing...if I could have given my own life to save Corinne that night, I would have done so in a heartbeat."

"I know, Josh." Thaddeus's light eyes were clouded. "We all know that. It's just...hard sometimes...."

Josh reached out to put a hand on Thaddeus's shoulder. "Yes, it is," he answered firmly. "Now, let's go get those crazy little brothers of ours."

Thaddeus nodded without speaking and walked over to the second boat, where Holstein was already waiting in the back poling position. "Let's get moving," the burly foreman said soberly.

It was slow-going. At first they hugged the shore with Holstein jumping out of the boat every few yards to pick up signs of a trail. After three stops, he gave a shout of success and came back to the boats with a resolute look on his face. "They've been through here, all right. It looks as if they're walking right along the bank. If they keep this trail, we'll have no trouble catching up."

Kari, Josh and Thaddeus all breathed a little easier after this pronouncement, and the afternoon passed almost pleasantly as they floated along a straight, flat portion of the wide river. But by the time Holstein said they would have to stop for the night, their spirits had dropped once again.

"There's no way to follow their trail in the dark, Josh," Holstein argued. "We could go right past them and never even know it. We'll start again at daybreak."

"How long do you think it will take to catch up to them?" Kari asked.

Holstein gave her a hand out of the boat, and Kari was grimly pleased to find that she could step over the water without a tremor. "They're healthy boys," Holstein answered. "Lots of energy. We might be another day or two yet."

He went off to collect firewood, leaving the other three standing on the bank, looking down the river, and thinking of their respective brothers somewhere downriver, alone in the Wisconsin wilderness.

"They're good boys," Thaddeus said.

Josh picked up a rock and hurled it into the river. "They'll be all right."

Kari said nothing. She shrugged off a shiver and started up the bank to go help Holstein with the fire.

By morning it had turned cold again. A light steam misted up where the warmer water met the chilly air. None of them talked much as they broke camp and slid the boats into the river.

"We know they've come this far," Holstein said. "Let's try catching the current in the middle for a ways before we stop to pick up their trail. We can go faster that way."

Josh nodded and they pushed out into the center of the fast-moving water. The river had narrowed and slowly the landscape around them was changing from level pines to rocky banks with occasional sandstone and limestone cliffs that shot straight up, higher than a building.

"They'll have to do some climbing here," Holstein shouted up to the front boat. "It should slow them down."

Midmorning, Holstein motioned for them to pull over to the bank. He pulled a small jar out of one of the packs and approached Josh and Kari's boat.

"You and I need some doctoring, little miss," he said.

"Doctoring?"

He pointed to his face, which was an even brighter shade of red than normal from being out in the open on the river. Kari had felt the heat of the sun's rays that morning on her own fair skin, but had been too preoccupied thinking about Arne to mention it.

Suddenly Holstein's thick fingers were rubbing an oily substance on her face with surprising gentleness. A pungent odor assailed her nostrils.

"Whew, Holstein," Josh said from the back of the boat. "What is that stuff?"

"Bear grease." Holstein grinned.

He held out the jar to Josh, but he waved it away. "I'll take the sunburn," he said quickly.

Holstein shrugged. "Suit yourself. But your lady here and I don't have any choice. We might be a bit smelly for a while but it's better than having your face peel off."

Kari wrinkled her nose. She supposed she'd get used to the stink after a while. And the sun did feel less strong. "Thank you, Holstein," she said, mustering a smile for the first time all morning.

He smeared a last dab on her dry lips, his own red skin darkening with a blush. Then he started back to his boat, carelessly slathering the grease over his face and neck. After Thaddeus politely declined the smelly protection, Holstein stepped back into the boat and they pushed off.

They had been going farther and farther between stops. On the last stop Holstein was gone for longer than normal. The three waiting in the boats began to look at each other uneasily, but no one spoke. Finally, Holstein emerged through the trees shaking his head. "It's so rocky now, it's hard to tell, but I think we've lost them. There's no sign of any fresh movement through here," he said.

Josh couldn't see Kari's face, but he could tell her concern from the stiffening of her back. "This could mean that we've passed them, right?" he asked his foreman.

Holstein scratched his day's growth of whiskers. "Could mean that . . . or it could mean that they've gone inland from the river. Or it might just be that I can't find the trail. We could go downriver a ways and I could check again. Or they could've swum across the river to the other side. We could check over there. . . ."

Josh felt sick to his stomach. He had a sudden memory of the night on the *Atlantic,* not knowing which way to turn to look for Corinne, going belowdecks when she evidently was already abovedecks. And in the end . . . too late to save her. At least this time he was not alone.

"Holstein, you and Thaddeus keep on downriver and see if you can pick up a trail on either side of the river. Kari and I will start back upriver by land and see if we've missed them." No one questioned his tone of command. "Take a bearing on this place . . . we'll try to meet back here by sundown."

Kari and Josh pulled their boat as far as they could up onto the bank. They left most of their provisions inside, though Josh grabbed his rifle and a knapsack of food. They watched as Holstein and Thaddeus pushed off once again into the river.

"Do you want to wait here, Kari?" Josh already knew what her answer would be, but thought he would at least make the attempt. "We may have to do some rough climbing around those cliffs we saw a ways back."

"You've never seen a fjord, Josh. I was *born* climbing."

A brief smile touched his face. After a moment's hesitation, he reached into the boat and pulled out a second rifle he had tucked under the gunwales. "Do you think you can carry this?"

"Of course. But what do we need rifles for?"

"We won't, I hope. But it never hurts to be prepared out here." He slung his ammunition pouch over one shoulder, the food pack over the other, and motioned for Kari to follow him up the bank.

"Do you think we'll find them, Josh?"

He turned back to meet her worried gaze. Pulling her briefly into his arms, he dropped a chaste kiss on her lips. "We'll find them, Viking."

They went slowly, Josh trying to look for any signs of recent travel, though he admitted to Kari that his tracking skills could not compare to Holstein's. "We'll pretty much have to blunder right into them for me to find a trail," he tried to joke, but neither could manage much of a smile.

Even with the sparse foliage of early spring, making their way along the bank was hard-going. Brush had completely covered the trail in most places. The only comfort was that this meant that no one had been through this way recently. Unless the boys had gone inland, they were still upriver from them and the two parties were bound to meet sooner or later.

Josh found himself cheered by the thought. "First thing I'm going to do when we find them is wring Davey's neck," he said.

"You'll do no such thing," Kari chided.

"Just watch me," he replied darkly.

The sun had reached its zenith and begun its descent. It glinted brightly off the peaks of rushing water. Neither

Kari nor Josh had spoken for the past hour, concentrating all their efforts on picking their way over the rocky shore.

"Let's stop and eat something," Josh said as they reached the edge of a rock that jutted out over the water in a bizarre formation resembling a giant bull's head.

Kari sank gratefully to the ground. Carefully, she laid the spare rifle she'd been carrying to one side and rubbed her shoulder. The longer they walked, the heavier the firearm had become.

Josh knelt beside her and offered her a flat, round piece of bread from his canvas knapsack. "Cookie's trail biscuits," he said, making a face. "They sit in your stomach like rocks, but at least you don't feel hungry."

Josh looked up at the sun. "We're good for a couple more hours, I would think. You're not too tired?"

Kari shook her head. "I just wish we would find them."

"I know—" Josh stopped himself in midsentence. He had been twisting the stiffness out of his neck, and suddenly he pointed to the top of the odd-shaped rock they were sitting beside. "Look!" he said to Kari, his voice hushed.

Kari craned her head upward and there, staring down with two coal black eyes, was the cutest little face she had ever seen. "Oh, the darling thing!" she exclaimed.

Her voice didn't seem to bother the little animal. Suddenly, it was joined by another, identical furry creature, and two sets of black eyes stared down at them curiously. "I've never seen a bear before," Kari whispered. The two were not much bigger than the piglet the boys had put into the kitchen back in Milwaukee. They were covered with soft, blackish-brown hair that stood out from their little bodies as if someone had just given them a good rubbing with a towel. "They're adorable!"

Josh had reached immediately for his rifle, and leaned over to hand Kari the one she had been carrying. "Take this," he said tersely.

"Don't be ridiculous, Josh," Kari said, laughing, still keeping her voice low. "They're not going to hurt us."

Josh slowly eased himself up, and the second cub scampered away. The first one held on for a few moments more, then with a last long look of its sparkling round eyes, it, too, ran off into the woods.

"Oh, Josh, you scared them away." Kari sounded disappointed as she stood up next to him.

Josh's face was grim. His eyes searched the woods around them. "Those were babies, Kari. At this stage, bear cubs never go far from their mother."

"Oh." Kari felt stupid. The little creatures had looked so lovable, it was hard to think of them as connected to danger. But Josh was evidently taking the threat seriously. He still scanned the shadows of the forest.

"The cubs are born during the mother's hibernation," he said. "They've probably all just ventured out for the first time. The mother bear'll be hungry, bad-tempered and definitely not in a mood for visitors with those young'uns around."

"What should we do?"

Josh looked downriver. "The best thing would probably be to head back the way we came. Bears stake out certain territories. The sooner we get out of this mama's territory the better."

"But we may still have missed the boys." The sky had clouded and Kari shivered. Her warm blue coat had stayed back in camp, still damp from her dousing in the river. She was wearing only the heavy wool shirt and cinched-in trousers one of the loggers had lent her.

"We'll go on," Josh decided. He checked his own rifle, then handed it to Kari to hold while he loaded the one she'd been carrying. "Keep a sharp eye," he said, handing the gun back to her and taking his own.

The woods took on a more sinister cast as Kari now saw creatures lurking in every shadow. The sun stayed firmly hidden behind the building bank of clouds. Even the river seemed more menacing. She nodded to him and they started moving. They climbed over the rock formation the bear cubs had been standing on, only to find an even steeper one beyond. This one they had to cross at times on hands and knees, and neither wasted energy talking.

Shortly after traversing this second formation, they came to an area where the river widened and the rocky shore gave way to a small swampy meadow, with the cliffs jutting back around it. The ground was spongy, but at least it was temporarily flat and clear of brush, giving them an easy walk for a change.

Kari shifted the heavy rifle to her other shoulder and looked up. At the far end of the stretch of marshy grass, she thought she saw a flash of color. "Josh, look there!"

He turned in the direction of her pointing hand, and now they both could clearly see movement and colors that were not part of nature. "Someone's over there," he said with restrained excitement.

They started across the bog at a half run, and Josh called out, "Davey!" Now they could distinguish two figures, one taller and one shorter with white-blond hair.

"Arne!" Kari shouted. The figures were waving their arms in the air and running toward them. But there were still only two of them.

At last they were close enough to see the two boys. Their faces looked scared and tense, and Josh felt a cold foreboding. "Where's Phineas?" he yelled sharply.

Davey kept on running until he reached his brother and threw his arms around him. "Criminy, Josh...I'm so glad you're here." He sounded out of breath and agitated.

Kari was enfolding Arne in a similar embrace, and tears ran down the younger boy's cheeks. "Cri-min-y, Kari," he said, parroting his friend. "I didn't mean to get anyone in trouble. I just got angry...and I wanted to go to Minnesota. I didn't mean to cause trouble." The tears came heavier.

"What is it?" Josh pulled himself away from Davey and took a firm grip on his little brother's shoulders. "Where's Phineas?"

Davey pointed across the grass to a ridge of rock. "He's there. We found a place up in the rock. He's awful sick, Josh."

Josh looked over to Kari. She and Arne were watching him, their identical blue eyes fearful. "Tell me what happened," he said to Davey, his voice level.

"It was last night, just before sundown. We'd decided to camp in this meadow. Arne and I went off to get some fish while Phineas built a fire. We were down at the river..." Davey's voice was shaking. "We heard Phineas scream. It was horrible!"

Arne had dashed the tears away from his eyes and pulled himself up straight. The broken English words tumbled from him. "It was dee black bear. It have grabbed Phineas."

"Dear Lord," Kari breathed.

Josh unconsciously tightened his hold on Davey, but he tried to keep his voice calm. "Then what happened?"

Davey swallowed. "I...I shot at it with my rifle. I guess I missed, but it ran off into the woods. We didn't dare sleep all night thinking it might come back."

"What about Phineas?" Josh asked.

"The bear had torn open his leg. We dragged him up to a place in the rocks we thought the bear couldn't get to, but Phineas woke up this morning with his leg swollen twice its size, and he's talking crazy-like."

Josh took a deep breath and released his hold on Davey. "Take us to him."

In solemn procession the four made their way across the clearing to the edge of the rocks. About two-thirds of the way up the twenty-foot-high cliff was a deep indentation in the rock wall about the size of a small carriage. Josh handed his rifle to Kari and started to climb.

"We pulled him up there, Josh. We were so scared…we didn't know what to do. We thought maybe the bear couldn't get up the cliff."

Josh looked back down at his brother. "Bears are good climbers. If she'd wanted to get to you up there, she could have."

"She?"

"Kari and I saw a couple of cubs just down the river from here. If this was their mama, it would explain why she attacked Phineas." He turned back to the rock and pulled himself up to the ledge the boys had indicated. Phineas lay on the ground not four feet from the edge. His face was flushed, and the left leg of his trousers hung in bloody strips.

When Josh knelt down beside him, Phineas opened glassy eyes. "How y' doing, Josh?" the boy said weakly.

At least the boy recognized him, Josh thought with relief. He took Phineas's hand and gave it a firm squeeze. "We've come to take you home, lad. Figured you might not want to wait around for another visit from that bear." He pulled away the torn material from Phineas's leg and winced as he saw the deep gashes running the length of his calf. They were puffy and red around crusted dry blood.

"The bear's comin' to tea, Josh. In the parlor." Phineas gave a crazy little giggle, and Josh realized that the boy was out of his head.

His stomach knotted with apprehension, Josh picked him up. "I'm going to have to put you over my shoulder to get us down from here, Phineas. You just hang on, all right? You're going to be just fine. . . ." He kept talking to the boy as he carefully made the descent to the ground, where Arne and Davey helped him move Phineas from his back.

"The bear's gonna sit on Ma's silk settee." Phineas had a silly smile on his face and Kari looked at Josh with alarm.

"His fever's up," he told her brusquely. "We have to get him down to the river and try to cool him off."

Phineas grinned up at Josh and his two shaken friends as the three carried him across the meadow to the edge of the river. Josh soaked his neckerchief in the cold water, then handed it to Kari. "Keep it on his forehead," he told her. "When it gets hot, get it cold again in the river." Then he peeled back the pieces of Phineas's trouser leg and pulled the wounded limb right into the river, letting the cold water flush out the nasty wound.

"Is he going to be all right, Josh?" Davey asked fearfully.

Josh had gently washed the crusted blood away from the scratches. "It's just these two here that are deep," he said, examining Phineas's leg. "Nothing that can't heal up. But it's the blood poisoning that's causing the fever. That's what we've got to worry about."

Tears were once again flowing unheeded down Arne's cheeks. "I didn't mean it, Kari," he said in a quavery voice. "I didn't know we'd get into trouble. I just wanted to get to Minnesota."

Kari reached over to give her brother's hand a squeeze, but just then Josh rose to his full height and walked over to the trembling boy. "I suspect you've learned a lesson about running away, Arne," he said gravely. "Sometimes it's better to hunker down and face whatever it is that's bothering you."

Arne looked up at Josh, his eyes swimming with remorse. "Is Phineas going to die?"

"I sure as hell hope not," Josh said firmly. "But I need your help and Davey's to get him back to camp." He leaned over and picked up the second rifle Kari had left on the ground. "This rifle belongs to you, Arne. Do you think you and Davey can keep an eye out for that bear while I carry Phineas?"

Arne's eyes had grown as big and round as two of Cookie's flapjacks. His pointed little chin bobbed up and down as he nodded vehemently. He reached out slowly and took the gun from Josh's outstretched hand.

"Good," Josh said, releasing the weapon into the boy's hands.

Phineas had started to shake. "I'm cold, Mama," he mumbled.

Kari kept the cold compress on his forehead, but she looked over at Josh with concern. "Isn't this much cold bad for a fever?"

Josh shook his head. "Not according to Holstein. At camp we have men getting hurt, ax cuts and the like, all the time. Holstein always says to keep the fever down with cold. And he uses lots of water to wash out the wounds . . . says water is God's medicine." He knelt down again beside Phineas and pulled the sick boy's leg deeper into the river.

The authoritative tone of his voice was reassuring the others. Some of the tenseness left Davey's and Arne's faces, and Kari gave Phineas a smile when he opened his eyes. "The tricky part is going to be getting him down-river to meet Thaddeus and Holstein," Josh said.

"I could stay here with him while you and the boys go meet them," Kari suggested. "Then you could bring them back here with the boats."

"I'm not leaving you alone here with that bear around," Josh said grimly. "We're still in her territory. We've all got to leave." His eyes swept the woods. "I'll have to carry him."

"We'll help you, Josh," Davey said. "Arne and I carried him up the cliff." He stopped and put a hand to his forehead. "I forgot... all our stuff is still up there."

"Hurry up and get it, then," his brother told him. "I want to get out of here."

Davey stood and started jogging across the expanse of meadow. He was still several yards from the cliff when a big black shape came crashing out of the woods opposite them... heading directly for Davey. Josh dropped Phineas's leg and jumped up, yelling at his brother, who apparently did not see the bear. The animal was running like a gigantic dog in a fast, even lope. Josh snatched his rifle from the ground next to Kari and took off.

At Josh's yell, Davey turned his head and saw the huge creature heading toward him. He stopped dead for a moment, then looked back helplessly toward the group of people by the riverbank. Finally, he turned and made a dash for the cliff. By now the bear was only yards away from him. From behind, Josh hollered and whooped, but the big animal didn't even turn a head in his direction... just kept running straight at Davey.

Josh's lungs were bursting and he had broken out in a cold sweat. Davey had pulled himself up a couple feet onto the rocks, but the animal was now at his heels. It reared up toward the boy, its wicked claws showing whitely against the dark brown rock. Shaking with fear for his brother, Josh knelt in the spongy grass and put his rifle to his shoulder. With all his strength he willed his body to be steady as he drew a bead on the animal's rolling black head. He pulled the trigger. The dull click of the misfire echoed in his ears as if it had been a volley of cannons.

The next few moments, standing there in frozen horror with his useless rifle, Josh would always remember as a blur. He watched as the bear reached out a massive claw at Davey's shoe, pulling the boy's foot out of its precarious hold on the slippery rock. Davey almost fell, then regained hold and began to scramble desperately up the side of the cliff. Suddenly, there was a deafening blast in Josh's ear. He watched as the heavy animal gave out a roar of rage, then fell backward off the face of the cliff. It rolled to one side, tried to stand, then fell again, this time with an almost human whine of pain. Finally, it lay in a great, still mound on the ground.

"Arne!" Davey shouted. He leapt from the rock, careful to land several feet away from the bear, and raced toward them. Josh turned to see that Arne had come up next to him. The boy's face was as white as his hair, and in his arms he held the rifle Josh had given him only moments before. It was still smoking.

Davey slowed as he approached them. His face, too, was pale. "You shot it, Arne!"

Kari had left Phineas by the bank and come up beside them. She looked at her brother with wonder. "How did you do that, Arne?"

Her brother looked down at the ground. The knuckles of his hands clenching the rifle were white. "Josh teached us," he said. "I have to save Davey."

Kari reached out her arms to give both boys a hug. Josh was reloading his rifle. He walked over to the motionless form of the bear and without hesitation put the gun to the animal's head. This time his rifle fired.

Epilogue

Milwaukee, Wisconsin
August 20, 1853

"You shouldn't even be here, Josh," Kari said with a little frown that did nothing to spoil the perfection of her appearance. She was dressed in a new peach-colored gown that matched the natural blush of her cheeks. The front part of her hair was pulled into a corona of braids on the top of her head while the rest of her flaxen tresses hung in shimmering waves down her back. "You're not supposed to see how I look until the ceremony. It might be bad luck."

"I'll tell you what's bad luck," Josh grumbled, closing the lock on her bedroom door with a firm click. "Bad luck is living in the same house all summer long with a beautiful, long-haired, long-legged—"

"Josh!" Kari protested.

"Long-legged," he continued resolutely, "temptress of a Viking, without ever being allowed to..." His words were lost as his mouth came down on hers in an impatient kiss that carried an edge of thwarted desire.

Kari joined in enthusiastically for a few moments, before she pulled away, her smile gone and her eyes aflame. "Please, Josh," she said huskily. "I have enough—how do you say it?—*butterflies* in my stomach today. You see? I don't even remember my English."

Josh pulled her back into his arms. "Viking," he whispered, "by the time tonight's over, you're not even going to remember your *name.*"

Kari felt a tingle of anticipation along her limbs, but she laughed lightly and pushed him away. "I've already forgotten it once in my life, remember? Just this time last year...."

Last year. They both became solemn as they remembered the tragedy that had taken place on Lake Erie just a year ago today. Planning the wedding for this day had been a compromise they had reached back at the lumber camp after a long, unhappy argument—and an even longer, much happier, reconciliation.

Kari had insisted that they wait out the year's mourning for Corinne before they married. Josh had finally agreed to wait the year...but not one day more. What he hadn't realized was that once he got his Viking back to the civilized surroundings of Milwaukee following the end of the year's log drives, she had insisted on observing what she called, with her musical inflection, "proprieties."

"You learned that word from my mother," he had accused.

"Nevertheless," she had said primly.

And that had been the way of it...for more than two months. Until he was half-crazy with waiting...and wanting.

"It's good for a bridegroom to be eager," Kari had whispered to him as they had said good-night last night after a wedding-eve supper. The soft words had turned his blood to lava.

"What about a bride?" he had responded.

She hadn't answered. She had merely smiled, given him a slow, sensual kiss, and closed her door in his face.

Now the waiting was over. In less than an hour they would be husband and wife. Stubbornly, he pulled her once again into his arms.

"Kari?" The pounding on the door mimicked the throbbing in the lower portion of Josh's anatomy, and he gave a frustrated groan. "Kari, are you almost ready?"

Kari pulled away, smoothed cool fingers over the scowling lines on Josh's forehead and walked over to open the door. "Come in, Elizabeth," she said warmly.

"Thanks for the interruption, Bethy," Josh said glumly, but he leaned down and turned a cheek for his friend's kiss and fluffed the heads of the three little ones who clustered around her.

"Didn't I tell you children to stay downstairs?" Elizabeth looked down at her pint-size attendants. Gently she shooed them out the door, then turned back to Josh. "Interruption, my foot. It's time for your wedding, Josh Lyman. You two will have a whole lifetime for this kind of stuff."

Kari smiled at the maternal bossiness of Elizabeth's tone. "We're so glad you and Tom could be here," she said.

"We wouldn't miss it. We're going to see that this big galoot does it *right* this time. No more..." As if she realized she was venturing into unhappy waters, Elizabeth changed her words in midsentence. "No more bears, that's for sure!"

Kari shuddered. "We were very lucky."

Josh grinned. "Arne claims it wasn't luck . . . just skill. He carries around that new rifle of his like a third arm. I think he even sleeps with the thing. And he's right about the skill. He's turning into a darn good marksman."

The slow acceptance that had developed between Arne and Josh since the near tragedy of the boys' river expedition was fast growing into respect and even affection. It warmed Kari's heart every time she saw them together.

"It was nice of you to ask him to stand up with you," Kari said softly.

"A man never had so many witnesses," Josh said with a false tone of complaint. "Davey and Arne wouldn't stand up without Phineas, now that he's hobbling around again on that bad leg of his. And none of them are legal age, so along comes Tom offering to sign the papers. Doesn't want to leave me any loopholes, he says."

The two women laughed. "Well, let's get down there, then," Elizabeth urged.

Both Josh and Kari had agreed that they wanted the wedding to be small, but the front parlor looked quite full as they made their way in for the ceremony. Daisy's beau, Charles, was there, looking ill at ease with a collar that rode too high on his neck. But Daisy sat beaming by his side, her curls springing out from her head with a life entirely their own. Mrs. Hennessey sat near them, her ample frame occupying the better portion of the silk settee.

Josh was surprised to see Theo Pratt sitting close to his mother on the sofa, and even more surprised to see a mischievous sparkle in her eyes as she looked up at the portly businessman, who had once been one of Homer Lyman's best friends.

But the biggest surprise was seeing Vernon Pennington, standing stiffly at one end of the room, flanked by Thaddeus, Chester and Emmett. Josh left Kari talking with his mother and went over to greet them.

"Vernon," he said heartily. "It was mighty good of you to come."

"We wanted to be here, Josh." Vernon's voice sounded older than Josh remembered. "We wish you well, we really do. And—" now there was a definite tremor in his tone "—and...I wanted to thank you again for bringing my boy back to me."

"We all brought him back," Josh said gently. "Thaddeus here, too."

The old man shook his head and fiddled with the chain of his watch. "Thaddeus says if it weren't for your doctoring...my boy would've died out there in those woods."

"We're all just glad he's going to be all right," Josh said.

Thaddeus thrust a hand out toward Josh. "Congratulations, Josh. I guess the best man won, eh?"

Josh grinned. "Sorry, Thaddeus, but there was never any contest." He shook hands with the other two Pennington brothers, then looked hastily around the room. After a moment's hesitation, he asked, "Myra?"

"Ma's got the headache," Chester replied.

Vernon looked soberly at Josh. "Give her time, lad. She did say I was to tell you thanks for everything you did for Phineas."

Josh nodded. His trips to the Pennington parlor were perhaps over for a while. But with the new partnership he, Vernon and Thaddeus had formed to open up more of the west for logging, the longtime relationship between the two families was far from ended. "It means a lot to me that you came," he said warmly, clasping the older man's hand in both of his. Then he turned to find his bride.

* * *

"You were almost rude to Mr. Pratt, Josh," Kari said with one of her musical laughs, snuggling up against him in the coziness of their feather bed.

"The man would have stayed the night if I hadn't given him a hand out the door," Josh said, smiling. He hadn't felt so charitable toward the elderly feedstore owner when he had lingered on nearly two hours after the other wedding guests had left.

"I think he's sweet on your mother," Kari said happily.

"Well, that's fine...but tonight's *my* wedding night, not hers."

"It was scarcely past nine when he left, Josh."

"But I'd been ready since nine this morning. Hell, I've been ready for two long months." He gathered her more closely in his arms.

"You did seem ...*ready*."

"Is that a complaint?" he asked lazily, too pleasantly satiated to muster any indignation.

"Hardly." Kari laughed. She stretched upward and gave him a kiss. "It's just that it seemed almost indecent the way you practically dragged me up here. The boys hadn't even gone to bed yet."

"Those rascals. One of these days I truly am going to wring their necks." They both were silent for a moment, remembering the boys' entrance during the wedding ceremony that afternoon. Tom had started to play a stately tune on his harmonica and Kari and Josh had taken their places in front of the fireplace. Elizabeth had moved up to stand next to Kari, and Helen had said in an undertone, "Where are those boys?"

Then the double doors had opened and Davey, Arne and a limping Phineas entered solemnly, each holding on to a piece of the cord which ended up around the neck of a nearly grown Porky. They had clothed the poor creature in one of Homer Lyman's old dress suits.

Josh turned toward Kari in their bed and chuckled. "Weddings can get kind of stuffy, I guess."

"Not with those three around," Kari said dryly. "But it was a beautiful wedding, Josh."

"The honeymoon's even better." He pulled himself up on one elbow and threw back the comforter to once again expose her long body to his view. His hand made a slow trail from her neck to the slight curve of her stomach. "Let's get back to it," he said huskily.

She was cool and silky—hair, skin and mouth—and he was hot and hard. He made it last this time...endless moments just on the edge...the tip of the breaker riding, riding...about to be smashed to pieces by an unyielding shore. Then release, relief, fulfillment, warmth...tears.

"Shh," Josh comforted her, drawing them back together into the cocoon of their bed. "I didn't know that Vikings cried," he said gently.

"We don't. I'm not."

Josh smiled and kissed the tears from her cheeks. "Oh."

He could just see the luminous blue of her eyes in the darkened room. "I love you, Josh Lyman," she whispered.

"I love *you*, Mrs. Lyman."

"Now I have an American name."

Josh shook his head. "There aren't any American names, Viking, except for the Indians. We've all brought our names here from other lands at some point."

"But now I will sound more American."

"You'll always be Kari Aslaksdatter to me. I think that sounds just fine. But the new little one that we're going to continue trying to make in a few minutes—" he wiggled his eyebrows suggestively, making her laugh "—now, *he* will be an American."

"Or she."

"Or she," he agreed.

Kari was silent a few minutes, looking into the darkened room. "What is it, love?" Josh asked.

"This is silly to think of right now...but sometimes I wonder about those two babies we saw by the river. The little bears. What would have become of them?"

Josh tucked her golden head under his chin and rocked her against him. "We killed their mother, Kari. They wouldn't have had any way of surviving."

"Oh, dear."

"It was the bear or Davey. We had no choice."

"I know, but it seems so unfair for the little ones."

"A lot of things in life seem unfair." All at once Josh sounded like he was talking more to himself than her. "But we have to just keep going, doing the best we have with the hand we're dealt."

Kari smiled in the darkness. She had learned this lesson the day her mother had died so many years ago, or perhaps the knowledge had always been with her as some kind of innate gift. But for Josh, so hardheaded and in control, this acceptance had been a struggle. A months-long battle that had almost cost them the happiness they were experiencing now. She knew that for Josh, the fight would never be truly over. He would continue to try to bend the whims of fate to his liking. But for now, as he lay with his strong arms enfolding her, he was at peace.

"'The hand we're dealt'...this is an American saying, Josh?" She felt the rasp of his whiskers as he nodded against her cheek in the dark. "I think we've been dealt a pretty good hand," she whispered.

"I do, too, Viking." He closed his eyes and let himself enjoy the warmth of her against him. "A very good hand."

* * * * *

Author's Note

My home state of Minnesota was largely developed by the energetic and positive people of the Scandinavian countries, who found here a land of pines and water similar to the homeland they had left behind.

There is hardly a Minnesota family that doesn't have a story about the incredible movement of Nordic people from one side of the world to the other, which began in the 1830s and to a lesser extent continues to this day. I thank one of the more recent arrivals, Synnöve Bakke, for her help with the Norwegian language in this story.

The genesis for this book came from an episode in my own family saga. My great-great-great-great-grandfather, Holstein Isaccson, came from Norway as a young man to establish a place for his family in the new frontier of Wisconsin. His family soon followed, but tragically, the last leg of their journey was the fateful voyage of the SS *Atlantic*. Holstein's mother, Kari, his father, Aslak, and his younger brother and sister all perished beneath the waters of Lake Erie in the early morning hours of August 20, 1852.

In spite of his loss, Holstein survived and flourished as a successful innkeeper and landowner in Wisconsin and, later, Minnesota. Like so many immigrants throughout the history of this country, he did what he had to do...he faced the challenges and heartaches of beginning a new life in a new land . . . and he triumphed.

HARLEQUIN SUPERROMANCE®

HARLEQUIN SUPERROMANCE NOVELS WANTS TO INTRODUCE YOU TO A DARING NEW CONCEPT IN ROMANCE...

WOMEN WHO DARE!
Bright, bold, beautiful...
Brave and caring, strong and passionate...
They're women who know their own minds
and will dare anything...
for love!

One title per month in 1993, written by popular Superromance authors, will highlight our special heroines as they face unusual, challenging and sometimes dangerous situations.

Love blooms next month with:
#553 LATE BLOOMER by Peg Sutherland
Available in June wherever Harlequin Superromance novels are sold.

THREE UNFORGETTABLE HEROINES
THREE AWARD-WINNING AUTHORS

Untamed

MAVERICK HEARTS

A unique collection of historical short stories that capture the spirit of America's last frontier.

HEATHER GRAHAM POZZESSERE—over 10 million copies of her books in print worldwide
Lonesome Rider—The story of an Eastern widow and the renegade half-breed who becomes her protector.

PATRICIA POTTER—an author whose books are consistently Waldenbooks bestsellers
Against the Wind—Two people, battered by heartache, prove that love can heal all.

JOAN JOHNSTON—award-winning Western historical author with 17 books to her credit
One Simple Wish—A woman with a past discovers that dreams really do come true.

Join us for an exciting journey West with
UNTAMED
Available in July, wherever Harlequin books are sold.

**Harlequin is proud to present our
best authors and their best books.
Always the best for your reading
pleasure!**

Throughout 1993, Harlequin will bring you
exciting books by some of the top names in
contemporary romance!

In June,
look for
*Threats and
Promises* by

The plan was to make her nervous....

Lauren Stevens was so preoccupied with her new looks
and her new business that she really didn't notice a
pattern to the peculiar "little incidents"—incidents
that could eventually take her life. However, she did
notice the sudden appearance of the attractive and
interesting Matt Kruger who *claimed* to be a close
friend of her dead brother....

**Find out more in THREATS AND
PROMISES...available wherever Harlequin
books are sold.**